THE
SCATTERED
BONES

THE
SCATTERED BONES

NICOLE SCARANO

CONTENTS

OVEC'S TEMPLE

SZENT

THE VESI

DEATH'S TEMPLE

AUTHOR'S NOTE

The Scattered Bones is a dark fantasy romance, and I recommend it for readers ages 16 and up. There are some darker elements to this book, and if you wish to go into it blind, feel free! But if you would like CWs, they are below.

This book contains scenes of fantasy violence and peril, a slightly oppressive but fictional religion, and some mild love scenes (definitely not hot chili peppers scenes, but not fade to black. They are very low steam, not graphic, and concentrate more on the romance.) This is a slight **SPOILER**, but there is also an on-page execution that lasts two pages.

ONE

My scorched skin and chapped lips blister under the enraged sun. Its molten rays burn me, feed on me, punish me as the singed wind beats my flesh. The whipping dust is so thick it braids into my hair, and I've become more desert than human, more sand than soul. Every breath feels like fire, and my water supply ran dry hours ago. I have no food. No water. No hope. I'm lost in the Sivatag. Hopelessly and irreversibly lost in this desert tomb. This wasteland grave.

There's a reason mortals never enter the Sivatag. None who cross its borders ever reemerge. Their flesh shrivels in this cruel temperature, their bones bleached white until they become grains of sand. There's no life in this desert, no food, no water, no shade. Just endless dunes, and a sun that plays tricks on its invaders. It's believed that the Sivatag hides its true form from its trespassers so that those foolish enough to step foot within its boundaries lose their way. This deadly stretch of earth has existed as far back as human memory stretches, but legend remembers the twin gods, even if their names are hidden from the annals, just as their corpses are buried in this desert. Hreinasta, the Pure One—the divine primordial goddess who turned her back on me—declared their names forgotten, her decree transforming their brotherhood into a cautionary tale. The histories recall little of those siblings, but the stories claim that while their appearances were mirror images, the brothers were polar opposites, each one jealous of the other. In the first days, the Sivatag was a lush beauty teaming with life, but the twins waged their war on this cursed land. Nothing within their reach survived the battle, and when the twin gods died, so did the land. A stain upon the realm to honor their shame.

It's why what I seek was hidden here. It was bound by magic and cast into the sands, and even if one could navigate this wasteland, what I search for is impossible to find. No living soul knows where it landed. Only the dead keep it company, and they cannot guide me. All they can do is welcome me with brittle arms when I succumb to the heat, and it won't be long before I join their eternal slumber. Dehydration has become my constant friend, and as I stumble through the sand, a hollow ache eats at my chest. I cannot call upon the gods for aid. Hreinasta abandoned me, ensuring no god will ever answer my prayers, and while I don't regret the actions that caused her shunning, I feel the absence of her blessing. I never realized how empty and dangerous the world was without the gods' grace.

Hreinasta is not the only deity our realm worships, but the Pure One is our greatest treasure. When she rejected me, the rest followed suit, and I have no one to ask for help as the sun eats at my skin. I cannot even beseech the god of death for aid. Hreinasta outlawed his cult when the realm was still young, but no one knows why. Some say it's because she loved him, but in his cruelty, he spurned her, inspiring her pledge to purity. Some believe his evil so outweighed her goodness that she refused to allow his malice to affect her flock. Still, others say they are siblings, and like the nameless twins, their falling out was so infinite that Hreinasta emerged as the ruler and obliterated him from history. Whatever the reason, his name is never spoken. It is forgotten, and worshiping even the memory of his spirit is forbidden. No deity governs the afterlife; therefore, no one will answer when I plead for death to avoid me.

But I cannot die. Not yet. This is only the first trial of my impossible journey. The Sivatag is merely the beginning of a daunting quest I refuse to fail. Worse fates await me if I escape this desert, but I must survive… for him. This is all for him. A thief who's only sin was stealing my heart and offering his in return.

"Please," I croak, my throat raw after weeks of disuse. I don't know his name, the man I beg for help. He's simply The Stranger. Unnaturally tall and handsome, his appearance was both elderly and youthful, his black hair and white eyes adding to his mystery. He stank of a dark and ancient magic, but he appeared in my time of desperation.

"My child," he'd said as he captured my frail hands in his powerful fists. "Give me your faith, and I'll return to you what was lost."

I shouldn't have believed him. I should have fled, for the more he spoke, the more he frightened me. Yet his solid white eyes stared into my crystal blues as he whispered a promise I wanted, no needed, to hear, and instead of fleeing, I listened. I obeyed. I accepted that handsome yet terrifying stranger's help, and because of him, I'll die in the Sivatag.

"Please," I cry without tears. There's no water in my dehydrated body to spill. No words beyond the simple plea, but he knows what I ask. He has to.

"You're not weak, my child." The Stranger's haunting voice whispers in my mind.

"Please."

"You know the agreement. You must do this on your own."

"I can't." I sink to my knees in the burning sand.

"Are you negating our covenant? Are you losing faith in my promise?"

"No."

"Then complete this task. It's the only way I can help you in the end."

"You can't help me if I'm dead." I cough on the dust.

"You won't die. You're stronger than you know."

"No, I'm not," I argue.

"Then lay down and give up." Even his harsh words sound beautiful.

"No."

"There she is. I knew you hadn't lost yourself."

I force myself to a stand, scanning the dunes for any sign of hope. "Promise me I won't die."

"Move, child."

The Stranger's voice vanishes, leaving me empty once again. After Hreinasta rejected me, the realm turned hostile. No one looks at me. No one speaks to me, which is of little consequence because I can't bear conversing with the living. The man I long to talk to is dead, and if I can't speak to him, then I prefer silence. His fate was my fault, yet he was the one punished. This solitude, this despair, this desert. This is my atonement, my debt to be paid. Only The Stranger bothers to acknowledge me, but his voice appears in my mind. His conversations never fall on my ears, but I hear him all the same. I ignore the implications of our unnatural communication. No mortal has the power to invade another's brain, which means my dark companion is either far more dangerous than I suspect or my grief has driven me to insanity. I saw him only once during our first encounter, heard him once, and I'm probably a fool for believing his promise, but I have to. If I don't, I have nothing. My thief has nothing.

I order my limbs to move, and while The Stranger cannot aid me—my faith must be absolute until I've found all I search for—I have a sudden sense in which direction to travel.

"Thank you," I whisper. The Stranger doesn't answer, but he doesn't need to. I see it. There, on the horizon, is a darkness that doesn't belong in this unending sameness. I shuffle toward it. The journey over those last miles feels as if it takes decades, but just as my blistered skin threatens to peel from my body, I arrive at the dark stain. It's an opening in the sand, a gateway lost in the desert, and my heart can feel it. It's here.

———————

MY BREATH FOGS as the frigid air burns my overheated skin. The instant I stepped within the gate, darkness swallowed me, the extreme temperatures shocking my system. It's cold. Too cold. Evil dwells in these walls. Dark magic stained the desert heat here, and I descend deep into the earth as the icy wind bites my skin. The coolness should be a welcomed blessing, but its aggression freezes the warmth in my lungs with every breath. Breathing stings my throat, and I decide I would rather burn under the Sivatag sun than endure this frozen death. This blackness is thick with malice, with magic so corrupt I fear I'll have no soul left when I emerge... if I emerge. The ice in this tomb makes no promise of survival. It only whispers pain and a frost-entombed slumber.

As I stumble down the steep staircase, I'm careful not to touch the walls. I tripped when I first entered the stairwell and made the mistake of grabbing the stones for support. The frozen blocks adhered to my flesh, and when I yanked my palm free, the outermost layer of my skin ripped off. The torn flesh will remain forever cemented to the wall, and the pain is unlike anything I've experienced, so I cradle my hand to my chest as I repeat his name over and over. He's why I'm here. He's why I willingly suffer, and so his name has become my prayer. I recite the syllables that are all that remain of the thief. The sound is my mantra, my reason to survive. So, I speak his name over and over and over and over—

The stairs come to an abrupt end, sending me sprawling, and my knees crack against the floor. My worn pants shield my skin from the frozen ground, but they do nothing to soften the impact. I have no tears left, yet I can't stop the soft sob that escapes my lips. I cry at the pain in my body. At the pain trapped in my memory, that gods damned memory. I mourn his suffering. A suffering so visceral and savage and slow, that no matter how the Sivatag tortures me, it'll never compare to what he endured. How he screamed and bled because of me.

I pray his name again. I won't stop reciting it until I'm dead. The dark magic they used and the absence of the god of death means there's no eternity for him. There's no afterlife where I'll see his face, kiss his lips, feel his arms. If I leave this world, we both end, and my stubbornness won't allow that.

So, with shaking limbs, I stand and walk. I walk and walk and walk. I freeze. I ache. I walk. The earth swallows me whole. The blackness eats at my sanity, and only when I've given up hope does the darkness lighten. I can barely move, the blood in my veins sluggish with this frost, but my feet refuse to surrender. The dimness turns an unnatural blue, and I follow it as fast as my battered body allows. It takes an eternity. It takes only seconds.

The blue light hurts my eyes, and I blink as I enter the central chamber of this underground tomb. Magic consumed this place, turning the desert cold and the sand to stone. I squint as my vision adjusts, and when it finally clears, I see where the light emanates from.

My cry is a chilling song of heartbreak and solace. It's here. What I seek is here, and I move so fast, I stumble at the base of the altar. My knees crack against the stone, but I don't register the impact. I feel nothing save the relief at finding it and the terror this object evokes. For a second, I'm no longer in a freezing tomb but in the past, standing before him as they begin, as he screams.

"Calm yourself." The voice is so quiet, I assume it's my imagination. Even if it's my mind conjuring The Stranger, it anchors me to the present, and I push to a stand.

I stare down at the altar, afraid to touch it. To touch him. I hate myself for being a coward. He wasn't a coward. He screamed, but not because he was weak. He greeted his punishment with a dignified rage, regretting nothing despite our brutal outcome. No, he was brave, his gaze never leaving mine so I wouldn't be afraid. I forced myself to watch everything they did to him so he wouldn't be alone. It took a long time, magic keeping him conscious to prevent oblivion from softening his suffering. He was awake until the bitter end, and I saw the agony and sorrow and love in his eyes until they blinked shut for the final time. Cowardice never marred his features, and I won't be weak now when he was remarkably strong.

With a fortifying breath, I pick the object up, knowing the frost will hurt, but I welcome the pain if it means I can hold part of him. Because of the ice, it's perfectly preserved. The blood is as crimson as the day it was spilled. I scream as black magic shoots through my flesh, but I clutch it to my chest, all the same, pressing the icy surface to my cheek so I can feel him through the ache.

I've finally found his second severed body part, and I cling to his leg, enduring the sting of its curse. Tears flood my cheeks as I embrace his thigh, the drops melting his skin where they land. It's just one leg. A single fragment of his once powerful form, stretching from hip to foot, but it's a piece of him. Along with his torso that I rescued from Hreinasta's holy fire, I have more of him than I did yesterday. I can do this because his love gave me faith. His training forged a warrior in my soul, and his death hardened my resolve. I'll find the rest of his scattered bones. I don't care how long it takes, how far I have to travel, or how much evil I must battle. I'll recover every severed limb, and then? Then I'll learn if The Stranger was telling the truth. If he'll keep his promise, or if I'm simply a foolish girl so desperate for hope that I've placed my trust in a madman.

THE OFFERING

SEASON OF THE HARVEST, CYCLE 78909

I was only ten cycles old when my parents offered me as a potential vessel to Hreinasta's temple. My father was a city magistrate, a man of immense wealth and prestige, and my mother had birthed him seven children. My older brothers would inherit his power. My sisters were betrothed to men who would further elevate our station, but many judged my family for not offering one of their offspring as a sacrifice to the gods. So when I was born, my future was clear. My siblings had their places in this world. They were on the cusp of bringing my father greater affluence, but I was destined for a holier purpose.

It's an honor to be chosen as an acolyte, though, and each god demands respect and worship, but Hreinasta? The primordial goddess accepts only the purest and most beautiful girls to be raised as her potential vessels, and my mother locked me away until my tenth birthday so that I might appeal to her. I was given every luxury my family could afford, but I was kept separate. The most prolific female tutors were charged with my education, and I was fed by the choicest cuts of meat and ripest fruits. But I was always alone, forgotten in my own home like treasure hidden away for safe keeping.

With my raven black hair and my crystal blue eyes, I was lovely even as a child. I was smart and healthy, devoted to my prayers, and my parents knew Hreinasta would choose me.

At the birth of mankind, the gods journeyed to Earth to live among their creations. Legend tells that when their feet first touched the dirt, the land bloomed with blessing, and ever since, Szent has been the capital of the realm, the high holy city. Every dwelling across the continent, from the greatest cities to the smallest villages, possesses shrines to the deities, but Szent houses the only temples the gods dwell in. Some temples are extensive, their followers forming entire communes, while some are so small only a single priest tends the altar.

Sato, the goddess of the harvest, farming, and livestock, has the largest cult. Her acolytes reject all wealth and outside ties when they enter her fields. They remain within her grace until they die, many creating new families, and their children often pledge their lives and fate to her provision. Some choose to leave her fields when they come of age at twenty-one, and some pledge their futures to other gods, but Sato is not jealous. Her followers never go hungry, and those who leave go with her blessing. Her acolytes live completely off the land, for Sato is kind, just, and loving, her harvest always overflowing. It's why Szent hasn't witnessed famine for centuries.

Valka, the god of war, is another deity whose cult is vast. Soldiers, assassins, guards, warriors, executioners. They all bow to his discipline, trained from adolescence in the art of bloodshed. Blasphemous as it is, I hate his sect. I despise Valka. It was his hands that broke my spirit and ruined my life. I refuse to speak his name.

Dozens of other gods dwell in Szent. The god of wine. The wed god and goddess of love, their power split between them as they bless all marriages pledged in their name. The goddess of children and family. The god of the weather. All holy. All worshiped, adored, served. Except for the nameless death. He has no temple. The land where his shrine once stood is now only blackened earth and rubble. It's forbidden to set foot on that scorched dirt. Hreinasta destroyed his altar when she banished his name from history, and despite the centuries, the ravaged land has never recovered. It's as black and singed as it was the day the Pure One obliterated it.

With the exception of the nameless death, it's the highest honor to serve the gods, to see them in the flesh, but my father refused to pledge his lineage to anyone but the almighty. Hreinasta, the high goddess, the first. Her cult is the most devoted. The virgin reigns over all, as she is the only remaining primordial after Death's destruction. When the gods first set foot in Szent, she lingered long enough to choose a vessel. She feared that her virtue would be tested if she dwelled among men, so she gathered the most beautiful women to her side. She confirmed their virginity, and after living alongside them for a week, she chose one to house her spirit. Hreinasta's physical body returned to the realm of the gods, but her spirit remained on earth inside her host. Ever since that fateful day, her temple raises the loveliest women to await her choosing. Her acolytes remain untouched until their twenty-first birthdays. Only then can she inhabit them, and while she resides within them, they may never feel a man's touch. If the goddess doesn't bless them with her spirit by the time they reach thirty cycles, they become virgin priestesses, tasked with raising the next generation of vessels. Hreinasta inhabits and vacates bodies as she chooses, lingering only until the flesh shows the first signs of age. For a deity sworn to purity, she's obsessed with youth and beauty. It's why her dwelling must always be filled with potential hosts, each girl more pleasing and younger than her last.

If chosen as a vessel, the acolyte experiences worshiped luxury. To serve Hreinasta is the ultimate honor, to be her host is the sign of transcendent favor. A favor my father craved for his family name.

On my tenth birthday, my parents delivered me to the offering ceremony. My feet didn't touch the dirt, servants bearing me within an enclosed litter so that no man saw my face. I wasn't allowed to emerge until we set foot inside the temple where only women served. My father and brothers were the only men I'd ever laid eyes on, but they kept their distance to avoid any accidental contact. Not even my important father was permitted to enter Hreinasta's inner court, so my mother, dressed in all her finery, led me to kneel in nervous prayer. I was finally going to look upon a god. She might choose me, honor me, love me. Her choice would force me to leave the home I knew, the family I loved, but not being chosen? That was a shame worse than death. I could never face my parents if Hreinasta rejected me, and so I prayed fervently for her favor.

And then the room stilled as Hreinasta's vessel entered, and the sight left me breathless. She was tall and strong, with tan and intoxicatingly smooth skin embellished with fragrant oils and sparkling jewels. Her white dress contrasted her coloring, and her long hair hung in intricate braids. She walked as if she wasn't of this world but merely floating through it, and my youthful heart longed to be like her. I believed I wanted to contain such beauty, for I was innocent then. I knew not what I craved.

We waited in silence as the vessel moved fluidly about the room, stopping before each kneeling offering. She chose some, and their joy was radiant. She rejected others, and their despair was so thick it tainted the air. I was the last offering she observed, and she paused before me, studying my face. I could barely control my anxiety, and my mother clutched my hand as we knelt, whether to still her nerves or mine, I didn't know. My heart sank. It beat wildly. It didn't beat at all. She was taking too long. She didn't want me. I'd failed my family, and we would leave in shame.

Suddenly, the vessel bent forward and gripped my jaw

with her velvet-soft fingers. She smelled of flowers and spice, and her golden eyes turned my insides liquid. She was so beautiful; her grip was both painful and pleasant, and my mother gasped beside us. She had graced no other girl with her touch.

"Divine," she whispered, Hreinasta speaking through her, and my soul exploded. "I accept your offering." She left without another word, but I knew. That was the moment I realized I would be her next vessel. She'd chosen me to house the Pure One's spirit.

TWO

R emember," The Stranger says, "while the sun travels the sky, you'll be able to leave the temple of your own free will, but as soon as the shadows swallow it, you'll be bound within its walls for all eternity."

I tear my sight away from the ruins and stare at The Stranger. He stands beside me in a shredded yet intimidating black cloak, his solid white eyes peering out from beneath the hood pulled low over his forehead. Wisps of his dark hair flutter on the breeze, and his arms hang crossed over his broad chest. He's a blackened stain on the eternal green of this lush jungle, and his presence is both a surprise and a comfort. I didn't expect to see him again, but after my days of solitude in the burning sands, his unnerving presence unexpectedly fortifies my spirit.

I remember little of my escape from Sivatag. I was submerged in the icy tomb, and then I was wandering through the endless heat. Stealing his leg seemed to break whatever evil had created the freeze, and with nearly frozen limbs, I stumbled through the sand until the desert gave way to life. The gods have abandoned me, yet I survived the scorched death. I emerged alive, clinging to what little of him remains, and before I threw myself into the creek where I left my horse, before I drank my fill and collapsed, I opened the heavily chained chest. I laid his leg to rest beside his torso and locked the box, unable to stand the sight of him in pieces. Then I slept. How many days, I don't know. I ceased to exist.

"Whose temple was this?" I ask The Stranger. He cannot help me beyond his promise. This journey is mine and mine alone; my faith required to be absolute, but when he promised to return what I lost if I found his scattered bones, he'd captured my hands. Something happened when his skin touched mine. A darkness dove deep into my muscles, ensnared my organs, flowed within my veins. He swore he couldn't help me, so I feared his touch was a curse. Yet from that moment, I could sense my thief's limbs calling to me. His shattered body, his broken heart. He wants me to find him, to make him whole. Or perhaps it's our vows that guide me, and that's how I came to stand before these ruins. Not even death can part us, for we are one.

"Whose do you think?" The Stranger's eerie hum answers. This is the second time I've seen him in person, but his visage is no less frightening. So, I look back to the crumbling temple hidden deep within the jungle, its broken stones entombed by vines.

"Death?"

"Death," he agrees. "No other god would leave his holy ground so empty."

"It's so far from civilization."

"Hreinasta wouldn't dare set foot close to his shame, and the realm followed suit. It's why the jungle surged around it. One day, the temple will disappear completely, a mound of greenery its tombstone."

"I should go before the sun climbs higher." I start to move, but his serious tone halts me in my tracks.

"My child, when Death left this tainted ground, the shrine called to the darkness, desperate to fill its walls. Absent power, an evil took up residence here without resistance." I stare at the Stranger. Concern is written in the line of his lips, in the emptiness of his white eyes, and he continues, "The dead crowd this temple, corpses of the unfortunate souls who couldn't escape its grasp before the shadows fell. What you seek will be concealed in plain sight, just another rotting bone scattered among this evil's victims. It's why he was hidden here."

"I'll know him when I see him," I say, and I almost pray I'm right before I stop myself. The gods have turned their backs on me. I refuse to offer them anymore worship from my lips.

"I hope you will, my child, but a word of warning." He pulls his hood back so I can see his chiseled cheekbones, his black hair framing his beautiful yet hideous face. "This evil lurks in the shadows. You can escape it while the sun reigns, but the malevolence will still hunt you as you move within those walls. Do not step into any shadows, my child. I know it'll prove difficult as the trees block the moving sunlight, but my warning stands. Avoid them at all costs. Do not give it a taste of your soul."

"I'll try," I promise.

"Do not try. Do." His expression almost softens. "I've grown fond of you, and your quest is only at its birth. It would be a shame to lose you so soon."

I nod, unsure if his words should encourage or alarm me. I linger amidst the foliage, but after a long silence, it's clear his warning is complete, so I turn toward the temple.

I DON'T KNOW what I expected to find inside this forgotten shrine to Death, but nothingness wasn't it. The Stranger's warning rings like a gong in my brain, but only peace and sunlight wait for me in the rubble. And bones. Hundreds of bleached piles huddle in corners and tangle in the vines, and it takes me a minute to realize that the human remains are concentrated in areas where the shadows fall first. It seems The Stranger's concern was well founded, and I swallow with a dry throat at the task before me. I'm hunting a single body part among thousands. Hidden in plain sight, yet impossible to find, much like his thigh in the Sivatag. Cast aimlessly, where no one would discover him.

I grit my teeth and leap over a small shadow created by a fallen boulder. That's why they hid him here. One could search for a thousand cycles and still not identify which bones are his. Cycles that trespassers don't have, for the moment the sun sets, the evil hiding in the shadows owns you. You can never leave, and judging by the piled skeletons in my path, many have wandered into these walls believing darkness wouldn't trap them, only to die alone in a jungle where no one could hear their screams. I'm well acquainted with evil. It craves destruction and pain, misery and violence. Whatever took possession of this temple when Death was banished has spent cycles beckoning travelers to its doorsteps. Each of these bodies had a reason to venture to this unholy ground. A reason encouraged by this entity so it might feed its hunger. That thought makes me shiver despite the humidity. Did my quest bring me to danger's mouth, or was it this evil tricking yet another sacrifice?

I say his name out loud, pushing thoughts of him to the forefront of my mind to drown out the dread. I say it once, twice, ten times, twenty. I picture his face, his hands, the flaw-less skin that stretched over a broad chest and abs. I imagine how its softness felt pressed against mine, the way his fingers pushed through mine. I picture his scars, his hair, even his feet. My memory recalls the sleek and dangerous clothes that hugged his powerful frame. It remembers him gloriously bare. *Thirty times, forty times, sixty.* Over and over I speak it because one day I woke to find my memory of his voice muddled. I couldn't recall its gravel, or how deep it sounded when he laughed, when he groaned, when he whispered his love into my ear. It was the first thing I noticed about him. How rich and low his voice was. It rattled my chest, embedded itself in my bones, and I can no longer remember it. The sound abandoned me, so I speak his name. I visualize him from his crown to his soles, and not the body I search for that lies in ruthless pieces. The body that was whole and imperfectly perfect. The body that worshiped mine. *Seventy-five times, ninety, one hundred.*

One hundred and twenty repeats later, I'm still no closer to finding him. Nothing calls to me. All I see are the hundreds who died before me and the empty spots where thousands will die after me. Dust and decay fill my nostrils, and then it strikes me. The air is silent. The sounds of the jungle have vanished. I see the greenery peeking through the collapsing walls, but I hear nothing. Not a bird, not an insect, not the wind.

"Stranger?" Panic lodges in my throat when he doesn't answer. He sometimes ignores me, but this silence is different. He's not ignoring me. He can't hear me. I'm utterly alone, cut off from everything outside these ruins, and as the sun flies across the sky, my time races with it. I leap over another shadow as fear claws at my throat. The day is fading, and I don't know where to search. Time behaves unnaturally here. The sun is farther than it should be, and his warning crashes into me tenfold. I'd wondered how so many could lose their freedom within these walls, but now I understand. Time obeys no laws in this temple. Its master is the evil that creeps ever closer.

I want to run, to race through the rubble in search of his bones, but anxiety cannot steal my control. I can't cave to insanity. I must be smart and act with intention, so I close my eyes. I picture his face, his chiseled jaw, his brown irises with their flecks of gold. My memory gazes into them, hones in on them, and begs them to lead me.

"I'm here," I whisper. "I've come for you like I promised I would. Guide my feet." I pause for a long moment, but I sense nothing. The evil has isolated my soul, hiding everything from me save the sight of the sun slipping lower through the trees. *Slipping, slipping, slipping.*

I move through eroded hallways, crouch under fallen pillars, and scale protruding boulders, but all the bones look the same. All the rotting corpses resemble each other. I'll never find him. For all I know, I've passed his limbs one hundred times over and never noticed—

I yelp as the ground gives way, and I collapse to my knees with a painful crack of bones, both mine and the dead's. My leg falls through an opening, but my foot thankfully lands in a patch of sunlight. One inch to the left, though. One centimeter to the right, and it would have touched the shadows filling this new hole.

I slap a hand over my lips and sit frozen in fear as an unseen thread pulls at my chest. My heart sinks like a battered ship in a storm. I know where he is.

I carefully withdraw my foot and peer through the opening. I hadn't noticed at first, but the collapse here is worse than in the rest of the temple. The vines that braid through the ruins are absent, as if this section hasn't stood exposed to the elements for long. My heart sinks further. This is where they laid him to rest. They placed him in the lowest part of the ruins and then toppled the stones above him. The only way I'll retrieve what they hid is if I descend into the shadows.

I shiver and check the sun's position. I won't be trapped until it sets, but The Stranger instructed me to avoid even the smallest shadow. I don't know what will happen if the lurking evil tastes my flesh, and I curse myself for not asking him to explain his warning.

Swinging to my knees, I peer into the shadows, and from what I can see, the cracked opening descends into a cavernous void. My guess is this was originally a cellar, and I pull my head back and scan my surrounding. With how fast the day is dying, I don't have time to clear the rubble to gain more sunlight. The fallen slabs of stone are too heavy for me to shift, anyway. I only have two options: admit defeat or brave the evil. I picture his face and know. He would never admit defeat. He never did. Neither shall I.

"I'm sorry," I say as I glance at where I left the Stranger in the jungle. "If I don't make it out, thank you." And then I drop into the blackness.

Chaos erupts around me in the form of a vicious wind. It batters my body and steals my breath, and I cough as my feet slip, the air's force too strong. The darkness is hazy, and I can barely see my own hands as they crawl over the floor. I think I'm screaming, but the violence silences any cries I make. It strips me of my voice, my hope, my courage. It replaces my every emotion with fear, and I want to lie down and die.

One, two, three times. I say his name even though I can't hear the words. *Ten times, eleven, twelve.* I crawl blindly forward. *Twenty times.* I do not stop. I never stop.

The thread in my chest tugs harder. Our vows, our promise, our love. It cannot be silenced. We're bound even in death, and that's why I still sense him. I move despite the pain. Despite the evil salivating to claim me. I've granted this entity more than a taste. I've given it my entire being, and it is ravenous. Its hunger pulses against my skin, through my bones, and into my soul. Its desire is impatient, raging that it must wait until nightfall to devour me whole, but damn the gods, it will wait. It cannot have me yet.

I lose track of how long I crawl as the wind whips and tugs at me, but suddenly my heart stutters. It misses a beat. And then a second and a third, and my fingers shoot out before me, searching the stone for what I seek. Minutes fly by, and my fingertips encounter nothing but dust. Despair rattles my chest. I need to find him. We're running out of time.

"Gods," I yelp as my knuckles brush against coarse fabric.

I seize it and peel away the burlap until I feel flesh. Cool flesh, and I don't need to see to know these hands. How many times did they wrap around my fingers, stroke my hair, caress my face? I would recognize them anywhere. I found him.

Folding his hands inside the fabric, I fling myself back toward the hole of light. It's dimmer now, and panic tightens my chest. The sun is too low; the daylight disappearing too fast. I scramble to my feet as the wind fights to drag me down, to keep me in its eternal embrace, but I refuse to surrender. This hateful world ripped him from me once before. Not again. Never again.

I push faster, tossing his hands up to the main level before climbing out to join him. Absent the wind, the silence is almost deafening, and my eyes scan the horizon. The sun is dangerously close to setting. I have minutes. Maybe less.

I launch into a run, barreling through the ruins as I disturb centuries of sedentary bones. I don't care to avoid the shadows, but each time my limbs pass through them, the evil pulls at my soul. Its rage bleeds into my veins. This entity refuses to relinquish me, and as if willed by its greed, the sun descends faster, forcing me to flee through more and more shadows. This time, when I scream, I hear my terrified voice.

And then I see the exit. Clutching his hands tighter to my breast, I push my aching legs to maintain the brutal pace. My lungs burn with exertion. My brow spills sweat. The wind howls through the darkening hallways as the sun burns her last rays. I'm so close, but I won't make it.

"Run!"

My gaze snaps to the temple's entrance. The Stranger hovers on the opposite side of the threshold, safe from the evil's grasp.

"Damn it, child, run!" His hands extend to me, his fingertips hovering just shy of the line.

I can barely breathe as I race for his open arms. I concentrate on his white eyes, and even though they're solid, pupilless orbs, I recognize the panic in them. It spurs me on, but then the sun sets. The light flashes one last time, and I'm too late. Through the haze of desperation, I stare in disbelief at The Stranger as he does the unthinkable. The dying sunlight still touches the threshold. One more second and it'll be gone, but he shoves his hand over the line. His fingers push as far as the light allows, and I dive. I throw myself at him, one arm clutching the bundle at my breast, the other outstretched. My fingers clasp his, and he yanks me hard just as the world goes dark.

I slam with a harsh thud against his chest, and we topple to the jungle floor. I can't stop the sobs that wrack my body, but to my surprise, The Stranger wraps his muscular arms around me. He says nothing as I convulse. He merely lays there and lets me cry as I catch my breath.

"You aren't allowed to help me," I whisper into his chest, my fingers clutching his cloak to assure myself that I'm safe, that I'm in his embrace and not bound to the shadows.

"I didn't." His ribs rattle my cheeks. "I simply held your hand."

"Thank you." Relief floods my words.

"We should go." He abruptly stands without ceremony, hoisting me to my feet as if I weigh nothing. "The evil has tasted you. We need to put as much distance as possible between us and it."

"It's all right," I say, clinging to the Stranger's cloak with one fist and hugging his severed hands with my other. "I don't think it liked what it tasted."

THE MEETING
SEASON OF ICE, CYCLE 78919

I jerked awake, adrenaline coursing through my body as my heart beat an uneasy rhythm. A distant commotion played out in the temple's lower levels, but the sound wasn't what woke me. It was the overwhelming sense that I wasn't alone. That someone was locked in my room with me.

Fear pulsed through my limbs, and I bit the inside of my mouth to keep silent. Hreinasta's temple had protected me for the past ten cycles, but I'd slept alone my entire life. I knew what solitude felt like. I was intimately acquainted with the presence of every priestess who served me, and the being hovering at the edge of my consciousness wasn't one I recognized. It wasn't someone allowed to be there, and for long and terrifying seconds, I prepared to die. I prepared for my innocence to be ripped from me, but as I prayed to Hreinasta for salvation, the presence didn't move. It didn't speak. It simply hovered in the shadows.

Gathering my courage, I opened my eyes and scanned the darkness. The hour was well past midnight, but as the commotion receded further into the temple, the feeling persisted. Someone was watching me, and when my sight finally found him, the earth shifted.

NICOLE SCARANO

A dark shape huddled in the corner, almost invisible inside the shadows. I might have missed him if I hadn't committed that entire room to my memory, but I'd memorized every angle, every curve, every imperfection of those chambers, and his mass protruded from the wall like a looming demon. He was dressed in the darkest black, his raven hair the same inky shade. Even his eyes were dark, as if he was born and bred of the night, molded to hide within the shadows. Despite his crouched position, I could tell he was massive, tall and broad and muscled. I'd never seen a man this close beside my father, but that was cycles ago. I could gaze upon him and my brothers when they prayed in the temple courtyard, but no man, not even my own flesh and blood, could touch my skin since I was pledged to Hreinasta. Men were forbidden from entering her inner sanctuary, and as a result, I'd never witnessed the finer details of the masculine features.

I scrambled backward across my mattress at the realization that a man hovered feet from my bed. My back slammed into the wall with a loud slap, and I opened my mouth to scream.

"Please, don't." He threw up his hands in a placating gesture, and I froze, my alarm lodging in my throat. His voice. Its deep rumble, even spoken in a hushed tone, was so fierce, so rough, that it shook the air as he pleaded. The sound rattled my chest, its gravel vibrating my bones, and my alarm heightened. It was as if a demon had whispered. It was as if beauty had come to life as words. I wanted him to speak again, to push that deepness against my skin and shake me to my core. It was both cruelty and seduction, jagged edges and blooming roses. I should have screamed. I needed to scream, to escape this intruder, but instead, I hovered on the edge of my mattress, craving the melody of his voice.

"I won't hurt you." He emerged from the shadows, and a tear escaped my eye to trail down my face. "I promise you're safe from me. I just need a place to hide."

Embarrassment flushed my cheeks, but I couldn't stop the

28

tears. I didn't know how to interact with men, and being forced into one's presence in the supposed safety of my own room shoved me off kilter. His closeness was overwhelming. It made it hard to breathe, and I knew I should run. I should have screamed for help, but I was frozen. I cried in fear. I cried because his voice was everything. It reached inside my soul, rewriting my definition of perfection. It strangled my erratically beating heart and coated my mind with its harshness. That sound. It could burn the world to ash with its power, and it terrified me how it erased the wariness of men that servitude had engrained in my being.

"I'm sorry." He moved forward, thought better of his actions, and then recoiled. "It's all right. I won't touch you, see." He sat hard against the wall and threw up his hands in surrender. "Please don't cry."

I hated myself for how easily his voice convinced me to obey, but I sank against my pillows anyway, mimicking his posture as I wiped the tears from my cheeks. From that angle, I realized just how large the young intruder was. He was a monster in the shadows, and I dreaded seeing him stand to his full height. He would tower over me.

"What are you doing here?" I finally gathered the courage to ask after minutes of tense silence. "Men aren't allowed in the inner sanctum."

"I know." He flashed me a smile, and my heart forgot to beat. His voice might have been rough and dangerous, but his smile? It was the sun. It shone with blinding beauty, and I blinked, afraid to look at the inviting curve of his lips. I was untouched, untainted, unmarred. Even my thoughts were pure, but staring at his smile was an unadulterated sin. I didn't realize an expression could hold that much magic.

"I'm pledged to the house of Varas," he continued.

"God of Thieves," I whispered.

"Yes." He smiled. He needed to stop smiling.

"If you belong to the Thief, why are you here?"

"To join his cult, his acolytes train under the masters for cycles. For our final test, we must steal an object from one of the other gods and bring it to his altar. He rejects your offering if you're caught, but if you are successful, he welcomes you into his guild."

"You're here to rob Hreinasta... do you plan to kidnap me?" My panic flooded back tenfold.

He chuckled, and I involuntarily leaned into the sound as if I might capture it whole and save it for eternity.

"I suspect Varas would be highly displeased if I brought you as my offering." He raised an eyebrow teasingly. "You were asleep, so I planned to hide here until the guards stopped their search. There was a slight wrinkle in my plan downstairs. The greater the god, the higher the honor the Thief gifts us, so while looting the other temples is a far easier feat, stealing from Hreinasta reaps the greatest reward. No one has ever attempted to plunder her sanctuary. The punishment inflicted on a man caught within her walls is unspeakable, but alas, what good is life without challenge? I intend to be the first to lay an object from the Pure One's inner sanctum at my god's feet. Then I'll be the greatest thief Varas has ever blessed."

"But you've been caught." I gestured to my chest.

"Have I?" The twinkle in his dark eyes lit up his beautiful face. The shadows cloaked him in mystery, but what little I saw convinced me that nothing in this world would ever compare to this intruder.

We drifted back into silence as I studied him. He remained pressed against the furthest wall to assure me he had no intentions of disrespecting my vows, and perhaps it was my naivety, but I trusted him. I was still terrified of breathing the same air as a man, but I knew the thief wouldn't harm me.

Realizing sleep wasn't in my future until he completed his mission, I threw my legs off the mattress. Careful to wrap my robe securely around my body so that my skin remained hidden, I walked to the chest at the foot of the bed. My anxiety flared at being so close to him, but I pushed down the rising sickness and lifted the lid, removing one of my robes. All Hreinasta's priestesses and acolytes wore white to signify their purity, but the potential vessels' dresses were inlaid with pure gold threads. White for virtue. Gold for priceless. The fabric was spun luxury, each dress tailored perfectly to the vessel, but their coloring was unmistakable. White and gold. Hreinasta's chosen.

I turned toward him, careful to keep out of reach, and set the garment on the floor. I retreated slowly, never turning my back to him, and when my calves hit the mattress, I sat, curling my legs beneath me so that not even my feet were on display.

"Offer that to your Thief," I said with an experimental smile, and as a reward, his entire face lit up. The room was dark, but his expression was the sun, bathing the winter air with its warmth. "No one will doubt where it came from." I shrugged as if it wasn't the most terrifying yet exhilarating encounter of my life.

"You won't get in trouble if it goes missing?"

"It's an old dress." I shook my head. "It no longer fits." He couldn't see the details of my frame with my outer robe wrapped tight, but my childhood beauty had morphed into the garden of womanhood. With every passing season, the current vessel watched me with more and more hunger. I knew it was Hreinasta anxiously awaiting my twenty-first birthday when she could finally inhabit my body. I grew tall and lean. My hips curved enticingly. The priestesses had designed new garments to protect my modesty after my breasts spilled out of the old ones. My pink lips were full, my blue eyes like priceless jewels, contrasting my midnight black hair. My food was carefully monitored, and my bathing rituals endless. For a goddess who devoted her life to purity and lived eternally as a virgin, Hreinasta certainly craved elegance and sensuality. Her vessels were only the most exquisite women the realm had to offer, and as I grew more and more beautiful with each cycle, it became painfully obvious I was her next host. She was merely biding her time until I was ripe for the taking. She'd set the law herself, declaring she would possess no woman before the age of twenty-one, and I was twenty. One more cycle until I was no longer myself but divinity bound in human flesh.

"Thank you." The thief stood, breaking my reverie, and I gasped, flinching involuntarily. "It's all right." He instantly recoiled. "I simply meant to accept your gift." He pointed at the gown I set too far for him to reach sitting down.

"I..." My cheeks flushed crimson, and I thanked Hreinasta for the darkness. "I know. It's just... it's nothing." Embarrassment flooded my veins. I hoped it would drown me.

"Go on. Say it." He pushed as he stepped forward to grab the garment. "Don't be shy on my account." His words only made my blush deepen.

"You're the tallest person I've ever seen," I said, his kind presence inspiring my bravery.

He threw his head back and laughed, and I wanted to live inside that sound. I hoped it followed me all the days of my life.

"Yes, I'm tall," he said. "Varas' priests almost turned me away when I first arrived. They claimed a boy my height could never work as a thief. I've spent the last fifteen cycles proving them wrong."

"So, you're good?"

"The best." The pride in his smile bloomed so strongly that I felt proud of him. "Well, I will be once I lay this offering upon the altar."

"I'm glad to have helped." I longed to step closer and get a better look at his face.

"Thank you, dear priestess." He bowed with an exaggerated flourish before turning to leave, and I was suddenly desperate to make him stay. It was foolish. It was a sin, but that mysterious man with the gravel deep voice had captivated me. As long as I didn't touch him, my vow was safe.

"How did you get in here?" I blurted before he reached the window, and he turned to meet my gaze. In the moon's light, I finally saw him in clear definition, and the sight ruined me. His face obliterated my heart. His eyes destroyed my spirit, and in an instant, the thief re-wrote my future. He stole my life and twisted it to his will. He was tall and broad, and his black hair was shaved close on the sides but left longer on the top. Flecks of gold swam in his brown eyes, and a long scar ran through the left side of his lips, top to bottom, as if someone tried to sever the corner of his mouth. It was unsettling to look at, and most people probably found it off-putting, but I had the sudden urge to feel the uneven skin beneath my fingers. None of the vessels had scars. We were locked away in velvet cages to keep our bodies flawless. I'd never seen someone with such a pronounced deformity, and it called my name like forbidden fruit.

"Wouldn't you like to know?" he winked, and it took me a moment to remember I'd asked a question. I frowned at him, and he leaned against the wall, staring at me with a curious smirk.

"So, you're one of the vessels?" he asked, and I couldn't tell if he'd decided to linger for my sake or his. Either way, a giddy surge of electricity ignited my nervous system. I'd been locked away from my siblings as a child, sequestered inside this temple throughout my adolescence. I'd never glimpsed the outside world, and now that it had come to me, I hated letting it disappear.

"Yes." I didn't tell him I was *the* vessel. The chosen one.

"What's it like? Living trapped behind these walls, never touching anyone?"

"It's an honor." I shrugged, but he glared at me as if he saw through my answer. Until that day, my belief never wavered, and I swallowed uncomfortably. I was holy and pure, selected by the primordial being herself. This honor was only gifted to the worthy, and she'd found me perfect. I devoted every waking moment to Hreinasta's service, as I had since my birth, and I believed with my entire spirit in the divinity of my path. But now? Standing in front of this enticing man who appeared a few cycles older than me, it suddenly sounded like a hollow lie. The world was at his fingertips. Every pleasure was available to him, and by this time next cycle, I would cease to exist for decades until Hreinasta abandoned my body.

"It's lonely sometimes," I added, and he nodded as if he recognized the truth. "But to serve the Pure One is a privilege." I couldn't abandon my faith completely, not even for a face more handsome than the wed gods. "One I accept gladly."

"I'm glad you're happy in your service, even if you're lonely." His words were genuine, but sadness bled through them. "Tell me your name." He demanded, and then his features pinched as if his outburst surprised him. "I'm Kaid."

"Kaid." I tasted his name, and it was more delicious than the ripest fruit on a summer's day. "Will you promise me something, Kaid?"

"Anything you want." His eyes spoke the truth. He meant every word.

"Tell no one you saw me. Tell no one I gave you my name."

"Then you'll tell me?"

"You must promise."

"I swear on Varas' altar." He knelt before me, and a thrill ran up my spine. "I won't tell a soul of this. Meeting you... I shall treasure it for myself."

"Sellah." I couldn't stop the smile that spread across my lips, and he looked stunned for a moment as he stared at my mouth.

"Well, Sellah." He shook his head, recovering from whatever trance had possessed him. "Now that we're acquainted and no longer strangers, you don't have to be lonely."

I desperately wanted him to be right.

"I should go." His expression sharply contradicted his words. "I can't get caught with you."

I nodded in agreement. Being caught in the temple was a punishable offense.

"Thank you, Sellah." He gestured to the dress before throwing open the window. A blast of frigid air assaulted my face, and I drew my robe tighter around my chest. Kaid seemed wholly unaffected by the icy wind, and he smiled that grin I was already addicted to.

"Who knows?" He climbed out into the snowy night, his gaze meeting mine one last time. My breath left my lungs, and he inhaled as if to capture the same air that had occupied my body. "Perhaps I'll see you again… so you don't have to be lonely." He shrugged mischievously. "I'm very good at getting into places I shouldn't."

And then he was gone, the open window the only proof he'd ever been there.

THREE

I haven't seen The Stranger since the jungle, so when the pull drags me north to a small hunting village, I find the presence of others unsettling. I haven't heard my own voice in weeks, not felt the vibrations of my vocal cords in so long that I worry they might tear if I speak above a whisper. I have not seen a human face in days save my own reflection in the streams that I refilled my water skins with. The only breathing creature I've had contact with is my horse, but he doesn't need my words, only my care. I enjoy his company, though. I wasn't raised around animals, and seeing him for the first time was like lightning to my chest. I was both in awe of his speed and terrified of his power, but now I prefer him to humans. He cares little about broken vows or mortal sins. His daily concerns are simply for the meals he'll consume, the water I'll lead him to, and my scratches behind his ears. He's all I have besides The Stranger... and the severed body in the trunk. But I never open that locked box unless it's to add another bone. I don't acknowledge it, either. It's like knives to the gut knowing that what lies inside cannot speak to me, so I don't talk to it. The memory of his voice faded despite my attempts to keep it with me, and I hate offering him mine if I cannot hear his. I miss the lightning that cracked over my skin at the sound. I miss everything about him.

After I found his hands in Death's abandoned temple, I woke the next morning to find The Stranger long gone. I never know what part of the realm to search for him. His executioners didn't provide me with a map, but The Stranger's promise stirred something in my soul. I walk without plans. I simply begin, and when I end, his scattered bones are waiting for me. So, with his hands locked away with his torso and leg, I strapped the cart to my horse and left the jungle. I didn't know where my wanderings would lead, but I'm both surprised and unnerved by the destination. This village at the base of snow consumed mountains is nothing more than a hunters' gathering. The air is all ice and sharpness, razor winds and painful breaths. It's a miserable stretch of earth, but its horrors come from the climate. No black magic hovers here, only nature.

I hate revealing myself to others, and without the thick oppression of evil that normally surrounds his preserved flesh, I'm confused about why the pull led me here. This far north, I doubt anyone will recognize me. I'm no longer the girl the gods declared an outcast and a heretic. She was soft and smooth, her hair long, her health vibrant. This Sellah is all muscle and bone, scars and ragged hair. I look nothing like the woman I used to be. She died the day he died. Sellah ceased to exist the moment his heart stopped beating, and now I simply endure. A wanderer. A godless traveler on the path of vengeance.

Still, I'm afraid of others. I witnessed firsthand how cruel mankind can be to their own, and I've chosen to spend many nights hungry rather than interact with my kind. I'm scared that outsiders will see past my dirt-caked skin to the girl who fled the gods' wrath. I worry they'll drag me before her altar and burn me alive for my betrayal, and if I die, then he's truly gone. So, I avoid civilization. I steal and hide and fight, and each time I take something that doesn't belong to me, I thank him for teaching me his knowledge and skills. My thief trained me in his god's ways; he tutored me on the darkest of nights to be like him, and it's because of his god that I'm still alive. Perhaps not all the gods have abandoned me. Maybe somewhere deep down, Varas smiles every time I play the thief, every time I honor his fallen acolyte.

But I have no choice now. His pull tugged me into the lands of eternal ice, and I cannot hover on the outskirts of the village. The cold will steal my breath in the night. The frost will plunder my animal companion for its hunger, and the unseen thread that stitched my soul to his has stilled. Its tug no longer guides my heart, but without the evil polluting the air, I don't know where to search. All I know is that as I approach, the hunters stare at me with unwelcoming glares. The North is a land reserved for those who live and die here. Outsiders aren't welcome, and only those born in the snow are given respect.

As I cross the village's threshold, a bloody altar crafted of bones and fur captures my attention. For a split second, I'm back inside Hreinasta's inner sanctum, his blood pooling on the temple floor, and I clench my eyes shut until I see swirling colors behind my lids.

"Please, no," I whisper, my voice hoarse and cracked.

"The Hunter demands blood," The Stranger's unnerving melody seeps through my brain, and though he tells me what I dread hearing, I'm relieved he hasn't abandoned me. "It is his way. It is theirs."

"But it's not mine."

"Open your eyes, child."

I obey, gagging at the sight of the crimson snow. Lovec, God of the Hunt. It's his altar that graces the village's entrance.

"All who come grant him an offering," The Stranger speaks in my mind. "He's not picky. He cares little who's veins spill in his name. All he demands is a sacrifice of blood. The North is harsh and barren and filled with beasts bred to slaughter. Humanity's survival rests on their hunters' shoulders, their skill at shedding blood the only line between life and death. Just as they bleed to feed their families, so must they bleed in service to their god." He pauses for a moment before continuing. "Do you see how they look at you? All who enter must bleed. It's blasphemy to ignore the offering."

"I am blasphemy."

"No, my child. You are a survivor."

I hate The Stranger. I hate that he's right. I hate that blood is the last thing I saw before his breathing stopped. *Red. Red. Red.* It's a color I never wish to see again.

"I'll offer him no prayer," I whisper defiantly.

"He does not need your prayer. Only your blood… or that of your beast."

I rest my palm on my horse's neck. "No. He can't have him. I'll do it."

The Stranger chuckles, but I scowl as I storm to the altar. I slip the blade from my boot and drag it gently over my fore-arm, where the slice won't hinder my movements. Crimson beads on my skin, and I tilt my arm, letting the drops roll onto the stained and frozen furs. Only three fall, but that's all I offer Lovec. I must bleed, and so I do, but he gets nothing more. *Red. Red. Red.* I hate this color.

I HAVE no coin to barter with, but currency is useless here. The North demands blood in all aspects of life, and the only payments those with lodgings and food will accept are that of flesh and bone. If they cannot eat it, carve it, or wear it, they reject its presence. I grind my teeth at their demanded price. It's much easier to steal gold than it is to hunt a beast. He taught me how to pick both pockets and locks. He did not teach me how to skin a northern elk.

My horse is my only possession of worth, but he isn't for sale. I'll make no bargains with my only friend; therefore, I have nothing to trade for a warm bed to survive the oncoming night. I have no food to fill my cramping stomach. No fire to thaw my stiff fingers. Damn Lovec and his blood demands, I'm no safer within the confines of this village than I was outside.

Villagers survey my beast as we wander in search of shelter, and I scowl at them until they look away in discomfort. Almost a cycle with only a white-eyed Stranger and a horse for company has turned me bitter.

My steps falter. *It's been almost a cycle?* How is that possible? I only knew him for the same length of time we've now been apart. A mere blink of an eye to the universe, yet every second without him is agony. How have so many seasons passed since I heard his voice? Saw his dark eyes? Felt the scar on his lip worship my body? This is why I forgot the deep tenor of his speech. Hundreds of days separate me from the last moment I listened to it. When we promised forever, I never realized the end would come so soon. I say his name. *One time. Two times. Ten.* Over and over. That I refuse to forget.

Burning orange captures my attention, and my eyes focus on a raging fire in the village square. The wood is piled high, the steepled peak reaching over my head, and it looks as if it has always burned and always will. These flames appear to belong to everyone and no one, so I lead my horse to the heat. The intensity thaws my face, and I realize just how cold I am. The sun's setting, and the night will only grow more frigid. Without this fire, I would not live to see the sun's rebirth, but perhaps that's why Lovec requires you to bleed. Maybe he keeps this blaze alive so that his people won't freeze. Fuel reserves don't surround the bonfire, nor do attendants feed its heat. It burns despite the howling wind. It rages in spite of heaven's frozen tears. None of the villagers turn me away when I sit on the logs before it. No one questions me for pulling my animal close to the warmth. Damn Lovec and his blood demands. I am safer within the confines of this village than I was outside. The Stranger chuckles. I tell him to shut up. He doesn't listen.

I JERK awake to the sound of a gut-wrenching scream. I don't remember falling asleep on the log, but my face is warm, and the fire hasn't waned despite the moon's reign. Heartbreaking wails echo off the distant mountains, and I push myself to a seat, my spine protesting from the unforgiving surface. It's a woman's voice, and I recognize that breed of sorrow. It's woven into my muscles, buried in my bones. It's the anguish of a lover's death.

I stand, my aching limbs forgotten. Soreness has become my old friend this past cycle, and I've learned to live alongside it. I search for signs of a threat, but the only sight that fills my vision is one that roots me in the snow. Suddenly, I'm no longer shivering in a hunting village but kneeling on the temple floor, his blood staining my legs as I scream for a man who can no longer hear me, for a man who was ripped to ruthless shreds. The white world of my present begins to spin. *Faster. Faster. Faster.* I'm going to be sick. I know this scene. It's my greatest nightmare. I say his name, but only once this time, because as the procession bearing a dead man's destroyed body passes me, it's the face I love—carved to pieces and lifeless—that stares back at me.

"Calm yourself, my child." The Stranger's voice slices like a sharpened blade through my panic, and my beloved's features fade from the corpse, replaced by that of a man twenty cycles my senior. My cheeks sting, and I realize I'm crying. The tears freeze to my skin, and I wipe them away as I weave my fingers through my horse's mane for comfort.

A group of hunters, armed and savage, carry the mangled hunter through the village toward Lovec's altar. A woman follows, clinging to his body, and I ache for her. The wife left behind. We are the same in that misery.

She wails as they lay him to rest atop the bloody pile of flesh and bones, and the crowd falls to their knees, praying that Lovec will accept the ultimate sacrifice of one of his fallen. The widow and I are the only two who remain standing. She's too overcome with grief to pray as she clings to her husband's brutalized corpse. She hugs his chest with inconsolable anguish, and my eyes flick to the box chained to my cart. There's a torso locked inside that I once clung to just as fiercely. It took The Stranger's promise to force my limbs to release it. Without him, I might have never let go, and I see by her distress, she doesn't intend to either. The eternal blizzard will freeze his body to the altar, forcing her to witness the man who once warmed her bed grow cold and pale. She'll cling to him until the new offerings bury his face. I don't know Lovec's nature. I was pledged to Hreinasta since birth, but I hope he's a kind god in this harsh place. I offer a half prayer to join my drops of blood. Not for myself, but for the woman who wasn't alone this morning but is now. I'm well acquainted with her suffering. She's at least twenty cycles older than me. How long was her husband her entire life? I shudder at the thought. Mine was ripped from my side at our beginning. How much pain would I feel if I'd been allowed to love him for decades?

"What happened?" I ask a young man who wandered beside me as an older woman pulls the widow from her husband's corpse. Her absence reveals the full extent of the hunter's injuries, and my stomach cramps at the sight. His flesh has been carved to ribbons, slashed and hacked and obliterated. Something sliced through him as if he was soft snow, the white of his bones and the curl of his intestines pushing through the wounds.

"In the days of old, my people dwelled in the mountains. Homes carved from the stone, they lived in a fortress of wealth," the man answers in a daze, and it dawns on me how simple and temporary this village appears, all wood and mud and hopelessness.

"Our people were skilled hunters, blessed by Lovec's presence. He lived among us, choosing to shed blood in the treacherous mountains rather than boast of comfort in Szent with the rest of the gods. Our people were proud. Our city strong. Our hunters brave, but one hundred cycles ago, Lovec fell in love with a human. He bedded her, blessing her with his child, but before she gave birth, hunters found her body ripped to shreds in the snow, the baby carved from her belly. Lovec went mad with despair. He loved her and his unborn son and vowed to avenge her death. He searched for the creatures that murdered his beloved, but what he discovered turned him against us. The city's chief had a daughter, but when he learned Lovec had wed another in secret, he was infuriated. Lovec's wife was a servant, a stranger living in our lands, and the North doesn't accept outsiders as its own. The chief was incensed that such a shamed woman was chosen over his daughter to bear the god's son, so he called upon the dark magic that lives within the mountain's beasts. Great white tigers, so pale they disappear in the blizzard, came and butchered Lovec's wife.

"Enraged by the injustice, Lovec resolved not to destroy the tigers birthed of blood and black magic. Instead, he abandoned the realm of men, retreating to the home of the gods. The creatures, left wild and hungry for human flesh, attacked the city. They slaughtered everyone their claws found, and those that survived fled down the mountain. This village was only supposed to be a temporary haven. Lovec vowed that if we cleansed the mountains of those beasts, he would return to live among us, but for one hundred cycles our hunters have ventured into the snow never to return. Malek was their most recent victim. He won't be their last."

The young man falls silent, and my heart thunders. I pray to no god, not after what they did to me, but I understand Lovec. He loved someone others felt he shouldn't, and now he must live without her. Perhaps he's a god that does not deserve my hatred. Perhaps he is one that might aid my quest. Our pain is not so different.

I leave the warmth of the flames and walk to the altar. The widow looks up at me in surprise, but her expression softens when she sees my face. It's as if she reads the loss I wear and understands that we're the same. Her, me, Lovec. We are all the same. I pull out my blade, and this time, I bleed willingly. I bleed for Lovec's lover. I bleed for the dead man carved to pieces. I bleed for the one I love most.

Despite the blood loss, I feel strong and warm. I say nothing, my voice still unable to verbalize a prayer, but Lovec knows my thoughts. He knows what my offering is for. The Stranger hums his approval in my mind, and the cold bites less as I return to my horse.

I'm glad Lovec accepted my sacrifice because, as soon as the young man told me of monsters formed by black magic, I knew. Evil always cloaks his body. Darkness always surrounds it, and I know where they hid his bones. I understand why the thread of fate pulled me here. In these mountains, there's a city ruled by man-hunting creatures. There are ruins guarded by black magic. Another piece of him is up there.

As I leave the village, I say his name five times, ten times, twenty. *I'm coming, my love.* I will kill those snow tigers, and then I'll be one step closer to hearing the voice I've forgotten.

THE BEGINNING OF THE END
SEASON OF ICE, CYCLE 78919

The thief did not return, and for two weeks, disappointment made its home in my gut. The streets outside the temple walls were as foreign to me as the distant lands of the realm. The Sivatag was just a legend. The snow-painted North merely a myth. All I knew were marble pillars, luxurious opulence, and restraint. I'd never witnessed men or animals up close. I'd never tasted wine or enjoyed the sun warming my bare skin. The last time someone embraced me was ten cycles ago when my mother—all pride and jubilance—hugged me goodbye and delivered me into the priestesses' hands. Joining Hreinasta's cult was an honor unmatched, and I devoted myself to that future. My faith was strong, my dedication unwavering, but the curious child that had been snuffed out long ago saw the thief as a window. A glimpse into a world I would never experience.

By the time a month had passed, I resolved not to think of him. His presence was a sin, and I threw myself into my prayers. Day and night, I knelt before the altar. I let Hreinasta's current host witness my devout resolution. In a cycle, I would come of age and bear the purest goddess' soul. I couldn't afford the distractions. It was better if he never returned.

By the time two months came to a close, I'd forgotten him... or so I convinced myself.

"Miss me?"

I yelped at the interruption, the unattractive sound spilling past my lips as I tripped off the mattress. The voice rumbled with laughter, and with as much dignity as I could muster, I whirled around, my balance teetering on a disaster.

"Got you." He winked as he climbed through my window before locking the cold outside. This Season of the Ice had been one of the most brutal freezes Szent had endured in decades, and prayers to Sato for the warmth's return poured from the city's lips.

Kaid slid gracefully onto the small cushioned lounge beside my window and spread his legs wide as he leaned against the wall. He took up the entire sofa. He took up the entire room, all the air meant for my lungs now flooding his, and I couldn't breathe. How did someone so tall and strong move so silently? He was all grace and stealth, power and strength, and unlike our first meeting, his face was stained. He wore the same midnight dark clothing that marked him as a thief, but his temples and forehead bore ash stains. His brown eyes with their golden sunlight flecks stared out at me, and the scar on his lip twitched as he let me drink him in. His chest seemed broader than I remembered, the arms crossed over it more muscular. My cheeks flushed four shades of red, but, thankfully, he made no comment. He simply sat there, consuming the molecules surrounding him like he owned everything in this room. Including me.

The sides of his skull were freshly shaved, but the raven black hair on the top of his head was longer, and he had it pulled back with a leather cord. Everything about him screamed danger. Every inch of him was designed for the darkness, yet he was devastatingly beautiful. I didn't remember him being that imperfectly perfect, and the fire I'd tried to smother in my chest sparked to life. How could someone so dark and scarred be that striking?

"Sorry it took so long to return," he said with a mischievous smile, and I slammed my mouth shut, realizing I'd been gawking at him. "I guess they learned their lesson after my first break-in. Took me weeks to plan an unseen path in and out of this temple."

"You've been trying to visit this whole time?" I asked in shock.

"Yes." He tilted his head at me, his expression falling. "You thought I forgot?"

"No," I blurted. "Yes." I sat at the top of my mattress, keeping the bed between us like a fortress wall.

"I keep my promises, Sellah." The way his voice rumbled through my chest as he said my name stole my breath. I would never tire of hearing it on his tongue, of watching his full lips form the sounds. "I told you I would return, and here I am." He extended his arms in emphasis as if he were a golden prize. "Unless you didn't want me to visit?" He hesitated, as if suddenly realizing that an acolyte of Hreinasta might despise his presence.

And I should have. I should have run from that room screaming, thrown myself before the altar, and begged forgiveness for his transgressions. Instead, I curled my legs beneath me and grabbed a pillow, hugging it like a soft shield. "I wanted you to visit." I'd spoken those dangerous words out loud. I could never take that confession back, but I didn't want to. Kaid had captured my spirit, and I craved everything he offered. I wouldn't touch him, but I longed to know what friendship tasted like. Even though this towering man oozed danger, his spark breathed life into the part of my soul that isolation had caused to wither and die.

"Good." He smiled wide, his scar stretching, and the expression ruined my world only to rebuild it brighter. No one had ever looked at me like that, as if their whole heart was happy to see me. Not the vessel. Me.

People smiled at me, but never like he did. I was a body destined to house a goddess. I was my parents' pride and a sacred object of our religion. But Kaid's smile reached past my skin and found the walled-off parts where I kept Sellah buried, and she blossomed to the surface.

I offered him a small smile as the silence stretched between us since I didn't know what to say. I didn't know how to hold conversations, and it struck me how lonely I was. People talked at me, never to me. One day, Sellah would step behind the veil, and Hreinasta would take her place. To most, I wasn't a person; I was the goddess' next choice. They worshiped me more than they spoke to me. My lack of experience reared its head, and the room spun with my panic.

Kaid, on the other hand, seemed unperturbed by the silence. He leaned confidently against the wall, drinking in the sight of my face, and slowly, his confidence bled into me. He didn't push; he didn't insist. He simply was, and that gave me strength.

"What is that?" I dragged what little bravery I had out of my spirit and shoved it into my voice. He tilted his head in question, and I pointed to the stains around his eyes. Black like soot, they matched his hair and his clothes, hiding his light skin in the night air.

His smile ignited with so much pride, it crossed the divide and expanded my chest. "The Marks of Varas. He accepted me into his house as one of his thieves." Kaid leaned forward, but when he saw the hesitation in my eyes, his arms twisted behind his back. "I won't touch you, I promise. You can come look if you want."

I shouldn't. I couldn't. I wouldn't.

I did. I crawled over the white bedding and slid my bare feet onto the cool floor. True to his word, Kaid's muscles remained frozen as he hovered before me, and I stepped as close as I dared. I noticed the finger strokes used to apply the soot. The ash intensified the gold specks in his irises as if they were on fire, and I read the cruelty of the scar that ran through his mouth. I'd never had the urge to touch anyone before. The priestesses touched me when they helped me prepare for worship, but that was the only time skin brushed against mine. I never stopped to consider the way someone's flesh might feel under my fingers, but standing temptingly close to Kaid had my fists clutched into balls in order to resist. I lied to myself, blaming the desire on the deformity. Hreinasta allowed none of her acolytes to wear blemishes. Therefore, I'd never seen what healed violence looked like. It fascinated and sickened me in the same breath. How did someone stare at that beautiful face and slice through his lips? Perhaps that's why they did it, to rob him of his beauty, but they failed. They only made him more intoxicating, and my thoughts lied when they claimed I wanted to trace his scar because it was interesting. I longed to touch his scar because it was on his mouth, and it was a mouth that could rearrange the heavens if only it smiled. If only it spoke.

"When I laid your dress before his altar, Varas was shocked," Kaid continued, and I jerked, forgetting I had asked him a question. "We're not permitted to dwell alongside The Thief until the day of our offering. If we're successful in stealing from another temple, he accepts us into his house, our position based on the difficulty of the shrine we stole from. That was one reason I was determined to visit you. I wanted to thank you for your help and prove I was skilled enough to break through Hreinasta's defenses again. I was sloppy when we met, and her priestesses learned. Far harder to slip in unnoticed this time."

"Yet you did," I said.

"Of course." He scrunched his eyebrows teasingly. "I had to show you the Mark of Varas. You're not permitted to stain your skin with the ash of his holy fires until he welcomes you as one of his Thieves. The stains help hide you in the shadows, but first, you must prove you have the skill to do it without his aid."

"I like it." I stepped closer but froze when his chest heaved at my movements.

"Thanks." His breathing stumbled, and my foot lifted to retreat. "Don't go," he whispered. "Stay. Please stay. My apologies. It's just the bed was too far from the moonlight to see you, and…" He trailed off. "Never mind."

"What were you going to say?" I shouldn't ask. I couldn't know his answer. The Marks of Varas was a safe topic. They spoke of devotion to our gods, commitment to our temples, but if he voiced what he was thinking, he could never take it back. I knew his words would alter me to my marrow.

He studied me for a silent moment, his eyes darkening. "I've never seen anyone as beautiful as you. I mean this in the most respectful way, but you are divinely lovely. I'm almost ashamed to share the same air as you."

It was my turn to laugh, and crimson stained my cheeks as dark as the ash staining his forehead.

"Sorry," he muttered, the bones in my chest vibrating with his voice's power. "I promise I won't say anything like that again. I didn't mean to disrespect your vows. I'm here because you helped me… and because I understand loneliness. I read it in your eyes. I saw someone who needed a friend, and I'm someone who could use the same."

"You're lonely too?" I sat on the edge of my mattress, tucking my cold toes beneath my skirts.

"All my life." His confession shattered me into a million pieces. "But that's a depressing topic, and I'm in a good mood. I was welcomed as a thief, and after two months of failing, I finally figured out how to break through your temple's defenses. I'm here to bring you smiles, not tears."

I gave him what he wanted, and the moon shone brighter at his returned expression.

"I wouldn't mind, though," I said.

"Mind what?"

"If you gave me your sorrows."

"Maybe I will." His smile changed from joy to genuine appreciation. "But I think we should start our friendship by celebrating."

"I would like that."

"Good." He leaned forward farther, his hands slipping from behind his back to prop himself up on his knees. "I leave for my first job next week. Want to hear about it?"

I nodded with enthusiasm, ignoring the warnings blaring in my mind, and his gravel voice launched into an exciting explanation of the city he was to travel to and the men he was commissioned to rob. He talked late into the night, his soft thunder a lullaby, and each time his story came to a close, I found another question to ask. Another reason to encourage him to talk, and he gifted me with everything I asked for. As night transformed to dawn, my eyelids grew heavy until I was lying on my mattress, barely conscious enough to decipher his words.

When I woke with a start, the sun was high overhead, and Kaid no longer watched over me. I was achingly alone again. The only proof he was there was the blanket that always sat folded at the foot of my bed draped over me.

THE REALIZATION
SEASON OF ICE, CYCLE 78919

K aid's absence was like a veil being ripped from my eyes. I'd always known I was lonely, a pure object placed on a pedestal not to be touched, but his conversations showed me the painful truth of my isolation. In the days that followed his return, I watched the priestesses with the other groomed vessels. They all congregated within their private friendships, and that was the moment I realized I belonged to no one. I was a holy relic, the sacrificial lamb, and whether it was born of jealousy or wariness, the others in the temple avoided my presence. They were polite. They were kind, but they never offered me their companionship or confidence. How had I never seen it? Even as a child, my family isolated me. I didn't remember the warmth of my mother's embrace or the tenor of my siblings' laughter. For as long as I could recall, it was only me and my destiny. I was Hreinasta's from birth, and it took a thief with a voice like a demon to show me how alone and starved I was.

A week later, my parents visited the temple. My father couldn't enter the inner sanctum, but they permitted my mother as she was a woman. She didn't touch me, though, for her smiles were focused on the other worshipers. I brought pride to my family. The Pure One's chosen acolyte, the holiest daughter in all of Szent. Tears battled my will as I watched her pray. I craved her affection, her attention, her acknowledgment, but she offered none. I was an object to her, and it carved a jagged hole in my chest. I didn't even need her to hug me. I simply hoped she would meet my gaze and ask me how I was, but she left with a prayer and a bow. Both aimed at the altar and not her daughter.

I waited until I was alone to cry. It was an honor that Hreinasta chose me. It was a privilege to be a part of her house, and I wished to serve her.

But I missed Kaid. I missed how his eyes saw Sellah and not the vessel.

I hated myself for those thoughts. I hated how I suddenly felt wrong in my own home, in my own body. I cried harder because a dangerous man was the kindest person I knew.

Through my tears, I caught sight of my father outside, and I crept closer to the balcony railing where I hid. It was frowned upon for an acolyte to venture this close to where the men worshiped, but after ten cycles, I desperately hoped one of my parents would show they cared. I silently begged him to look up at me. To prove he loved me.

He talked to the other men, praying at the outer altar; his pride so inflated, I was surprised he didn't float up to the sun and burn alive. After long minutes of waving my hand through the slats, hoping to catch his eye, I sat down in defeat. My father worshiped at the temple where he had abandoned his daughter, yet he never intended to lay his eyes upon his own flesh and blood. He wanted the praise of his peers, not me. Never me. He left without noticing I was mere feet above him, and I clenched my eyes shut, forcing the tears back as Kaid's face filled the darkness. In my imagination, he stood below me at the outside shrine, and I knew that if he'd come to pray, he wouldn't leave until his gaze found mine. Until his scarred lips twitched upward in a smile that could shift Earth's axis.

I started sleeping facing my window after that. I wished to be ready when he returned, if he returned. Varas had sent him on a dangerous mission. The object he wanted stolen was one that no thief had managed to capture. I wasn't familiar with Varas or his ways, but I prayed to him every night for Kaid's safety. Even if he never scaled the temple walls again, I wanted the man shrouded in both darkness and light to be alive and safe.

For three weeks, I prayed. For three weeks, I felt his absence with an intensity I didn't believe possible, and then at the dawn of the fourth week, a blast of icy air pummeled my face just as I drifted off to sleep. The smile the frozen wind brought to my lips was of pure joy, and when my eyes fluttered open, Kaid's large frame climbing through my window lit up my world.

"Hello, friend," he said as he collapsed on the sofa, his hair escaping the leather cord to fall into his eyes. "Miss me?"

"Maybe," I teased, but by the look he gave me, he recognized the lie. I missed him to the point of pain.

"Well, that was an adventure," he huffed, brushing back his escaped locks. "And by adventure, I mean I never want to do that again. On Varas' name, that was the worst three weeks of my life."

"That hard of a job?" I asked.

"That dangerous of a job."

"Do I not want to know?" I needed to learn everything about him, but I worried if he told me of the danger that nightmares would plague my sleep.

"Probably not." He shrugged. "But I'm going to tell you anyway, because I haven't had someone kind to talk to in three weeks, and I like when you listen to my stories."

"I enjoy hearing them."

"Except I'm always the one talking." He leaned back, a

god-king on his throne, and I involuntarily leaned closer to him, his gravity that enticing. "One of these days, you're going to have to tell me one of your stories, my friend."

"My life isn't adventurous like yours."

"I don't care." He shrugged. "I still want to hear about it. If I tell you, do you promise to tell me one in return?"

"Deal." I put my hand up as if to make an officially binding oath, and he laughed so beautifully at my awkwardness.

"Wonderful." He pitched forward, excitement electrifying the golden flecks in his eyes. "It was a disaster from the beginning, and my bad luck all started with a loud and stubborn donkey."

FOUR

S tranger?" I ask as I trudge through the snow. "If I don't
return, will you take what little of him I've found and
lay him to rest?" I left my horse and the chained chest
with a bewildered villager before I set my sights on the mountain, but if I don't survive this evil, I don't want his final
resting place to be a locked box. I want his body surrendered
to the earth in a real burial.

"Of course, my child," his silent voice answers.

"Thank you."

"Although I would prefer you returned."

I laugh. "Not even Lovec's pledged hunters can reclaim
their city. I am no hunter. What chance do I stand?"

"You are not a descendant of the people who slaughtered
his wife."

He has a point.

"But the gods turned their backs on me all the same."

"Grief calls to grief, and you wear yours like a cloak.
Lovec carries his like a shield. You're not so different from one
another."

"You think he'll help me?"

"No." His chuckle is soft. "You know he cannot. You must

do this alone."

"Then why bring him up?" I feel annoyed.

"Because he's free to move atop this mountain," The Stranger continues. "Hreinasta cannot forbid that, and is it aiding your quest if he happens to walk before you? If he pauses in the only spot in the blizzard that blocks you from evil's view?"

"Just like holding my hand." I smirk as I repeat his words from the temple.

"There are no laws against holding your hand or walking or breathing. So, no, he won't aid you, but I sense a touch of luck on this mountain."

"I hope you're right." I don't feel lucky. My fingers are already brittle with cold. "I don't want to end the day in shredded pieces... If I die, will you bury me beside his parts? I want to rest in the dirt with him."

"Of course, my child." His voice is soft, almost affection-ate, and it surprises me. "But stop asking me to bury people. It's exhausting."

I laugh, shaking my head as the distant ruins come into view. "I wish you were here."

"I am here. I am always with you."

"You know what I mean." I'm afraid. I don't want to be, but I am.

The snow whirls on a gust of wind to my right, and my heart stops beating. The tigers? Have they found me already? The city is still a long way off.

"You aren't alone, child," The Stranger says as the snowflakes settle with an unnatural twirl, but his tone is not urgent, not worried, and I understand. I'm not alone. Lovec is here. He won't set foot in our realm until his temple is cleansed, but his spirit is watching. I am glad I bled on his altar.

I FINALLY REACH the abandoned city, and even crumbling under the weight of one hundred cycles of snow, it is breathtaking. Carved from the very mountain itself, it's one with nature, a home intended for a god, and Lovec's desire to return hangs thick in the air. The village I left behind is a sad imitation of this looming structure, and I try to picture what it looked like before evil stole its magnificence.

The grey stone is smooth in some places and razor-sharp in others as it protrudes through the ice. Some structures are small and humble, while others tower high, disappearing into the blizzard. My imagination dusts the piled snow off the streets and sprinkles life throughout the vacant windows. I allow myself a moment to picture the Great Hunter walking among his people. I pretend the Northerners welcomed his secret bride with open arms instead of allowing magic to carve her into pieces for scavengers to find. Lovers embrace in my imagined scene. Children play. Animals roam free. It's a beautiful sight. One I would have loved to see, and I wonder what he might think if he were here with me. I was never permitted beyond the temple walls. My knowledge of the realm came from his stories. His tales of rich merchants and their hidden jewels, of assassins and their weapons, of lands I couldn't fathom. He enjoyed telling me as much as I relished hearing them, and now our roles are reversed. I'm witnessing the wonders and horrors of this world, and he lies locked in a box. I shudder, but not from the cold.

A low roar rips me from my reverie, and I stiffen. The entire mountain stills, as if even the storm fears the predators, and I climb up a barren tree for a better view of my surroundings. More of the city becomes visible, and I wish it hadn't, for I see how close the monster drifts. Pure white with thin streaks of black, so tall its shoulder blades would reach my chest. The tiger is all grace and violence, a malicious beauty. It's one of many beasts who knows the taste of human flesh. One of many monsters who craves it.

A second rumble answers the first, and subtle movement disrupts the snow further within the city. I hope they haven't caught my scent on the wind. If they hunt me, I stand no chance, and my eyes frantically scan the frozen buildings. A piece of him is there somewhere, but I don't have the luxury of time. These beasts will never allow me to search their territory. My only hope of survival is to slip behind their ranks unnoticed. The breath is icy in my lungs. The tree rough against my back. Where is he? Where did they hide him?

A swirl of dancing snow catches my attention, and my stomach pitches. I recognize that pattern. I know who walks there, and I know why he does, but the realization ties my insides into knots. The swirl falls into nothingness before the furthermost structure. Lovec's true temple. That's where his bones rest. Its entrance was carved directly into the mountain peak at the city's back. The sheer cliff's smooth stone and imposing height make flanking this city impossible. To reach it, I must traverse the convoluted streets, and no one can survive a trek that long with bloodthirsty carnivores on their tail.

The Stranger's voice penetrates my brain, but I don't hear his words. I'll never make it. The distance is too great, the enemy too brutal. For a second, I cannot comprehend how they hid him here. In the Sivatag? In Death's invaded temple? These places of unspeakable horrors, but then I see War's blood-soaked face, and I understand. Valka delivered his bones himself. It is fitting since Valka carved him to pieces, and I gag at the memory. Of course, War and his love of brutality walked unscathed within these—

"Damn it, Sellah, Run!" I register panic in The Stranger's voice, and I nearly fall out of the tree at its urgency. "Why aren't you answering me, girl? Move your feet!"

The low roar is all the warning I receive before a tiger leaps onto a branch behind me. The monster is all grace and hunger, and without thinking, I throw my body to the ground.

My ankle twists, sending a shooting pain up my leg as my palms scrape against ice, and I scramble forward, the beast's anger rumbling at my back.

I am a fool. A gods damned fool. I was so worried about the creatures at my front that I never noticed the one flanking me, and now I'm boxed in on all sides. I'll never make it.

"Run, damn it," The Stranger bellows into my brain, but the snow is too thick, too deep, too unforgiving. The tiger leaps from the tree, landing without a sound, and I grit my teeth, preparing for death.

Snow swirls to my right, and without hesitation, I lunge for it. I move through the drifts toward a structure missing a door. I don't know how running through it will save me, but if Lovec walks before me, then I shall follow.

The tiger roars a war cry, a savage scream of hunger, and three other rumbling voices answer him as I dive for the opening. I feel the wind at my back, the hot breath on my skin, but the second my body crosses the threshold, the entire house trembles. When no teeth carve through my flesh, I spin, coming face to face with white irises. My fear is a punch to the gut, and if I was half a foot closer, this monster's fangs would sink into my face. But for all its snarling rage, it cannot reach me. The doorway is too narrow for its shoulders to slip through. Fissures in the stone spiral out from his impact, but the creature is stuck. I burst into ugly tears as the tiger pushes against the structure. And pushes, and pushes, but it's no use. He cannot fit.

"Run, child," The Stranger orders, and I flee.

Returning to the blizzard, I race through the empty streets. My brain tries to picture the path to the temple, but the convoluted maze of homes is a twisted skeleton. I don't know where I am, and the roars have only increased. Three, four, six. They're closing in. My lungs hurt.

I shove my fingers into my boot and pull out my dagger. Its blade is no match for their fangs, but the solid weight anchors me. I cling to it as if it's his hands, as if it is his warm skin dragging me forward and not my spinning fear. I notice movement above me, but I don't look up. The tigers are stalking me from the roofs. What small and easy prey I am. I say his name over and over. If I must die, I'll die with him on my lips.

The tiger above leaps off the roof, and I fling myself sideways. I break through a rotten door and barrel through a house that's sat untouched for a century. The air is stale and ancient, but the lack of snow has me careening unrestricted across the floor for the opposite exit. In seconds, I burst back out into the cold, but I barely make it three steps when I freeze in my tracks. I curse with a laugh before retreating within the confines of that home-turned-tomb.

There, collapsed in the corner, is the corpse of a hunter, his body perfectly preserved. His intestines spill from his gut encased in crimson ice, and his once blue eyes gawk at me in their eternal sleep, but it's not his shredded gore that draws me close. It's the weapon frozen in his grip. For one hundred cycles, this man lay cold and alone, his sword at his side. My soul sings as I break it free from his icy hold with a few well-placed kicks.

"Thank you," I say to the dead. I say to The Stranger. I say to Lovec. The blade is still razor sharp, and I shove my dagger back into my boot. I'm no swordsman. I was not bound to Valka and his love of war. I wasn't raised by Lovec and his demands for bloodshed, but I was baptized in the fire of despair and heartache. Reborn in torture and anguish. Come, oh ancient evil. Take my head from my body. I will return the favor.

I say his name twice as I race out into the cold, but a tiger blocks my path. By the growl at my back, a second cuts off my retreat. I say his name a third time, a fourth. I beg his memory to stay with me and give me strength. I say his name a fifth time, and then the monster charges.

I'm too stunned to move as I watch the creature plow through the snow. He's as tall as I am, his muscles greater than anything I've witnessed. He'll kill me in seconds. Snap my bones like twigs, and I shut my eyes to picture my beloved's face. Not his beautiful face, complete with the soot markings. No, I picture his face in the end. The pain. The torture. The agony. I recall his screams. I visualize how Valka forced him to remain awake until it was over. That's what my mind conjures, the destruction of the man I love, not the beauty of his smile and his scarred lip, his flashing eyes and their golden flecks. Bile rises in my throat. I never replay that moment. I never let myself remember that day. It haunts my nightmares, but now I force myself to. I smell his blood and the black magic. I dwell within his fear. It fills me with an unholy rage, and then my eyes open.

The tiger is upon me, leaping for the kill, but with the grace he taught me over a cycle of stolen midnights, I lunge low and shove the blade high. The tiger roars, and I split him apart, throat to gut, his innards raining down on me. When he falls to the snow, everything is stained crimson, but it's his blood, not mine.

"That," I say loud and clear for the mountain to hear, "was for Kaid."

I stand and meet the stare of the second animal, the gore already freezing to my skin. Revenge is in the beast's gaze. Revenge is in my entire body, woven through the cells that build my being. We are not the same. I have a reason to survive, to kill, and steal, and hurt, and rage. It consumes me. Owns me. Drives me. I need to live more than this creature needs to feed. It was born of evil. I was born of love. We are not the same.

I scream a war cry as I flee from my new enemy, leaving a trail of carnage in my wake. The tiger snarls behind me, answered by two other voices, and I veer to my right, leaping onto a toppled wall and climbing up to the roof, just like he taught me. From this vantage, I can see Lovec's ancient temple. I'm so close. I'm too far.

I push my legs faster. Two tigers hunt me from below. Three track me from the roofs, but I don't stop. A divide approaches, and I leap, but the snow crumbles beneath me. I slide off the edge, catching myself before it's too late, and as my frozen fingers haul me to safety, pain lances through my calf. I scream in agony, cursing and spitting and raging. Blood pours from my veins in ugly pulses to freeze in the pure white snow, and I almost laugh. Once pure, I'm now tainted. My sin has stained my soul, just like my oozing blood stains the earth.

"Eyes up, child."

I jerk at The Stranger's voice in time to watch the tiger who savaged my calf leap to the roof. Mangled leg forgotten, I grip the sword, angling it above me at the monster. It punctures the beast's jaw and punches out through his skull, killing him as he lands on my prone body. His unbearable weight crushes my chest, but after desperate minutes, I escape his corpse. My ankle gives out as I try to flee, and with a sinking sensation, I realize how badly the beast shredded my calf. Adrenaline allowed me one final kill, but this evil will win in the end.

"And that," I spit with angry tears, "was for Lovec's wife." I rip the sword free from the animal's brain with a sickening crack. These tigers are here because black magic ripped a wife to shreds. I'm here because a god ripped a husband to pieces. At least, I offered both their souls some vengeance before I die.

The snow whips into a frenzy, and my breath stills. Another tiger. I don't have the strength to fight anymore. I can already feel the blood loss blurring my edges.

"Stranger," I say. "Goodbye." He doesn't answer. His silence hurts.

I grip the sword and twist my aching body toward the commotion. I wish there was an afterlife. I wish Hreinasta hadn't banished Death. At least then, the end wouldn't be so cruel. My soul could join his. Eternity would be ours, but nothingness will greet me, just as it did him.

I brace for death, but no tiger appears. As the snow whirls, a form takes shape, and as if emerging from thin air, a man steps onto the roof. My gasp catches in my throat. He's the tallest being I've ever seen, even taller than Kaid. His head reaches at least seven feet, and his build is broad, all strength and grace. His long, ice-blond hair hangs down his back, half of it tied up by braids and cords. He's terrifying and beautiful, his massive body dressed in fur and leather, and I can't breathe. I've never felt power this intoxicating. I have never seen beauty this magnificent. His blue eyes are so light they're almost white, and for a moment, The Stranger's eyes flash through my memory, but while his are solid and blinding, this newcomer has faint irises and pupils. A jagged scar runs down his throat, and a second one consumes his hand. I stare at them, but all I see is a scar that severed perfect lips. Lips that worshiped me, praised me, comforted me, and I know who this new stranger is.

Lovec. The God of the Hunt has returned to the realm of men.

I look down at the blood pooling beneath the tiger, and as if Lovec is reminding me, I recall the villager's words. He vowed to return only after the evil who took his bride was destroyed. There are other tigers. I hear their hunting roars, but when I killed this monster, I pledged it to Lovec's wife. The first kill to Kaid. The second to her. This was my sacrifice for both of our lost lovers, and to my shock, I realize it was the godless girl who returned the Great Hunter to our land.

As my blood leaves my veins, stealing my life with it, I smear my fingers through the tiger's death. Lovec demands offerings of the flesh, so on unstable legs, I approach the god. With shaking hands, I mark each of his cheeks. He's so tall he has to bend so I can reach, and when I'm done, he surprises me by capturing my hand in his. I yelp in fear. No deity has ever touched me in their true form, but he merely wipes the excess crimson from my palms. I expect him to keep the blood for himself, but he raises his fingers, and starting at my forehead, he drags three lines down over my nose, lips, and throat. Painted in blood, I understand. I am his hunter now. Lovec has bestowed his favor on me. The godless girl, the sinner, the unholy. The woman who understands his heartache, who gave his pain revenge. We are the same, and I belong to him. Warmth fills my chest, and my calf stops hurting. I look down, seeing nothing but new skin. His blessing made me whole, and suddenly I feel the Stranger's presence. I had no one. Now I have The Stranger and the Great Hunter. Soon I'll have my thief.

Lovec strides past me without a word and seizes the discarded sword. With grace and strength only a god could possess, he drops from the roof and settles before the gathering tigers. At least a dozen man-hunters are chasing my scent now, and with an expert swing of the blade, his strong voice roars through the city.

"Run."

I run with everything I have left in me, and Lovec follows my lead, cutting down beast after beast. I grin at the Stranger's words. The god isn't helping me. Not truly. He is simply standing behind me in the blizzard so that the creatures cannot see me.

"You're not out of the fire yet," The Stranger's voice says. I roll my eyes at his choice of words, but I heed his warning and push through the endless white. My lungs burn from the icy air, my legs burn from the exertion, and to the song of snarls and death, I explode upon the temple. I race inside, my heart singing with joy at finding another piece of him, but that excitement dies before it can take root. I just stumbled into the tiger's den, the dozen outside merely a taste of what waits in here.

THE FRIENDSHIP
SEASON OF THE THAW, CYCLE 78920

The soot around Kaid's eyes did little to hide the bruising. He'd barely spoken more than a handful of words since he climbed into my room, and my fingers itched to brush back his hair and wrap him in my arms. Not because I wished to sin. Not because he was forbidden fruit, lingering just out of reach. I wanted to hold him because every inch of his body whispered of the pain he'd endured. I longed to bring him comfort and steal his suffering. He normally spoke of his adventures when he visited, but he said nothing as he leaned against the wall. Only that he'd completed a job successfully, but at a cost.

Without a warning, Kaid stood and opened the window. Dressed in black, hair as colorless as the midnight sky, forehead painted in the ashes, he was a demon in the night, an angel of grace. He moved with agility and power, his forceful presence almost unnatural. Everything from his scarred lips to his hardened muscles to his gold-flecked eyes sang of danger, wove tales of darkness. Yet I could watch him for the rest of my days and never be afraid. He'd become my favorite part of my existence, breathing life into parts of my soul that had died. In such a brief acquaintance, this breathtaking man had carved a jagged hole in my heart and buried himself inside it. It was crude and bloody, still raw where it tore, but I held the pain close. I never wanted to be free of him. I couldn't explain his importance to me. He was a thief. A stranger. A sinner, yet he called to me in ways I didn't know one soul could beckon another. Perhaps it was my naivety and loneliness, but something had bent inside me. Bent and cracked and shattered. I would never be the same.

My heart sank as Kaid climbed out into the night air. His visit had been too short, barely a breath in my stifling week, and I wasn't ready to release him into the world. I braced for the dreaded goodbye, but then his tired gaze met mine.

"Come on." He gestured for me to follow him. "You should be able to manage the climb now that the ice has melted."

"Climb?" I balked. "I can't leave the temple."

"We're not leaving. I want to show you how I get in." He curled his fingers, enticing me closer. "Let's climb up to the roof. There's a flat section where no one will notice us, and you can see most of Szent from there. Come with me, Sellah, please."

I would have gone anywhere with him if he only asked.

"I'll show you how to climb," he said as I moved for the window. "I'll teach you anything you want."

I wanted him to teach me everything, but I was afraid to leave my room. Every second I spent with him was an act of defiance, a rebellion against the calling I was bound to, yet the lonely ache in my heart had burned a hole into my soul, a hole that Kaid's presence filled so thoroughly the edges ripped.

"I won't let you fall." Desperation brimmed in his eyes as he begged me to trust him, and for the first time, I had the distinct impression that Kaid needed me far more than I needed him.

"It's not that," I said, stepping closer. "You can't catch me, but that's not it."

He flinched, my words reminding him of how solitary my life was. "I'll leave then."

"I'm afraid," I blurted before his black hair dipped from sight. "This…" I gestured between us, "…is not who I am. I'm meant for Hreinasta, and every time you offer me your friendship, I feel my soul being pulled in two. The goddess has already claimed me. I can't give anything to you."

"I don't want to take anything from you." Conviction fortified his voice. "I want to give everything to you. I'm not here to break your vows. A lonely girl simply helped a lonely boy, and I love the light in your eyes when we're together. How can that be a sin? How can wanting to be your friend be wrong?"

"I must remain pure." My walls were crumbling.

"And you will." He smiled. "I won't take that from you. I won't take anything from you that you don't willingly give. If you want me to leave, I will, and despite my disappointment, I won't come back."

"Why do you visit me?" I searched for any reason to accept his offer. To send him away and forget his scarred lips and sunshine smile.

"There is cruelty in this world. Cruelty you've never seen, but I have. Hatred and death and destruction, but there's peace too, and I find it with you. You're the first real friend I've had."

"You are the only friend I've ever had." I crumbled under that confession.

"So, climb with me. Just to the roof." He beckoned me forward. "I swear on Varas' holy fire I won't touch you."

'Be brave!' my spirit screamed. *Be brave. Be brave. Be brave.* I stepped to the window.

"Place your hands and feet where I put mine," Kaid instructed. "This climb is easy."

He pulled heavenward, his powerful body scaling the

temple walls as if he was made of smoke, not flesh. I ignored the plea in my gut, begging me to return to safety, and followed him. He was all grace while I was a disaster, but his words were true. The ascent was an easy challenge, and within minutes, we stood below the star-studded sky.

Cool air brushed against our limbs. The ice had finally relented, and Sato, Goddess of the Harvest, surrounded us with the slowly thawing breeze. The ground was still bleak, the trees empty, but they hummed with anticipation as she prepared for the oncoming harvest. Earth had died, readying for her rebirth, and that was how I felt standing on that roof next to the towering Kaid. Meeting him had birthed something unfamiliar inside me. I only hoped the harvest would be a blessing and not a curse.

"Did you always want to pledge to Hreinasta?" He asked, breaking the silence.

"My parents promised me to her at my birth and then surrendered me to her protection when I was ten."

He looked at me in shock. "This wasn't your decision?"

"Of course it was." I stepped back, the space a defensive barrier as I detached from my emotions. "It's a privilege to serve the Pure One. How could I want anything else?"

"I didn't mean it like that," he soothed. "Pledging to the gods is a lifelong commitment. It's an honor and a sacrifice, and Hreinasta's priestesses are called to a holier living than most. It's a lot for a child to be forced into. Most temples refuse children, urging them to wait until adolescence before voicing their intent to pledge when they come of age."

"I wasn't forced," I argued

"So, you're happy with your calling?" I could tell he didn't believe me, but he dropped the subject for my sake. "That's good."

"Yes," I said aloud. *"No. I want to touch your scarred lip and feel the disfigured flesh beneath my finger,"* I screamed silently.

"Is it… Never mind." He sat down.

"Is it what?" I followed his lead, keeping my distance.

"Is it true that when Hreinasta inhabits a body, the vessel's soul ceases to exist until she vacates it?"

"They do not cease to exist."

He heaved a relieved sigh. "Thank Varas."

"The soul doesn't disappear but slumbers. Hreinasta doesn't like other beings sharing her body and mind, so the human spirit retreats within itself until the goddess deems their servitude fulfilled." I explained, and he looked at me in horror.

"You call it slumber, but in the end, it's all the same. The women vanish for decades. One day they are, and then next they aren't."

"All gods demand sacrifice," I said. "To serve the primordial requires all of oneself. If Hreinasta demands that of me, then it will be an honor to gift her my body."

"But she may not choose you." Hope flushed Kaid's face. "There are other vessels prepared here."

I didn't want to tell him the truth. Anxiety wafted off him, and for the first time in my twenty cycles, I truly considered what submitting to Hreinasta meant. In less than a cycle, I would come of age, and the goddess was merely biding her time as she waited. In a few seasons, I would vanish. I would sleep for decades, experiencing nothing, feeling nothing, and then one day I would resurface in a body too old for my young soul. Hreinasta would abandon me for someone younger and more beautiful, and I would wake up aching and grey. I wouldn't recognize myself. My raven black hair would be gone. My smooth skin wrinkled, and my joints stiff. I'd never allowed myself to picture the future awaiting me. I was born for this purpose, saved for this goddess. It was all I knew, all I would ever know, but Kaid's dread leaked into me, poisoning my spirit. For the first time, apprehension seeped into my cracks.

"You'll always be her priestess, but she may not choose

you?" Kaid repeated, and I longed to lie to him. To bring my friend peace and ensure him he wouldn't lose me.

"She already claimed me," I said. I had to tell him the truth. It was for the best. Perhaps it would keep him from returning, from tempting me with a life filled with more than emptiness. "When I come of age, Hreinasta will inhabit my body."

"How old are you?" His voice was so low it was barely audible.

"Twenty."

He sucked in a sharp breath. "You have one cycle left."

I nodded, but he said nothing. He sat in the cool breeze under the moon, the dim light clothing him in beauty, and I stared at the demon in the night who'd stolen my soul and captured my longing. I stared at the sinner who made me acknowledge the truth about my future, at the caring friend I'd lose in a cycle.

"I'll help you live an entire lifetime in the coming seasons," he whispered. "I'll make them the best days of your life."

———

KAID KEPT HIS PROMISE. As Sato thawed the land, my thief returned as often as he could, silently slipping past every defense Hreinasta's temple offered. He truly was blessed by Varas, worthy of the Great Thief himself.

Kaid broke into my room whenever Varas did not demand his services, and some nights he came to me full of vibrance and life. Other times, the soot around his eyes had rubbed off. His limbs were filled with exhaustion, his body colored by bruises. Yet still, he came. He told me every story he owned. He made me climb to the roof so we could see all of Szent as he whispered the holy city's secrets. The more we climbed, the stronger I grew, and we explored more, dropping into the gardens, balancing on the rafters, hiding in the alcoves. Each night was an adventure, and while we never left the temple grounds, he showed me things about my home I'd never noticed.

Kaid lay beside me under the waning moon. The sun would rise soon, and we were pushing our luck. I'd yet to sleep. The priestesses would come for me in a few hours, but I couldn't pull away. It had been a month since he first encouraged me onto this roof, and something had changed between us. He was no longer the forbidden stranger hiding in my room. He was my life and breath and hope. My best friend, and it made my heart ache. The only other person I'd been in close proximity to was my mother. She cared for me in those ten cycles before the temple took me, but I don't remember her possessing warmth like Kaid. His affection bridges our physical distance, but my mother had none, even when she touched me. Perhaps it was because she knew my future. She knew the soul I'd lose to become Hreinasta's. Maybe she was afraid to grow attached, reluctant to love a child only to banish her. Ever since Kaid barged into my life, I wondered if my father had pushed the offering on her. His status centered him in the public eye, and many had shamed him for not pledging one of his children to a god's service. Had he given me to my mother just so that my sacrifice would appease the people?

I shook away the thought and twisted toward Kaid. He was so much larger than me, and the scar severing the left side of his mouth captured my attention.

"You can touch it." He laughed, his smile shifting the uneven flesh. "If you wanted to, that is. I know you aren't supposed to touch anyone, but you can touch me. Even if you never do, you have my consent. You're safe with me."

"I know," I said as I rolled to my side, inching closer to his face. "But I can't."

He shrugged good-naturedly as he looked at me. "You always stare at it."

"We can't have scars," I explained. My gaze shifted away from the disfigured skin in embarrassment. "If an acolyte or priestess becomes scarred, she is dismissed from service, so I've never seen one before, especially not like yours."

"Look at me," he commanded in a gentle tone, and my eyes dragged back to his handsome face. "Don't be ashamed. I have nothing to hide from you."

"Does it hurt?" I blurted before I could stop myself.

"It did. Gods, it did. But not anymore."

"Is it the only one you have?"

"No, but Hreinasta would frown on us if I showed you those."

I laughed, suddenly curious where on his sculpted body those blemishes hid, and he winked at me as if he knew exactly where my mind had gone.

"How did you get it?" I asked, trying and failing to force the blush from my cheeks.

"I..." He trailed off. "That's not a story for you."

"Why not?" I couldn't stop the question from escaping.

"You..." He paused as if to organize his thoughts so he wouldn't hurt me. "You are innocent, surrounded by beauty. Everything about you is lovely and kind and full of wonder. My story is ugly. I don't want to stain you with my past. You don't deserve that darkness."

"Don't," I whispered. "Don't do that. Don't cut me out of your life because you think I can't handle it."

He looked at me with sorrow in his eyes. I hated it. I wanted to shake him, but I clenched my fists instead.

"I'm a person," I begged. "Treat me like one."

"Sellah..."

"I am not a thing." I sat up, anger pulsing through me. Not at him, but at how inhuman everyone made me feel until him. "I am not empty, not yet. I'm still me, still a human. Everyone else cut me out of their life. My parents. My siblings. Even the other vessels, because they're jealous of my station. I'm a thing to everyone but you." Tears threatened to spill down my cheeks. "I feel real to you, so don't turn me into an object to be admired and polished. Not yet."

"Sellah, I…" He sat up and shifted closer until our shoulders almost touched. All I would have to do is lean, and we would be joined.

"My father was an important man in Szent. He still is." Kaid surrendered the truth. "But my mother was no one. Someone he used and threw out like trash. She died when I was a child, confessing on her deathbed whose seed had fathered me. She hoped if I went to him, he would take pity on his son and save me from poverty. She was wrong, and I'm glad she wasn't alive to see it."

"He gave that to you?" I stared at his lips, his perfect lips with their long white scar that begged for my fingers.

"No." He shook his head. "He turned me out onto the streets to fend for myself. I stole to survive, always destined to be a thief, I guess." He chuckled without humor. "When I was a teenager, still scrawny and lean, I stole from the wrong market vendor. I was too hungry to think straight and didn't plan my actions. It cost me. The vendor was a gargantuan man, and he caught me as I tried to escape with the food. He…" Kaid trailed off and fingered his mouth.

"If it's too painful for you, you don't have to tell me." I offered. "I only meant I didn't want you to hide from me."

"I want to tell you." His expression swallowed me whole. "I want you to know everything about me. I want you in every part of my being. You're the only person I have." He blushed at the sad truth. "You're the only friend I have. The only person since my mother that cares whether I live or die, and I want you to know me."

I pressed my palm to the roof, dangerously close to his. "I would hug your pain away if I could," I whispered.

"I would like that." He flattened his hand so that our fingers were centimeters apart. "The vendor pinned me to the ground, and I begged for my life. I was still a boy, a starving boy, and he was too heavy. I screamed for forgiveness. Plead my case with tears. I was hungry, so hungry, but he drew a knife from his belt saying, 'Then I shall relieve you of your mouth'."

Kaid's fingers lifted and trailed over the long scar. "He sliced through my lips. I think he meant to carve them off completely, but a stranger pulled him off me. He beat the man into the dirt, then left without a word. I followed my savior, bleeding and crying, to the House of Varas. It was the last time I saw The Great Thief until he officially welcomed me into his guild. I didn't realize it, but it was the god himself who saved me from that vendor, and he told me if I was going to steal, I should do it properly."

Tears escaped my eyes, and I wiped them away before placing my hand back on the roof. The wetness stained the stone, and careful not to touch me, Kaid brushed his fingers over the teardrops.

"That's why I strove to be the best. I longed to be worthy of Varas. I didn't know he'd been the one to save me until I offered him your dress, and he was there. He saved me, and I wanted to be like him. A thief and a warrior. Someone no one could hurt." He looked at me pointedly. "I have scars from those who tried, but as the cycles passed, less and less could wound me, but your tears? They hurt worst of all. Out of everyone in my life, you have the power to hurt me the most."

"Why?" His words alarmed me.

"Because I finally found a soul that sings to mine, a friend unlike anyone I've ever met, and I made you cry. I can't take you away from here. I cannot touch you, and in a cycle, I'll lose you."

His words reminded me of my mother. Was this why she held me at arm's length? Kaid had thrown himself headlong into our connection, and he would emerge burned. I wouldn't emerge at all, not for decades at least. My mother was smart. She saved herself from the pain.

"The sun is coming." Kaid stood abruptly, signally our time was over.

"Will you come back?" I asked, suddenly afraid he would protect himself like my mother did, distancing himself from the misery of seeing my body without my soul inside it.

"Of course." He smiled. Sad, but true. "I'll even return when you're old and grey and Hreinasta abandons you for another. It may take a while, but I'll always come for you."

FIVE

Out of everyone in my life, you have the power to hurt me the most. And I did hurt him. I killed him, and now his bones lie across a long stretch of floor guarded by beasts born and bred of evil. Blood coats their white fur. Hunger lingers in their eyes. I'll be dead before I step ten feet into Lovec's abandoned temple.

The tigers stare at me as I hover in the doorway. They do not move. They do not roar. They simply study the foolishly brave girl hovering on the threshold. The desperate girl fueled by love and anger and hate. I should turn back. I should flee to the safety of Lovec's sword, but he cannot help me. Not with this. But I need his help. Especially with this, for there sits his arm. Shoulder to wrist, it rests atop the altar like an offering, but his beautifully powerful limb is no gift. Valka didn't leave it here to honor the Hunter. No, War left it here as sacrilege. A taunt. A sacrifice of flesh on a shrine Lovec no longer lays eyes on.

I'll always come for you. The promise he cannot keep. The oath he broke because of me. I uphold it for him now. I claimed his words as my own. I'll always come for him, and the marks from Lovec's fingers burn my face. The Hunter reminds me of The Thief. Blood and soot, they offer blessings and protection. They do not take; they do not hollow out and consume. The blood burns white hot on my skin, and I can no longer stand still. The pain is too great, and I stride forward.

The tigers tense, readying their attack, but they don't move. Instead, they study me with wary eyes and predatory snarls. The blood burns hotter, like my flesh is being flayed from my skull, and I force myself to walk. With every step, the pain on my face lessens, and I understand. Lovec marked me, blessed me, claimed me. Like Varas marked his thieves with the soot of his holy ashes, the Hunter baptized me in blood. I am his now. A hunter, a warrior, a priestess. The gods turned their backs on me, but out here in the wilds, Lovec understands. He's felt the loss of love. He had a spouse ripped from his side. We are the same. Perhaps, here in the frozen lands, I am not cursed for loving someone unconditionally. I am anointed. I am favored. I am marked.

I race through the horde toward the altar. Fangs gnash at my ankles as my feet pound the frosted stone. Throats snarl bloodthirsty cries, but I do not stop.

Run faster. It's not The Stranger's voice, but rather his thoughts that push into my mind. I want to obey. I try to run faster, but my legs are exhausted. The frigid air stings my lungs. The blood on my face burns.

I scream the moment my fists close around his frozen wrist. The arm that used to love and teach me is now hardened flesh, the black magic keeping decay from consuming him. My hands burn where his dead skin touches mine, but I hold it to my chest despite the agony. Another piece. Another scattered bone. I'm one step closer to ending this nightmare, but then I notice the tigers' movements. They allowed me to reach the altar, but it wasn't a blessing. It was a trap, and they've cut me off from the exits. I search wildly for an escape, but there's nothing in this vast temple save drifting snow.

A monstrous tiger prowls forward, readying for the kill,

and I close my eyes, letting the dark magic on his skin sting my throat.

"I love you, Kaid," I say his name so I don't forget. "Lovec? Help me." It's the first time I've prayed since his death. It feels wrong on my tongue, but right within my soul. The swooshing air of the tiger's attack is the only answer I get, and I brace for impact.

The animal lands with a harsh thud, but not atop my body. I feel no pain, no claws or rancid breath, and my eyes snap open. The creature lies at my feet, a spear protruding from its chest. I reel back in surprise, but I hear them before I see them. The villagers surge into the temple, weapons thirsty for bloodshed, and the tigers forget about me as they race for fresh meat. It's a cacophony of blades and fangs, a hunt within the Hunter's temple, and the air surges with power. With every drop of blood, Lovec's bond to this altar grows, and as man and beast fight and die, Lovec steps over the threshold for the first time in a century. His almost white eyes meet mine. The scar on his throat ripples as he welcomes the sacrifices, and his presence expands, consuming the sanctuary, the city, the mountain.

"Go, child," The Stranger's voice echoes through my mind, and I obey without hesitation. I weave through the carnage, his arm plastered against my breast. Death dances around me, yet no harm comes to me as I skid to a stop before Lovec.

"Thank you for helping me," I whisper over the bloodshed.

"I did not help you, little hunter." The hulking god stares at me as if he sees the deepest parts of my soul, every moment of both my past and my future, and my heart swells. He claimed me as his. I hate the gods. I don't want to serve them, but this brokenhearted husband? I will worship him. We are the same.

"You're the one who helped me," Lovec continues,

hoisting his bloody blade, readying for the kill. "You returned my city to me." He steps forward, violence flashing in his eyes. "Go, little hunter. Go before I decide to keep you for myself."

And then he's gone, sword swinging with power, and I obey his command. I flee out into the blood-soaked snow, and my lips repeat his name against his arm. *One time. Two Times. Five.*

"Valka made a mistake hiding him here," The Stranger says as I make the frigid journey down the mountain. "You must do this alone. You cannot accept aid, yet the moment the villagers heard you meant to slay the evil, they followed your lead. When they saw Lovec had returned to his city, they rallied in your footsteps. Only they didn't protect you. They didn't help you. Your quest was to find him, and you did that alone. They fought to end their exile, and you helped them break their curse, leading them to victory. Yes, Valka made a mistake hiding him here."

THE LESSONS
SEASON OF THE THAW, CYCLE 78920

The footsteps drew closer, and while he didn't speak, I heard him all the same. *'Hurry up.'*

My fingers ached, the picks clicked, the footsteps echoed like a deafening countdown, and I felt alive. My skin crackled with electric energy, my breathing coming in short huffs. I'd never been so nervous. I'd never experienced such an intense thrill, but if I didn't get this door open before they detected us, Kaid would endure the brunt of the punishment. I threw him a panicked look, but he slid his skilled hands behind his back, his message clear. *'Only you can save us now.'*

I forced myself to focus despite my anxiety, picturing what would happen to my friend if they caught us together. The image spurred my fire, and I twisted my fingers until I heard the telltale click of triumph. With as much stealth as I could muster, I shoved the heavy door open and rolled inside. Silent and deadly as a shadow, Kaid slipped in behind me, and we pushed the door closed just as the female guard rounded the corner. I slapped a hand over my mouth, afraid my heart would beat out of my chest and fall off my tongue if I didn't, and the second the footsteps faded into nothingness, I collapsed on the floor in a fit of laughter.

"You're learning fast." Kaid crouched elegantly before my prone form.

"What if I didn't pick the lock in time?" I giggled between my fingers. "Were you really going to just sit there and not help?"

Kaid stood without an answer and shrugged, mischief in his eyes. I'd asked him on a whim to teach me the ways of the thief, but he took his role as teacher seriously. He pushed me to learn everything he had to offer, and together, we were working our way through the temple. Each night, I grew stronger as we climbed further. With each adventure, I opened more complex locks. We stole nothing. I didn't want to. I only wanted to use my hands as he did so that his skills would forever live within my muscles.

"You should pledge to the House of Varas. You would make a worthy thief," he said as if I had unlocked gold. "It smells like you in here." He took a deep, reverent breath. And that's when I noticed it. The fragrance. This was no treasure horde.

"Incense," I explained, pulling myself from the storeroom floor. "They burn it at the altar."

"I like it." He inhaled again, his body angling toward me.

"Here." I grabbed a few sticks. The priestesses would never notice their absence, and I extended them to Kaid. "We broke in. Might as well keep something for our efforts. Take these to remember me by."

"I need nothing to remember you." He accepted my offering, his hand engulfing the incense until his fingers were a hair's width away from mine, and suddenly there was no air left in the storeroom. It was only him and me and the fraction of an inch separating us. One move, one simple shift, and I would know what his skin felt like. His palms were calloused from his service, and I spent too many nights wondering if his touch would be as rough as his hands. Or would it be gentle, full of warmth and care?

Kaid pulled the incense from my grip and turned his back on me, and the air painfully inflated my lungs. If I hadn't seen his features, I would have been heartbroken at the rejection, but I'd seen his face. Desire filled his eyes, a heat unlike anything I'd witnessed before. Yearning battled restraint, and his face was a painting of war. His heart challenged his mind in his expression, his dedication to my purity beating his own hunger bloody. It was the first time I ever noticed his control slip. The first time I saw craving in his eyes, and the storeroom shrank. I felt claustrophobic, suffocated, crushed. Standing feet from Kaid, knowing that beneath his surface ran a burning longing, frayed my edges. There was no window, no escape. Just me and the man who had become my best friend. The man I couldn't stop dreaming about. He kept his back to me, his dark form so much taller than mine, but I refused to look away. I didn't want control or order. I didn't want loneliness. I didn't want my spirit snuffed out the moment I turned twenty-one, leaving him to mourn my disappearance.

I stepped forward without thinking. In the darkness of the storeroom, we weren't a vessel and a thief. We were Kaid and Sellah. Friends. Confidants. Hunger. Why was it wrong to know what his touch felt like? Why was it a sin to witness the smile that engulfed my being? If they caught us together, they would torture him for staining a sacred vessel, but he hadn't stained me. He made me whole and happy and beautiful. He made me Sellah. Kaid was the only person who let my true self bleed to the surface.

"We should go before the guard circles back." His voice broke the spell as he reached for the door, and I followed with burning cheeks.

"You did well," he said as he twisted the handle. "Thank you for the incense. Maybe you can practice what I taught you and steal more for me? Enough to last the cycles that Hreinasta keeps you. Then I can burn it whenever I miss you."

I would steal this entire storeroom for him.

SIX

"Can you swim?" The Stranger's voice is full of doubt.
"No." I shake my head even though he isn't
here to see me. I grew up in Szent, locked away in
my parent's home and then the temple. Land surrounded the
holy city, so it was a lesson Kaid never taught me.

"You'll need to learn," The Stranger says, his sentiment
painfully obvious. "Oh well, no time like the present."

An unseen hand shoves me, and I tumble chest-first into
the cool, crystal water. My lungs restrict, my body spasms, and
an unpleasant rush of water shoots up my nose. I cough,
inhale more, and sputter as I flail and kick and roar. That gods
damned man. If I ever lay eyes on him again, I'll gut him like
I did that tiger.

"What's wrong with you?" I scream as my head pierces the
surface. My spastic limbs seize hold of the stones, and I haul
my soaked body out of the water. The Stranger doesn't
answer, but I feel his chuckle ripple through me.

"I hate you," I spit.

"Come, come, my child," he laughs. "Did you drown?"

"I could have!"

"But did you?"

"No," I concede.

"You did well." His voice in my mind calms to a serious tone. "You didn't drown, and you kicked your way to the surface. I believe you'll learn quickly."

"But you didn't need to push me." I'm all salt, both my emotions and my water-coated skin.

"Your instincts are strong. Fear drove your limbs, and it taught you how to move. I think it was wise to push you."

"No, you thought it was funny," I pout.

"It was." The Stranger huffs good-naturedly. "Want to try again?"

"Keep your gods damned hands off me," I snarl.

"All right, all right, it's lost its charm, anyway."

I wish he was here. I would slap him. "Don't let me drown?"

"You know I cannot help you."

"Fine. Have fun watching me swallow water."

"Oh, so dramatic, my child. You'll be fine. You're always fine."

"Until the day I'm not." My mind turns to Kaid. He was resilient, always finishing on top... until he didn't. Until the day his luck and life expired.

"I have faith in you." From the tenderness in his voice, I believe The Stranger. "Today is not the day I watch you die."

"Any tips for me?"

"Don't swallow water."

I call him an insulting word as I drop back into the gentle waves to try again.

"WHAT HAPPENED HERE?" I ask as I survey the Vesi, my skin drying against the heated sand. Simultaneously, a lake and a sea, the Vesi is an enormous stretch of water encased by sheer rock cliffs on all sides save for this lone beach, as if the earth had collapsed, giving way to water. This blue expanse is out of place in the wilderness, but it's the sunken city that's the most perplexing. Stone homes lay along cobbled streets, colliding with massive temples. An entire life buried beneath the lapping waves.

"How do you mean?" The Stranger's voice sounds in my head. He's been teaching me to swim these past few days, if abandoning me to struggle and cough is considered teaching. Szent is landlocked, and until this moment, the largest body of water I'd seen was the pool in the temple gardens. If only I had asked Kaid to teach me in that fountain. He was a far superior tutor to The Stranger. It's because of his lessons that I still draw breath.

"The city," I say, soaking in the sun's warmth. After the constant snow of the North and the scalding heat of the Sivatag, the Vesi's temperature is glorious. I never felt the burn of toasted sand or the sting of salt water before, and I like them. I wear nothing as I sun myself, completely alone save for the comforting voice in my head, and I picture Kaid's powerful body dripping wet. I imagine him swimming through the waves, his muscles curling and flexing as he dives deep. I feel his sun-kissed skin against mine, sliding against my sweaty body as our pleasure builds.

A soft cry escapes my throat as I fight back tears. I miss Kaid more than I can bear, and I hate that he's in pieces locked in a box and not naked on the beach beside me, black hair glinting and smile engulfing. This is the place where I miss him most. This is the place I want him to see, to experience, to enjoy. I wish we could share the sweet fruit that grows wild and free here. I want him to watch me peel off my clothes before I drop into the water and revel in the way his dark eyes flicker gold. He loved every part of me, body and mind. I adored all of him, soul and form, and my heart breaks all over again.

"What happened to the city? Why did it sink?" I ask,

forcing the pain down. Missing him does nothing. Finding his scattered bones is my only hope, and I silently beg The Stranger not to comment on the despair coating my voice.

"No evil befell the sunken city," he answers. "Udens, god of the sea, is neither man nor woman, but a beast of the depths. When the gods descended to our realm, most took up residence in Szent, but some ventured throughout the land. Lovec chose the North, his blood thirst driving him into the wilds, but Udens is bound to the water. Sailors pray to him, fishermen sacrifice to him, but he craved sacred waters, a temple in our realm while still in the sea. He longed to claim a dwelling among the people like his brethren had. His cult built the Vesi. They carved every stone, paved every street, erected each looming tower, and when construction completed, Udens sank it. The solid rock cracked, and the city plummeted as the earth flooded. Both a lake and a sea, and then again neither, the Vesi became his holy grounds."

"Then why would Valka hide him here?" I ask. "In an uncursed place?"

"Darkness may not have carved these cliffs, but it dwells within these waters," The Stranger answers, and his tone causes my stomach to clench in trepidation. "To kill and be killed, to eat and be eaten. That is nature's way. Life demands death, and Udens understands this. He doesn't wish to alter the cycle of life, but every creature of the sea caught by men to be consumed, every monster slain to ensure a ship's safety, every plant uprooted for its healing properties, drove him to despair. The beasts of old were savage monstrosities. Tentacles and eyes and scales and fangs, the ocean depths once teamed with unspeakable horrors, but humans eradicated them in their fear. They consume fish by the thousands, disrupt the corals for medicinal use, and Udens mourns each loss. When the Vesi sunk, he declared its waters holy. Mankind may dip beneath his waves, but they are not to touch those who live below the surface. All here are sacred to Udens, and while the creatures feed on both the vegetation and one another as nature requires, he forbids humankind from causing harm."

"I don't intend to kill anyone," I say in confusion. "I only mean to retrieve what was stolen."

"My sweet child, you do not understand. The monsters your ancestors eradicated still live in the Vesi. Beasts larger than Hreinasta's temple with a thirst for blood. Fangs that remember what human flesh tasted like. This shore where you bathe and practice is safe. Udens feeds off your pleasure in his waters, but the depths are filled with sights no human has seen in centuries. You'll descend into a pit of horrors to find his bones. The swim will test your stamina as you're hunted. Udens allows no violence against his kind. If you kill any of his creatures, even in self-defense, he will punish you. He tolerates such behavior in the oceans since that is its way, but not here. The Vesi is his. You cannot harm anything, not even the seaweed ensnaring your ankles as you drown."

"I surrender and die, or I fight and die?" I scramble to my feet, white sand clinging to my back as I pull away from the water.

"It is the way of the Vesi," he answers. "It's why Valka placed what you seek here. Your only hope of survival is to out-swim Udens' monsters, out-swim creatures who have lived below the surface for hundreds of cycles, all while never spilling a drop of his sacred children's blood."

THE TOUCH
SEASON OF GROWTH, CYCLE 78920

K aid wouldn't meet my gaze as I mimicked every thrust of his dagger with my own. We stood side by side, movement flowing in a dangerous dance beneath the moon's light, yet his eyes never sought mine. Smiles didn't curve his lips, and his voice had turned darker. It was always filled with danger, but the new tone was colder, the affection he saved for me absent. He'd been training me for weeks, joining me on the nights his god didn't demand his skills. He taught me to steal and fight. He taught me to be a friend, but tonight was different. The Kaid I'd grown irrevocably attached to had vanished, leaving a shadow of the thief in his place.

"That's all for tonight," Kaid said, his tone bled of all warmth, and despite the night's heat, gooseflesh pricked my skin.

"Would you like to do something else?" I was angry at my voice for wavering. Always so free with his words, this quiet stranger before me chilled my spirit. He'd taken to training me with the blade, but our lessons were stilted. We couldn't spar for fear of being discovered, for fear of touching, so we stood side by side, violent movements forming a dance. I lived for these moments, where my world learned parts of his, where my body experienced what he felt. I hadn't seen him for a week, so when he climbed through my window, my spirit soared, only to crash against his demeanor. My friend had disappeared, and an intimidating thief had assumed his place. For the first time, I was afraid of Kaid. Not because he would harm me, but because my heart sensed the shift. I was terrified of how I'd grown to love him, and that gave him the power to break me.

"No... I should leave. It's late," he answered without meeting my gaze. It wasn't late. He had only just arrived.

"Is...?" I was scared to ask. I didn't want his words to confirm the truth hanging thick between us. If he remained silent, I could clench my eyes and pretend this was a nightmare.

"Is everything all right?" My whisper was barely audible.

"Yes." His answer was too swift as he started for the roof's edge. "I should go."

"Kaid." I despised the desperation on my tongue. "Don't..." *Don't lie to me. Don't hide from me. Don't leave me.*

"Sellah." My name sounded like an apology as a tortured war fought in his expression. "I... I can't do this. I'm sorry. I have to go."

"Can't do what?"

"Sellah, please."

"Can't do what?" I repeated. My mother had abandoned me ten cycles ago, and I'd let her walk out of my life without so much as a word of protest. I wouldn't let him leave without a fight. He was all I had; all I would ever have as my twenty-first birthday crept closer.

"I..." He turned and strode across the roof, pausing at the edge before whirling on me so fast, I stumbled backward. "I can't do this anymore. I can't sit here and wait for you to leave me. Every time I look at you, I see the end of the greatest thing in my life. You're my best friend, my confidant, my heart. I love you, Sellah.

My emotion swelled at his confession. Kaid loved me, but my voice caught in my throat, threatening to choke me.

"Every night I spend with you, I love you more," he continued. "I'm filled with broken and jagged edges, but your softness and warmth fit perfectly between those sharp pieces. You make me whole. You're what my life was missing, and the longer I stay at your side, the more I love you. Varas may be the god I've pledged to, but you're who I want to swear my future to. You're the altar I pray at, the deity I worship, and I would sacrifice my life for you, but you don't belong to me. You never have, and you never will. You've belonged to Hreinasta since birth, and I can't watch the person I treasure most in this world lose herself to a selfish goddess."

"Kaid!" My voice pitched at his blasphemy.

"I don't care," he growled. "Gods be damned, but I do not care. May they strike me down, because my heart belongs to you, and I cannot stand by and idly watch your life be stolen. You didn't choose this. If you'd been of age when you swore the oath or if you'd sent me away when we first met, I could respect that, but you were born to appease your father's guilt. You were sacrificed before you understood what this meant, and in a few months, your soul will vanish. You'll sleep for decades, and I'll have to watch Hreinasta parade around in the body of the woman I love. I can't sit here and witness that happen. It's too painful."

"I was chosen as a child," I whispered with a weakness that disgusted me. "It's how it must be."

"Exactly," Kaid spat. "You were a child, a soul unable to choose for itself, and a predator came along to snatch you up."

"Kaid!"

"It's the truth and you know it. Stealing beautiful children to inhabit and forcing their own souls to vanish is predatory."

"Hreinasta is the Pure One," I argued, afraid the heavens

would open and strike him dead for his venom. "Our sacrifice is to keep her sacred."

"She's a selfish and cruel goddess," Kaid bit back, all rage and conviction. "The other gods came to the realm in their true forms. They subjected themselves to mankind's ways and lead by example. Valka leads his men into battle. Sato plants the fields alongside her harvesters, the sun blistering her skin as it does theirs. Varas steals just as we do. He saved me from death with his own hands." He gestured cruelly to his lips. "Elskere lives together as husband and wife as an illustration of a loving and faithful marriage. Each god fights and sweats and toils among their people except for Hreinasta. If she truly wanted her acolytes to remain pure, she would be here in this temple, leading by example. She would resist temptation first so that her priestesses could follow in her footsteps, but no. She hides in the gods' realm so that she doesn't have to practice her own doctrine. Purity is facing temptation and remaining holy, not enslaving young girls to hide behind."

"You shouldn't say that." Tears bathed my cheeks.

"It's the truth." Kindness disappeared from his features, and I saw the terror every other person he encountered must face. "She's selfish, coercing others so she doesn't have to resist herself. And even if I could ignore that, I cannot overlook that this wasn't your decision. You were forced into this life. You only believe it's your destiny because they gave you no other choice. If you had joined the temple at eighteen, fully aware of the path ahead of you, it would be different, but when you were ten cycles old, did you understand Hreinasta would shove your consciousness away? Did you know you would cease to exist?"

"No." The confession felt dangerous.

"If you knew then what you do now, would you have accepted this fate?"

"Don't make me answer that."

"Sellah." His voice was tortured. "If you'd known, would

you have chosen this life? Is Hreinasta the goddess you would have pledged to?"

"Yes." The lie escaped out of habit, and his features fell like crumbling rubble.

"I see." He turned away from me. "Then I must go, because I can't watch this. I won't survive losing you. As it is, I already feel as if a dull and rusted knife has pierced my heart, the pieces jagged and oozing." Sorrow wove through his voice. "I love you, but I won't come back. If I do, it'll destroy me. I don't want to live in a world without you, but I have to. I might as well get used to it."

Kaid dropped gracefully off the ledge, and panic washed over me. I couldn't breathe. I couldn't see. I couldn't hear. My heart was breaking, my soul was dying, and it was as if some deep part of my spirit took control of my body. I was no longer commanded by my limbs. My desperation ruled me, and I was across the roof before I registered my movements. Kaid fell to a decorative balcony below, and I vaulted down after him. He'd trained me well. I was strong. I was fast. I was feral.

He heard my feet land behind him, but he didn't turn. He didn't acknowledge my alarmed chase, and he gripped the opposite wall to climb out. One swift movement and he would be gone. He would no longer exist within the temple. He would belong to Szent, and if I allowed that to happen, his presence would never again grace mine. I couldn't describe the sheer terror in my gut. All I knew was I couldn't let him leave, so I ran.

I ran with loud steps and louder breaths, and as he gripped the ledge, I threw myself at him. My fingers captured his hand, my fist closing around him, and the world ceased to exist. The moon disappeared. The stars vanished. Szent fell away, and the wind stilled. There was nothing. There was no one. All that remained was the warmth of his skin against mine, the roughness of his palms scraping against my fingertips, his pulse jerking through the pressure point at his wrist.

I'd touched him. I had touched Kaid, and it was beautiful. The moment was sacred, destined to stay with me until death claimed me. My hand clutched him tighter as tears blurred my vision, but I didn't let go. I couldn't form words, so my hands spoke for me. They told him everything in that touch. One deliberate touch, and I'd chosen. He was what I wanted to pledge my life to. I was trapped in this temple, my future not my own, but my love was mine to give, and I offered it to him. I gave it to him with all of my heart.

My thief stared at our joined hands, and the pain on his face wasn't what I expected. It was excruciating, as if my touch was acid burning his flesh. Tears ran down his cheeks, smearing the ash, and then he pulled his hand free and climbed over the wall. He vanished into the night like a shadow, leaving me alone in my grief. At least I'd experienced his touch before he ripped my heart from my chest.

I LEFT MY WINDOW UNLOCKED, but he didn't come. I waited for three weeks, but he never returned. Kaid was gone, and he took my will to live with him. At the dawn of the fourth week, I resolved to close off my heart. I was a shell, my soul with the thief who stole it. It was for the best. I was already empty for Hreinasta to invade.

THE OVERWHELMING SENSE of being watched washed over me, and I jerked awake. Sleep had eluded me for days, but my body had finally succumbed to exhaustion. I'd been oblivious to the world, sensing nothing until his eyes found me in the darkness. I'd memorized the way his gaze trailed over me like a touch. I knew his scent. I recognized his presence. He had burrowed so deep within me that even the sound of his breathing had been ingrained in my memory, and I twisted on the mattress to stare at the sofa beneath the window. *His sofa.*

"Hi." He smiled hesitantly, his expression asking for forgiveness.

"Hi." I offered it wholeheartedly.

"Fifty cycles ago, a thief stole jewels from Varas' temple and sold them to a warlord. The thief was punished for the crime against his house, but the jewels were never recovered since no one could infiltrate the warlord's camps." Kaid looked at me with hope in his eyes. "Until now."

"You?" Pride swelled in my chest.

"I recovered every last one." He extended his fist. "I asked Varas if I might keep this, and he gave it to me with his full blessing." Kaid's hand unfurled, and the smallest jewel I'd ever seen sat on his palm. It was a vibrant emerald, flawless and sparkling despite its size. "I stole this for you." His voice was nervous, as if he was offering me his beating heart and not a gem.

I climbed off the bed and stared at his apology before plucking it from his palm. My fingers grazed his skin as I accepted it, and his chest rose with an unsteady breath.

"It's beautiful. Thank you." I gazed at him, tears blurring my vision. He'd come back to me. He knew the future we would face, and he had returned.

"Do you want to hear how I did it?" He leaned forward in anticipation, his question not really about telling me a story. It was a plea to stay. To return to the friends we were.

I didn't answer him as I walked to the sofa. I hovered before him, and then my gaze drifted to the space beside him. He shifted sideways, understanding my silent request, and I sat on the vacated cushion. The sofa was small, but a fraction of air separated us. We weren't touching, but I felt the heat from his body, the breath escaping from his lungs to brush against my ear as he regarded me with relief. I'd never sat there with him, and his expression was one of shock and excitement. Leaning my head against the wall and crossing my ankles, I clutched the jewel to my heart and then gazed at him expectantly. I didn't need to speak. He read the words in my eyes.

"You've heard of the Sivatag, right?" His question tumbled out of his mouth. I nodded, and he continued, "The warlord's camps border the desert. It's why he's not easily invaded. A wasteland at his back and an army at his front. For fifty cycles, thieves have been trying to return Varas' stolen jewels, but they either returned defeated or not at all."

"The warlord killed them?" I raised my eyebrows.

"And then sacrificed their corpses to the Sivatag," Kaid confirmed, and I shivered. The final resting place of the twin gods. The stretch of Earth so corrupted by war, an inescapable desert had dried out the land. I wouldn't want to enter its borders, even as a skeleton.

"I spent three weeks observing his camp," he continued, and I mentally acknowledged the length of his last absence. He hadn't been avoiding me. His god had sent him far from my side. "Three long, hot weeks. I don't know how the warlord lives so close to the desert. Even outside of its border is gods damned unbearable, but I sat there, day in and out, discovering why no thief survived this mission. I learned why no one escaped his hold, and then I saw it. I found my opening."

SEVEN

I already know where they hid him. A tower so tall that its base rests on the deepest silt and its peak pierces the water's surface stands in the center of the Vesi. There'll be no cheating, no shortcuts. It's a long and dangerous swim, and I know that's where he was laid to rest. Whether I wade into the water from the beach or travel days to dive off the opposite cliffs, the journey is the same. Open waters and monsters with a taste for human blood.

I stand, naked and tanned, in the sand, the gentle warm waves lapping at my toes. The sun has bronzed my skin. The swimming has strengthened my muscles, and the fruit trees bordering the beach fed my belly. I look healthier than I have since it happened, which makes my heart ache. My reflection stares back at me from the crystal waters, and I hate how my eyes sparkle in the sunlight. I should not look well. I don't deserve to be healthy. Not while he's in pieces.

"You're no good to him ill," The Stranger's voice pops into my mind, and I flinch.

"Stay out of my head."

"I don't need to be in your head. I can read your thoughts

on your face. The color in your cheeks would please him. It does me."

"That's why it hurts. He is pale and lifeless, and I am——"

"Beautiful." The Stranger cuts me off. "You should take pride in that. Not because it makes you superior or because it makes you selfish, but because when you find all of him, you'll be a welcomed sight. Think of how he'll blame me if you look like a skeleton when he returns."

"I may be a skeleton after this dive."

"True."

"Thanks." I scoff. "I appreciate the confidence."

"Someone has to keep you humble, my child. At the rate you're going, your feats of victory will outweigh the gods'."

"Do you think they've noticed me? What I'm doing?" His comment coils concern in my chest.

"Undoubtedly." His answer chills me despite the sun's caress. "But they do not know what I've promised you. They simply mock your foolish pursuits."

"I hope my trust in you is not foolish," I say. What he's promised me is impossible, but I'm desperate enough to believe him.

"You shall have to wait and see."

"Will you send me off with well wishes, at least?" I ask. "Even if they are lies?"

"I don't need to wish you well." His melodic voice bathes my mind. "I watched you train these past weeks. Your lungs are strong, your muscles powerful. Swim fast and swim well. Perhaps Udens will take pride in your new skill."

"Is he here?" I ask. "In these waters? Or do only his monsters dwell in the depths?"

"His soul lingers in every sea, every lake, every ocean and river that dampens this realm. He is here."

I step further into the water until my ankles are submerged, and I nod. I don't know what else to say.

"Do not forget," The Stranger continues. "He allows no

harm to come to his children in the Vesi. No matter the darkness, no matter the evil, you must not cause any living creature to suffer. From the smallest fish to the sea plants to the monsters."

I gesture to my bare body, absent my dagger. I go in alone, not even a garment to shield me.

"Swim swiftly, my child," he says. "May Udens watch over you."

"The gods have abandoned me," I say.

"Have they?" The Stranger asks, and my face burns where Lovec marked me as his own. But we are the same. Both tainted by loss, and as the warm water pulses around my skin, another thought occurs to me.

"May Udens watch over me," I repeat, the words almost choking me. It's been so long since I prayed, it feels like a betrayal to him. But Udens didn't carve him to pieces. No, the god of the sea simply guards him from me.

THE SWIM IS EXHAUSTING. Water is everywhere, but there's nothing to drink. The sun beats down on my bare back. The salt stings my lips and eyes. I left the shore at dawn to ensure the daylight granted me her long hours, but as fatigue settles in my bones, I wonder if it's enough. I don't want to be trapped floating in the Vesi overnight. Thankfully, some of the sunken city's roofs loom high, and I've found three perches so far to rest upon. I still have to stand, though, my chin just reaching the surface, but they were welcomed reprieves from the endless strokes.

I teeter on one such roof now, catching my breath as I wait for the call of black magic. The darkness draws me to him with a sickening pull, but beneath the sulfur and stench, another thread tugs at my heart. I often wonder if Elskere, the wed gods, stitched it there for me to follow. Most would claim our binding incomplete since tradition dictates the ceremony be held before their altar. Ours was pledged under the moon, but there are no two hearts as woven together as Kaid's and mine. Except for maybe Elskere, and the burning lines on my face taught me I'm not as forsaken as I once thought. I would like to trust that the wed gods—the husband and wife who forsook their own names to be referred to as a single deity—mourn my loss with me. They are nothing without each other. I am hollow without Kaid, and his fractured spirit calls to me. Begs me to find his severed body.

Something brushes against my bare calf, and I yelp as I throw myself into the water. My panicked eyes snap to the spot I vacated, bracing for my doom, but when I see the slimy creatures that assaulted me, I laugh so hard that I snort salt water up my nose. I sputter unattractively as I swim back to the roof, my toes finding purchase, and a school of neon-colored fish swarms my legs. They weave in and out, dancing in colors and grace. They're stunning, hues I've never seen in all my twenty-two cycles. I wore white trimmed with gold. Kaid always dressed in black, and now I wear what I find or nothing at all. My life has been temples and locked rooms and deadly landscapes, but this? I burst into tears as a pink fish bumps my thigh.

A yellow creature dances around my wrist, and a red one with orange fins nibbles gently on my belly button. My hands move of their own longing, and a blue fish with a bright green friend slip and slide over my fingers. I can't stop the smile that spreads across my face as the emerald color reminds me of the jewel Kaid stole for me. I left it behind when I fled, but seeing this emphasizes all the precious things I've lost.

I simultaneously laugh and sob. "I wish you were here," I tell him. I wonder if his thieving ever brought him face-to-face with such beauty. I hope it did. His life was filled with violence. His lips. His—I cut that thought off at the root. I can't think about that day. It destroyed me, and if I let the memory play out, I'll drown.

My attention returns to the vibrance surrounding me, and an orange and white fish darts through my legs like a spear through the water. His speed carries him far, and as if controlled by one mind, the school surges after him. Their rainbow vision weaves through the waves, leaving me mesmerized but alone.

"*Go.*" The order comes from nowhere, but it's not The Stranger's voice. It's an instinct, a feeling in my gut urging me to follow the colorful waters, and its urgency is so strong, I cough as if it punched me in the stomach.

Without considering if this impulse is a trap, I dive after the fish, their beauty captivating me in a trance. The farther I swim, the deeper they descend. The longer I chase, the more entranced I grow. Their colors and elegance are the only things I notice. I want to become a part of their lives. I long for my body to shed its flesh and bloom again with neon scales. I do not hear The Stranger banging at the gates, begging for entrance into my mind. I don't sense his worry wrapping around me. All I see, feel, know is exquisite color. All I desire is to become like them.

The vibrant school dives deeper, their swarming bodies closing in on the sunken city's center, and I've lost all track of the day. I know not what I seek. I exist for this beauty, crave this splendor. My lungs cannot feel the lack of oxygen burning through my chest. My skin doesn't register the drastic plunge in the water's temperature. My eyes don't sense the encroaching darkness. The need to follow is all-consuming.

Something seizes my ankle, and I jerk to a halt so violently that it throws my oblivion off. It disappears into the shadows with the school of fish, leaving me alone in the sudden cold. Panic floods my limbs as I realize just how deep I've fallen, just how loud The Stranger is screaming for me to wake up, but before I can angle for the surface, a second grip ensnares my wrist, a third wraps around my waist, and a fourth captures my thigh.

My vision snags on the writhing seaweed choking my skin, and pain blisters over my body as it constricts. I thrash against its hold, but its organic chains do not yield.

"Stop!" The Stranger's voice registers in my head. "Stop moving!"

I freeze, my lungs screaming for air. My suffocating brain cannot comprehend why he's begging me to surrender, but then I see it, and my veins flood with ice. A ripped sliver of seaweed floats past my vision, and my heart stills. I harmed one of Udens' children.

A massive shadow moves to my right, and I strain against my bonds. I can't control the fear rippling through me. I need to scream, to release what little air I hold into the darkness. But somehow, I manage to keep my lips clenched shut.

Tentacles thicker than my torso snake around a sunken building, and an enormous mass pulls itself from the shadows. Before the monster enters the dim light, movement below captures my attention. Crustaceans as large as rowboats crawl in hoards over one another, and this time, I do scream before I remember to clamp my mouth shut. My sight is burning, my body suffocating. I should open my mouth and swallow. I should drown before the massive tentacles suction my flesh from my bones because that monstrous beast moving closer is not one I want to face. It's the stuff of nightmares, and my heart feels like it'll explode from the fear pumping through my veins.

Neon colors fill my vision, and the school of fish that led me to my watery death swarm before my face. They've changed, though. Their faces are no longer the sweet creatures that flirted with me, but gaping mouths filled to the brim with needle-sharp fangs. There are hundreds of them. Thousands surround me, tasting the water as if to sample the flavor of my flesh. I twist against the seaweed as another arm of green wraps around my throat, and the sickly-colored fish close in. It was a trap. It was all so Udens' children could feast on human flesh. I hate myself. He deserves a better rescue, for I am a fool. I say his name even though it releases the last of my air into the darkness. I say it so that I die with him on my lips.

The scene before me blurs, and my thought from earlier pricks my memory. Lovec and I are the same. That's why he blessed me, claimed me, protected me. We're both intimately acquainted with loss. But so is Udens. His children, his creations, were slaughtered so that mankind could rule the seas. He and I are not so different, and I force my limbs to go limp, my struggle to evaporate.

"Please," I say in my mind because if I speak, the last of my oxygen will vacate my lungs. I stare at the hideously colored fish, the encroaching crustaceans, the behemoths with more tentacles than I can count. "Please," I silently beg Udens as I surrender wholly to these monsters. "I just want him back."

Nothing happens, and I hang my head, death closing in thick and oppressive. I won't kill his children. I won't harm the beasts Udens' fought so hard to save. I understand him in that respect, and this is a battle I cannot win. Any harm I cause will do nothing to save my life.

I can no longer hold my breath, and I convulse, inhaling a lungful of water. I cough and choke, trying to expel the salt, but I only swallow more. Fear consumes me. Mine and The Stranger's, and an odd emotion bleeds from him into my mind. The Stranger is afraid. He's afraid to lose someone he cares for, and I silently extend my apology to him and to Kaid. *I tried, my love, my heart, my husband. I'm sorry I failed you.*

As my vision dulls, the colorful fish before me morph, my dying brain playing tricks on me. They pulse and vibrate, losing their color, and slowly they collide with one another, their flesh tearing open. The water churns bloody, slabs of carnage ripping free in a violent display of death, but as they shred apart, their bared muscles fuse together. It's a terrifying sight to die to as they shed and mutilate, as their exposed sinews graft into fleshy, oozing strips. The water frenzies, air bubbles exploding in the chaos until a large one collides with my lips.

Oxygen floods my lungs as I swallow the bubble, a second slamming into me a moment later, followed by a third, a fourth, a fifth, until I am no longer filled with water but air. Glorious, beautiful air.

My vision clears, and the surrounding horde of monsters should frighten me, but they pale in comparison to what hovers inches from my face. It's terrifying, but not the kind of terror that makes you scream. It's an all-consuming fear that locks you within your body, and its power is deadly enough to still even the strongest heart.

The colorful fish have vanished, leaving the water bloody in their deformed wake, and in their place is the largest creature I've ever laid eyes upon. It resembles a shark, but it's too massive to be one. His razor-sharp teeth are as long as my arms. Scars the length of my torso score his leathery face, and his eyes? They are almost completely white like The Strangers, but his irises have the faintest hint of green, much like Lovec's were tinted blue, and I know who looms before me.

"Udens," I say, out loud this time, and a bubble of air floats toward me to replace what I expelled. The hideous god stares at me, his mouth wide enough to capture me whole, and I'm not sure if he means to devour me or speak to me. None of the creatures move, but my heart pounds viciously.

After an eternity, Udens looks over my bare body to where the seaweed restrains me. He sees no weapons. He registers my position of surrender, my refusal to harm his children even though it almost cost me my life, and then with an unexpected speed that rips a scream from my mouth, he unhinges his bloodied jaw and lunges.

I brace for a pain that never comes. Feather-light caresses consume my body instead. I part my clenched eyelids and watch in wonder as Udens explodes back into the colorful fish, their fangs gone, their beauty returned with almost blinding perfection. The seaweed retracts, leaving purple bruises and red welts where it strangled me. The crustaceans crawl back beneath the silt as the tentacles return to the shadows, and the gorgeous fish swarm and dance and play around me. My body aching in more places than I can count, I angle for the center of the sunken city, and resume my swim.

The school accompanies me as I dive, no longer possessing me, but eager to help. Their tiny fins beat the water, and pockets of air float into my mouth so that I don't drown. These aren't fish. They are Udens. They are him when he's at peace. When those he loves aren't threatened, and I can't resist touching him as I swim. My fingertips brush every fish I can, and they revel in the attention. He saves his monstrous form for his enemies, and I understand why Valka sunk his bones in the Vesi. Most wouldn't surrender. Most would fight and slay and butcher. The water would run red with blood, but I know what it means to lose what you love most. Udens and I are alike. Perhaps I'm not godless because Kaid was right. Selfishness warped those in Szent, but these wild gods that few remember? The ones no one taught me about? They only want true devotion. The kind you give freely.

The pink fish twirls before my face, fins brushing my cheek in a kiss, and then I see it. A calf, foot to knee. What was once the city square before it sank now lies at the deepest part of the Vesi, and the ancient cobblestones are void of silt where his limb rests. I wouldn't have survived this dive. It's too deep and cold. My lungs would have burst, and as if reading my fear, the pink fish slaps his tail against my cheek, forcing an air bubble into my nose.

I smile as I run my fingers over his small body, and then I plunge. The depths are icy, the lack of light oppressive, but

Udens swarms me, keeping me warm, and after a swim that has turned my muscles useless with exhaustion, I seize hold of his calf.

A soft cry of relief escapes me, and then I choke before Udens forces more air into my lungs. My lips clench shut as I throw the pink fish a thankful glance, and I hug his calf, kissing his dead skin in spite of the magic's burn. Udens hovers protectively, his body heat keeping me warm, but the school falls still, granting me a private moment to process my emotions. I hold him against my chest until I can't bear the sting, and then I nod to signal my readiness. In a tornado of color, the god of the sea whips into a frenzy and delivers me to the distant surface, the sun warming my cold skin as I crawl onto the steeple protruding from the waves. It's a long swim back to shore, but I can't find the will to care. Another piece of him is in my arms, and despite the colorful bruises on my body, I'm alive.

The school swirls around me while I catch my breath, and when my heart rate normalizes, they dive toward oblivion.

"Wait!" I yell, but they ignore me. They disappear into the depths, and it takes a moment for me to realize the pink fish still hovers in sight.

"Thank you," I say, and I can tell by his eyes, he understands. "When my quest is complete, if I succeed, may we come back here?" I ask. "I want him to see you, to see this."

The fish stares at me and then dives with no indication he heard my question. I sigh, disappointed until I hear that same voice as before. The one that urged me to chase the swarm.

"Yes."

THE KISS
SEASON OF GROWTH, CYCLE 78920

K aid did not return, and unlike his last absence, his fear of losing me wasn't to blame. I sensed it in my bones. Something was wrong, and as each night passed without him appearing in my window, my dread grew until cold sweat coated my skin and uneasiness greased my stomach.

———

THE MATTRESS DIPPED, yanking me from sleep, and I rolled away from the intruder so fast, I almost fell off the bed. Relief flooded my body when I realized who lay next to me, but it was short-lived when I saw his face. Perspiration beaded on his brow, smearing the ashes framing his exhausted eyes. Tension gripped my muscles at his expression, for he'd never touched my bed before. My emotions wanted to revel in this broken barrier, but his rigidity screamed alarm, stealing the joy I felt at waking to find his head on the pillow beside mine. His massive frame consumed the mattress. His anxiety consumed me, silencing my greeting, and all I could do was stare at his profile.

"Did something happen?" His dangerously low voice finally broke the silence, but he refused to meet my gaze.

"What do you mean?" I whispered, my concern making it difficult to speak.

"The temple's security changed, and I couldn't sneak in. I tried for two weeks before I found a crack in their defenses, and my success was only because of Varas' blessing."

"I don't—"

"Do they know? Do they suspect anything?" He cut me off.

"I don't think so." I longed to wipe the unease from his creased forehead. "All is as it should be, and Varas hides your movements from Hreinasta, doesn't he?"

"Yes." He gestured to his stained skin. "But, Sellah, I don't like this. There's been a shift in the temple's atmosphere, and I don't know how often I'll be able to slip unseen through the seams. I would never forgive myself if my actions endangered you."

"They don't know about you, I swear. Everything is—" My voice died in my throat, strangled by dread.

"What?" He twisted to look me in the eye.

"The claiming." The words turned to bile on my tongue. "I turn twenty-one this Season of the Harvest."

Kaid's body went rigid. "The Harvest is..." He didn't need to say it. We both knew how rapidly it was approaching.

"As Hreinasta's soul departs one vessel to enter another, her spirit becomes vulnerable. The transfer takes seconds, but those moments leave her bare and unprotected. The temple is preparing for my claiming."

Kaid's breathing faltered, and he turned his stressed gaze back to the ceiling, his hulking frame suddenly small beside me. His despair was palpable, and I could no longer resist his gravity. My fingers reached out of their own accord and trailed over his cheek until they found the scar on his lips. My breath caught at the sensation of the rough imperfection mixing with the softness, and it was both everything I imagined and nothing like I expected.

"Don't." Kaid gripped my wrist and pulled my hand from his face, his graveled voice thick and harsh.

"I'm sorry." My chest deflated at his rejection. "You told me once I could touch it, but I should have asked first." I tried to pull away, but his grip refused to yield. His fist chained my arm against his chest, his heart beating violently below my palm.

"Not there." He said, as if the words pained him. "Anywhere but there."

"I'm sorry," I whispered, embarrassed I'd brought his scar shame. "I wasn't thinking."

"It's not that…" He struggled to enunciate clearly, his tone rougher than I'd ever heard, and for a moment, neither of us spoke. Neither of us moved as he restrained my fist tightly against his thundering heart.

"You don't understand how badly I want to taste you," he confessed, his face twisted as if he wasn't speaking but ripping out his heart. "You don't understand how desperately I crave your lips on mine, your body pressed against me. My control teeters dangerously on the precipice, and the only way I can stop it from plunging over that edge is by keeping my distance. I refuse to take something from you that I can't return, and while I believe your vows were forced upon you, I won't be the one to break them. You're pure with me. Safe with me. Protected with me, but please, don't push. I won't be able to resist if you push." He turned toward the opposite wall as if even seeing me from the corner of his eye was a temptation. "Not there. Not my lips." His chest heaved as if I'd punched him. "Anywhere but there or I'll break. I can't break, but I'm afraid because I'm so close to surrendering."

"Kaid?"

His fist tightened around my wrist as he struggled. "Please don't. I can't love you. Not like this. Not when I'll lose you."

He shoved my hand off his body, the absence of his touch more painful than his grip, and losing his warmth convinced me to change everything.

"Kaid." I slipped my palm against his cheek and pulled his face back to me.

"Sellah, stop." He was begging, shaking.

"I love you," I said with conviction. Raw and strong and unbreakable. "Loving you isn't a sin, nor will it make me unworthy. Loving you is the only choice I've ever made for myself, so when I say this, understand it's with my whole heart. I choose you, and I cannot go into my future without knowing what loving you tastes like. You've filled my heart so completely, there's no room for anything else."

"Sellah…"

"I love you." I smiled softly, the moonlight dancing on our skin as we lay so close, yet too far apart. My heart threatened to beat out of my chest, but my nerves were nothing compared to my longing. For the first time in twenty cycles, I dictated the path I would travel, and life had never been so beautiful.

"Did you hear me?" I whispered when he lay frozen against my touch. "I love you, Kaid."

Kaid lunged for me like a warrior on the battlefield, and his hand gripped the back of my neck with inescapable force. For a moment, he surrendered his control to his desire, but then his better judgment took charge. His movements slowed as he pulled me gently against him, and when our chests collided, the breath rushed from my lungs.

"Is this too much?" He asked, cupping my face in his powerful hands. His heart beat against my breast, and the headiness of that moment threatened to drown me. It was both too much and not enough, and I experimentally gripped the front of his shirt, feeling the muscles that hid intoxicatingly below the fabric.

"Yes," I confessed, but when he started to retreat, I leaned in closer, refusing his escape. "Do you love me?"

"You are my goddess." His low admission rumbled through his ribs, vibrating against my skin. "You are what I pray to, what I worship, what I adore."

"Then show me," I challenged, and it was all the permission my thief needed. He closed the divide between us, and his lips were on mine like a man starving, the kiss soft and holy. An unexpected heat curled in my chest, and I gasped, the need in my voice surprising me. Kaid deepened the kiss at the sound, his heart rate thundering dangerously. His touch was reverent, respectful, loving, but I sensed the war waging in his chest. His longing fought to escape, but he didn't act on his desire, and my love swelled with the knowledge. He promised me I was safe in his presence, and his kiss sealed that oath. He did not push. He did not steal. He did not disrespect. Kaid worshiped me with the innocence of that embrace, and it was the purest form of ecstasy I'd ever experienced. Tears pricked my eyes at the beauty, and I released his shirt to capture him in a hug.

"I'm sorry." Kaid jerked back as my tears splashed onto his cheek, assuming I'd let go of him to escape and not pull closer. "I didn't mean—"

"Don't stop." My fingers tangled in his black hair, weaving through the soft locks, and I sighed with pleasure. How often had I stared at him, longing to brush the hair from his eyes? The desire filled my dreams, but my imagination paled compared to the reality. "Never stop."

He granted my wish, tasting me in ways I never dreamed a man could kiss a woman. My chest heaved against his, our breathing becoming one until I didn't know where I ended and he began. His hand left my face to hug me close. My fingers tightened in his hair, and I knew that was where I belonged. He was my world, and I was his home.

"This is the moment I'll take with me to my grave," Kaid

spoke against my lips before pulling back. I instantly missed him, but I understood his retreat. Our kiss was magic. It promised I was at home in his arms, but even its innocence was too much for me. My cheeks were flushed, my heartbeat erratic. I couldn't handle the emotions flooding my spirit, and he sensed my need to process. Most would have been disappointed by such a chaste kiss, but my world exploded the moment our lips touched. My body burned with a fire I didn't understand, and I wanted more. I wanted everything with Kaid, but the tears wouldn't stop. The dam inside my soul had broken, and I understood for the first time how beautiful love was. I'd lived so long without it, its sudden presence left me weak.

"Don't cry." He brushed the dampness from my cheeks. "You did nothing wrong."

"That's not why I'm crying." I curled against his side, and he instinctively wrapped an arm around me as if we'd always existed like that. "My mother rarely hugged me before she surrendered me to Hreinasta." Kaid stiffened uncomfortably at my revelation, and I pulled him close, unsure if it was for his comfort or mine. "Once I was accepted as an acolyte, she stopped touching me altogether. I haven't received affection in so long that I forgot what it feels like. There's no love in this temple. No warmth or fondness. Not for me at least, so I'm not crying because of guilt. I'm crying because I finally know what it means to be important to someone for more than just my appearance."

I expected Kaid to respond, but when only his silence answered me, I shifted so I could see his face. He stared at the ceiling, refusing to meet my gaze. I opened my mouth to ask what was wrong, but I paused when I saw them. Tears. His eyes brimmed with them, and they smeared his already blurred ashes. I watched him cry in silence, the power of that moment burrowing deep inside me to never leave. Kaid was the first person to shed tears on my behalf, and I gave him the space to suffer through the weight of my confession. I watched every tear land on my pillow, his sadness more precious than the smiles of the faithful worshipers who passed me daily, and when I could no longer bear his pain, I pressed my lips to his damp cheeks. They tasted of salt and sorrow, and as much as I wanted to erase his anguish, his grief proved how deeply he cared. It was humbling, and when he finally captured me in his arms and pulled me against his thundering heart, he kissed my head with heartbreaking tenderness.

"I love you, Sellah," he whispered into my hair. "You own me. All of me. Forever."

THE REQUEST
SEASON OF GROWTH, CYCLE 78920

I was in Kaid's arms the second his tall frame pulled through my window, and it was liberating to touch him so freely. He captured my waist, hoisting me off the floor as I hugged his neck, and I buried my nose against his throat. I would never tire of his scent. Incense coated my skin from its constant burning in the inner sanctum, but Kaid smelled of freedom. He smelled of the outdoors and sweat and the food he passed in the market, and it was my obsession.

"May I?" he asked as he lowered me to the ground, but he barely spoke the words before my mouth found his, his lips against mine in desperate hunger. His chest was solid beneath my curves, so much stronger than I'd expected, and I couldn't stop the soft moan that escaped me. I hadn't seen him in four days, not since our first kiss, and I felt his absence in every cell of my body.

"Sellah," he whispered into my mouth like a prayer. "You're so beautiful." He set me down on the ground and brushed my flushed cheeks with his thumbs. "I know you hate being valued for only your appearance, but I love all of you. You're still my best friend, but gods, you are perfect."

"I missed you." I smiled wide at his praise, noticing the

customary ash was missing from his eyes. "What happened?" My fingertips trailed over his temples. I would never tire of the sensation of his skin against mine. I could live forever in his arms and never grow tired of the fire he stoked within me.

"I washed my face." He gripped my jaw with gentle owner-ship and leaned forward, kissing me until I saw stars. "I wanted to kiss you and didn't want my ashes to stain your skin... well, I do." He pulled back so I could see the tease in his gaze. I'd never seen that expression before, and my cheeks flushed red at its meaning. "I would love to mark you with my ashes, to form a path of my every touch over your body, but I won't put you in harm's way."

"Thank you." I blushed at the image his words painted, and for a second, I allowed myself to imagine what I would look like bare, wearing only his ash stains.

"Stop," he groaned, and I jerked free of my imagination. "I can read what you're thinking, and I'm trying to exhibit control, but if you keep making that face, it will shred quickly."

"I'm—" I started.

"Don't you dare apologize. Never be sorry to me," Kaid interrupted. "We're just in uncharted waters. I love you, but I won't take anything you can't willingly give. Your situation..." His expression darkened. "I won't compromise you."

"You aren't." I cupped his jaw softly, forcing his gold-flecked eyes to mine. "I choose you, remember? I have no guilt or shame because you can't compromise what belongs to you."

"Sellah?" He gripped my hand, lacing his strong and calloused fingers through mine as he pulled me to a seat on the mattress. "You can leave, right? I've heard of acolytes dissolving their pledges when they changed their minds. You can renounce your vows and pledge to another god. It's not against the law."

There was such hope in his eyes that tears rose to my

surface. "No, it's not against the law," I whispered, forcing them down. "But the claiming is soon. Hreinasta announced her intentions on me almost eleven cycles ago, and once she claims a vessel, there's no undoing it. She won't let me go. I belong to her... my body does, at least."

"So, if you renounced her tomorrow?"

"She cannot harm my body, but there are other ways to punish a person."

Kaid flinched. "Have you seen that happen?"

"Once," I nodded. "When I was fifteen, they caught a priestess alone with a man and made an example of her. She was in her forties, well past the age of a vessel, but even the priestesses must remain pure. Perhaps she was merely comforting the man. Perhaps they were old friends or family members, but all she did was touch his shoulder. The chains they used on her were padded so that they didn't mark her beauty, but they tortured her mind for a month, and he was flogged for his sins. The priestess returned after her thirty-day penance, but she was never the same. Something had snapped inside her, and she died shortly after."

Kaid released my hand, pulling his fists into his lap, and I read fear in his rigid stance. We'd done more than that priestess, and the consequences of our actions terrified him.

"I shouldn't be here." He stood, but I captured his wrist with both my hands before he could run.

"She may not let me leave. She won't allow me to renounce my devotion, but she cannot steal my mind. Hreinasta will consume my flesh, but this?" I pointed to my heart and then my head. "They're mine, and they belong to you."

"I don't want her to punish you." The heartbreak on his face was enough to rip me to shreds.

"She already has," I answered solemnly. "She'll inhabit me sooner than I'm ready for. I'll disappear for decades. I've already been punished, so don't deny me the only thing in this life that's mine, and mine alone."

Kaid turned around and knelt before me, his elbows digging into my thighs as he cupped my face. "I won't, I promise." He kissed me reverently, worship in his touch as he remained on his knees. "I don't want to risk your safety, but I won't be like your family or this temple. From now until you disappear, every choice and decision are yours. Whatever they are, I'll obey."

"Then love me, Kaid." My fingers laced through his hair. "Love me enough for a lifetime."

He groaned, pushing further between my thighs until his chest pressed against mine. I gasped at the contact, my legs instinctively tightening around his ribs, and I drank every ounce of pleasure he offered me. The kiss was holy. It was destruction, and I burned in its desire.

"Sellah," he moaned into my mouth before biting my bottom lip softly. "Did you mean it? Do you really want a life-time of my love in these next weeks?"

"Yes." I could barely speak as something foreign and wickedly delicious curled in my belly.

"Gods be damned," he cursed. "I want to taste you." He pulled away, holding my jaw firm as he studied my face, searching for hesitation, but I was his, body and soul. "Please let me kiss you the way you deserve."

"Yes." I nodded, and he must have read the resounding consent in my eyes because he gripped my chin harder and slammed his mouth back to mine. The kiss was rough. Hungry and full of aching desperation. He uncurled his fingers from around my face and placed them on my thighs, sucking my bottom lip between his teeth. His calloused palms rubbed my legs for a moment as if to prepare himself, and then he settled on his heels. With slow movements, he bunched up my skirt until the hem sat on my knees.

A shocked gasp escaped my mouth as his fingers brushed

against my bare skin. No one had ever touched me there. No one other than myself had seen my legs since my childhood, and he stared mesmerized at my heaving chest.

"Do you want me to stop?" His deep voice was low and harsh, as if it struggled to escape his throat.

"Never." It was the truth. I would never ask him to stop.

He smiled at my answer, his scarred lips so intoxicatingly beautiful, and he shoved my skirt up further to rest his palms on my bare thighs. I felt drunk on his caress, and I swore the room was spinning, glowing, floating. Or maybe I was the weightless one, my spirit soaring as my heart raced. Kaid watched my chest heave at the sensation, and then he leaned forward as if unable to resist my gravity and kissed my clavicle.

"Remember." His moving lips tickled. "I only take what you give willingly. You're in control. Promise you'll tell me if you need me to stop."

"I promise." I wrapped my arms around his neck, clutching him to my chest as I buried my nose in his hair. He responded to my tenderness with a soft kiss pressed against my flushed skin, dragging his lips down until they reached the top of my dress.

"Good girl." He smiled like I'd granted his every wish and slipped his hands behind my thighs. In one swift movement, he hoisted me off the bed and slammed me against his chest. "You're so beautiful. No one should be this perfect."

My legs instinctively wrapped around his hips, our bodies so close, not even air could pass between us. I gasped at the contact, pulling a groan from him at the sound, and he slid his hands further up my thighs, making it impossible for me to escape. He didn't kiss me. He simply held my gaze, watching my reaction.

"My goddess," he growled, capturing my palm and shoving it against his thundering heart. "Do you feel what you're doing to me?"

"Yes." His roaring pulse forced a smile from my lips.

"Good." He released my wrist, his hand returning to my thigh, and I thought I might pass out from the feel of him so dangerously close to my center. "I can't wait any longer."

He sank to the mattress, shifting me so that I straddled him. His hands left my legs and slid up to my hips as his mouth captured mine. His body was impossibly strong, every inch power and grace, but I could barely concentrate as he used my hips to yank me close. I was naïve and innocent, and the feel of him between my thighs made me want to scream. Not in fear, though, never in fear, but in desperate desire. I didn't understand my body's reaction, but I craved it all the same. It was overwhelming, but I wanted to drown in it.

"Touch me," Kaid demanded as he nipped at my lip. "I want your hands on me. I need to memorize your caress."

I chose to ignore the heartbreaking reason behind his request and slid my palm up his chest. We were both fully clothed, and while I was curious to see how beautiful my thief was bare, I was thankful for the barrier. The sensations were too great as my fingers found every hard line and soft curve of his form. He was a work of art, a priceless jewel in my eyes, and I didn't think I would survive anything more intense than this kiss.

"Open for me." Kaid brushed his thumb against my mouth, and I pulled away in confusion. I instantly regretted my movement because seeing his face undid me. His expression was pure obsession, a devotion not even the gods experienced from their faithful, and he looked like he wanted to devour me, body and soul.

"Come here," he coaxed, realizing he needed to guide my movements. He kissed me gently before continuing. "Open for me, goddess. I want to taste you." His tongue licked the seam of my mouth, and I couldn't stop the obscene moan that escaped me. Kaid smirked against my lips before slipping his tongue against mine, and I froze at the foreignness of his affection. I'd seen my parents kiss in the courtyard below my room as a child, so I understood the concept, but this? This felt dangerous, and I wanted more.

I fumbled through the movements, but Kaid graciously guided me. His tongue explored every inch of my mouth, pulling pleasure from me I didn't know existed, and I tentatively brushed my tongue against his, savoring the exhilaration.

Kaid cursed violently at my touch and wrapped his arms around my waist. His control evaporated, and my sweet and gentle thief disappeared with it. His kiss turned primal, and I surrendered to it. I let him take everything with that kiss, and within minutes we were sweating and moaning and writhing together. Desire fueled us, but beneath the passion, beneath the arousal, was a love forceful enough to alter my destiny. Our romance wasn't based on lust, but friendship. I'd spent seasons learning every fiber of this man's being, growing to trust and care for him, and even though his longing was thick between my thighs, it was his love that undid me.

He bit my lip and pulled away with a proud smirk, both of us realizing we were in danger of plunging off the edge. Part of me wanted to protest his departure, but I recognized his control was for my sake. I detested his discipline, but he knew my body almost better than I knew myself. Kaid's care was absolute, and he understood I needed to process my emotions, to calm my racing heart, and think through my decision. With a sweet kiss on my cheek, he pushed me back until I sat on his knees. We were still touching, but I could no longer feel his arousal, and my pulse calmed.

"I love you so much, Sellah." He stared into my eyes. "You've ruined me. I'll never be the same."

"Neither will I," I whispered.

"Did you like it?" He traced my lips with his thumb, and I nodded emphatically as I kissed his fingers. "It wasn't too much for you? I don't want to frighten you, but I lose myself in your presence."

"Your tongue?" I asked, my embarrassment flooding my cheeks, and he laughed at my bright coloring. "Is that... Is that something lovers normally do?"

"It is." He brushed my hair behind my ear. "The tongue can do many things. Things I wish I had the time to show you."

"Don't." I pressed my hand to his mouth, silencing him. "Not tonight. Can we pretend my future doesn't exist tonight?"

"I'll do anything for you, you know that."

"Good. Then love me and forget my fate for a few hours. I want a lifetime of your kisses before the dawn sends you away."

He wrapped his arms around my shoulders, and I let myself imagine a life where I didn't disappear. Where I could leave and spend every night in Kaid's arms. I wanted him to show me all he could do with his tongue. I wanted to see him bare and feel him between my thighs. I wanted a future.

"I could live forever in your embrace and die an old man between your legs," Kaid whispered my own thoughts out loud, yanking me closer now that my heart rate had calmed. "Tell me truthfully, did you really like that kiss? I know it shocked you, but don't pretend on my account."

"I loved it." I peppered tiny kisses all over his jaw until he laughed. "It was surprising, but kissing you is better than I imagined."

"Then may I do it again?"

"You can do it all night," I teased, and he granted my wish, kissing me so hard my lips bruised.

EIGHT

The imposing cliffs loom so high, their greyness blots out the sun. Nothing touches this land, save rocks and shadows. No vegetation. No life. No color. Just harsh stone and jagged edges. Yet this task is one I don't fear. The threads binding our hearts led me here, and for the first time, I stare at the danger with confidence. I can climb and climb well. How many nights did we spend skirting the walls of the temple? How many hours did he train my fingers to hold the small ledges and crevices? He prepared me for this quest, gave me the tools to face a peril most never lay eyes upon, and I silently thank him for his training. My love didn't send me into the darkness unprepared.

"What's up there?" I ask the empty air. "What's on the other side?"

"No one knows," The Stranger answers in my mind. "No one's ever crossed the Verdens Kant. It is the end of the realm. The edge of our world."

"Not even the gods?" I ask. The Verdens Kant is a stretch of uninhabitable mountains and cliffs that mark the boundary of every map known to man. No one has ever climbed these ridges and survived to discover what lies beyond, but because his pull dragged me here, Valka at least ascended part of the way to hide his bones. Perhaps the realm of the gods hides behind this natural fortress. Perhaps I'll find Hreinasta's true form waiting for me. Oh, to see her true self face to face and let her witness what became of her favorite vessel. I'm scarred and starving. Sunburned and frost kissed. I'm not the beauty I was when she claimed me. I am a savage. His savage, and if my fall from grace returns him to me, I'll accept every blemish and disfigured scar this brutal life offers. May the Pure One look at what I've become with shame. Shame that it was her selfishness that brought me so marred to her feet. I would allow her shock to settle before I strangled her, though. Blasphemous as it may be, I know it in my soul. If I ever lay eyes upon the true form of Hreinasta, I'll test just how long the primordial goddess can survive with my fingers around her throat.

"Who's to say what the gods do and do not know," The Stranger answers. "Their minds and knowledge are not for us to question."

I snort at his comment, but his tone is playful as if he only half believes his words. "Is this truly the end of the world?"

"Climb and find out, my child."

I strain my neck to see where the monotone peaks disappear into the colorless clouds. To scale this height will take days. Days where my entire survival will rely on what I can carry on my back. The Verdens Kant is a barren citadel of stone. No life grows along its harsh ridges. No fresh-water pools in its crevices. My only hope of water is the rain, but if the heavens open up and weep, I won't count that as a blessing. Rain will make the rocks slick and my fingers unsteady. To quench my thirst means to sacrifice my security, so I must pack enough supplies to last the climb. If I bring too much, it'll weigh me down, the razor-sharp peaks offering me no comfortable rest, but if I carry too little, my shriveled bones will join his atop the greyness. My confidence suddenly vanishes. These heights care little for my skill. Their intensity will break me the same as all who came before me, hoping to defy the realm's borders.

"You'll stay with me?" I ask as I step to the rising cliffs.

"I'm always with you, my child." His answer is instant. I've lost track of how long it has been since I fled Szent in disgrace. I think it's been over a cycle. Maybe longer? And during these painful days, The Stranger's been my only companion, my only constant. If not for his voice, I would have descended into silent madness. This cloaked and hooded man I've barely seen tethers my voice to this earth. The more of his bones I find, the closer I get to discovering if the Stranger is capable of his promise, and it's a true testament to my brokenness that I dread our time together ending even if he's lying. I don't want him to leave me.

"Always?" I ask because I'm tired. I'm scared. I'm weak.

"You know the answer to that already," he says, and I pause, my fingers inches away from the sharp stone. "Do not delay, my child. The Verdens Kant is adversary enough. Don't allow foolish thoughts you know are lies to add to your trials."

"Can I do this?" I ask as I begin the endless climb no mortal has survived.

"Can you?"

"I have to."

"Then you will."

I CLIMB until my limbs are numb, and then I climb more. My fingers bleed. My biceps shake. My feet blister, yet I'm barely a fraction of the way up this cliff. I pause often to breathe and listen, hoping his pull will guide me to his bones. The pack's weight cuts mercilessly into my shoulders, my skin red from the straps, but every time I'm tempted to lighten it by drinking, by slipping the dried fruit and nuts into my mouth, I look at how distant the heavens are. The Verdens Kant is endless. Perhaps this is the edge of the world because the cliffs extend eternally into the sky. The mountains have no peeks, therefore the fools who dig their fingertips into the crevices die of old age, unable to reach a top that isn't there.

So far, the weather has blessed me. The sun shines, but not too hot. The wind blows, but not too harsh. There's no rain, no threat of storms on the horizon, but night's fast approaching. I don't understand how the sun is already falling from the sky. This morning feels like only minutes ago. My journey into the heavens just began, so how can darkness be upon me? The day slipped carelessly by, the stress on my muscles causing me to lose time, and that worries me. Perhaps that's why no one survives the Verdens Kant. Perhaps the struggle passes so swiftly, the climbers find themselves trapped on the cliffs for cycles on end. We're destined to experience days as moments, cycles as hours. How old will I be when my feet finally kiss the earth again? Will I be grey and wrinkled? Will I be nothing but falling bones for the wind to scatter?

"Night is fast approaching." The Stranger's voice slips inside my mind, and I grunt as a sharp rock slices my already bleeding thumb.

"I have eyes."

"Then use them to find your rest. You cannot climb in the dark."

"There's nothing here but edges and spikes," I growl. "Unless you wish me to skewer my flesh to sleep, then I must keep climbing."

"You don't have time for arguing, my child," he reprimands. "Cynicism does not become you in this predicament."

"Then find me somewhere safe."

"I cannot help you. You know that."

"Then don't tell me of the danger I'm in. I'm well aware." He goes silent, and I instantly regret my callous words. "I'm sorry. I'm afraid. I'm always afraid."

"I know, my child." His voice sounds broken. "Do you think I enjoy watching you suffer? I've grown attached to you in these dark days. You're perhaps the only thing my calloused heart can care about."

"Then why can't you help me?"

"Because…"

"That's not an answer."

"Because that's the way it must be. You'll understand in the end."

"If I survive that long."

"Sellah." It's the first time The Stranger has called me by my name, and instead of echoing in my mind, his voice sounds in my right ear. The surprise jerks my head to where I half expect him to be clinging to the cliff, but the rocks are empty.

I tilt my forehead, wiping the sweat on my sleeve when I see it. A ledge. It juts out from the mountain, its surface large enough to hold my sleeping form. It's a decent distance from where I hang, and it'll be a race to reach it before the sunset bathes the realm in darkness, but it's there all the same. To my right. Where The Stranger's voice sounded loud and clear.

I smile at his unhelping aid and angle for it. I move as fast as my bleeding fingers allow, but I can't compete with the sun. She falls and falls and falls, and my limbs shake. I have to reach the ledge before the light fails me. The crevices are too small to find without her guidance.

"Tell me I'll make it." I groan, needing to fixate on something other than my seizing muscles.

"Hurry, child."

"Tell me I'll make it," I repeat.

"Only you can know that."

"Is this why you never show yourself? Because you frustrate me and are worried that I'd slap you for your constant annoyance."

"I would like to see you try."

"I would too." I laugh. The Stranger is taller than my towering Kaid, and though I've never seen him without his black cloak, I have no doubt he's well-muscled. My starving skeleton would be no match for his power.

"But see how your irritation erases your other thoughts?"

He's right. The more my body experiences aggravation, the less it notices the unbearable desire to let go and fall. "Tell me I'll make it."

"You have to," he says. "I do not wish to carry your splattered limbs from this place."

"Then order the sun to stop moving." It's setting too fast. I'll never reach it.

"My child, if I held the sun's fate in my hands, I would."

I believe him. Deep down, I trust The Stranger would do anything I asked if he could. I suspect something keeps him from helping me, from protecting me, but the way his voice always caresses the words *'my child'* makes me feel like that's what I am to him. A daughter. It's sad to admit, but this man I rarely see with the eerie white eyes and the ability to speak into my mind is more my father than the one who birthed me.

"You're almost there," he encourages, and he's right. The ledge is so close I can almost feel its security, but those feelings are hopeless dreams now.

The sun has set. I'm blind and trapped on the sheer side of the Verdens Kant with nothing but my fingers in a crease to hold me above the world.

THE LOVERS
SEASON OF THE HARVEST, CYCLE 78920

Lightning broke apart the sky, and the heavy rain cast the world into darkness. It was as if the gods raged in the heavens and punished us on earth with this vengeance, so when Kaid pounded on my window, I stood motionless in shock, convinced I'd imagined him. He beat on the glass again, timing his strikes with the storm's power, and only then did I realize my thief hung outside in the flesh and not in my mind.

"What are you doing here?" I asked as I flung open the window, water pelting my face. I had to shout to be heard over the downpour, but thankfully, its violence concealed our voices.

"I figured tonight was the perfect time to visit." His smile twisted his scarred lips, and gods, was his smile enough to light up the world even on this stormy night. "It's growing increasingly difficult to find cracks in the temple's defenses, but right now the guards are huddled away from the rain."

"For good reason," I said, the cold droplets pelting my face as the Season of the Harvest stole the Growth's heat. "Only a fool would venture out in this weather. You could've been struck by lightning."

"I don't care." He leaned forward, pushing his dripping head into my room. "Kiss me and then I'll leave."

"Leave?" I asked as I captured his chiseled jaw in my hands, and I noticed the rain had washed his temples clean of Varas' ashes. I hoped his god's protection hadn't abandoned him because of it. The stains helped him remain hidden, and while his skill could elude any mortal, I worried it wasn't enough to hide him from Hreinasta. He needed his god's shielding.

"I'm soaked," he said against my mouth as I tasted his icy lips, and I kissed him deeply as if to force my warmth into him. "My clothes will drip all over your floor if I come in," he groaned as my tongue licked the seam of his mouth. I'd grown bolder since our first touch, but no matter how many times I had his hands on me, his body pressed against mine, it was never enough. I was starving, and only he could satisfy the hollowness in my chest.

"So, take them off." I pulled against his jaw, urging him inside.

"Sellah." My name was a warning on his tongue.

"I'll wrap you in a dry blanket," I said, even though the thought of covering his body disappointed me. I was curious to know if he was as beautiful as I imagined.

"I'm not sure…"

"The storm will shield us," I urged, kissing him again, and he lost his will to fight. He pulled himself through my window, and I shoved the couch out of the way to save it from the rain. Kaid peeled off his shirt and hung it out of the window so it wouldn't trail puddles over the floor, but he froze when he caught me staring.

I'd never seen a man's skin before. I'd never witnessed the curve of a man's chest, the plains of his abs, the hard ridges and magnificent contours of his muscles. It was exquisite, and my fingers itched to run along his biceps, to brush against his peaked nipples, to trace every line of his stomach, every blue vein that rose on his forearms. He was divine, otherworldly, and he was mine.

"Sellah," he chuckled so low my chest vibrated. "Do you want to turn around?"

"I..." My voice faltered. I didn't know how to ask him for this favor. "Can I... never mind." I turned away, but Kaid's wet hand captured my wrist.

"Don't be afraid to voice your thoughts." He pulled me to face him. "You can trust me with them."

"I want to see you." I blushed with a soft giggle, and Kaid smiled silently, granting me the space to gather my confidence. "I'm afraid to ask because my entire life has taught me to fear touch, but I don't want this anymore. I have no choice. I'm trapped in a life that was decided before I was born. You asked if I had known the truth about my pledge, would I have chosen differently? I have your answer now, Kaid. I would. I don't want to disappear. I want friendship, love, a family. So may I see you?"

"You know I cannot refuse you anything." With slow, deliberate movements, Kaid reached for his pants' laces and undid them one by one as he kicked off his boots. My mouth went dry as the waist fell below his hip bones, baring the angled muscles of his pelvis. The cool night suddenly burned dangerously hot, and I couldn't breathe. I was suffocating as I watched. I knew Kaid was my male perfection, but seeing him like this was like witnessing a god among men. None of the deities compared to the man before me, and I wanted to worship him with my hands, my mouth, my body.

"Sellah?" he whispered, the word a plea. His pants hung dangerously low, his arousal evident. He'd explained one night while we lay wrapped in each other's arms the beauty of love, and so I understood what I saw beneath the fabric, but nothing prepared me to actually witness him.

"Tell me to stop," he begged. "Tell me to leave."

"Why?" My voice emerged raw and thick. Just moments

111111

---

ago, he'd been eager to grant my wish, and I couldn't imagine why he suddenly wanted to escape my presence.

"Because if I do this…" He tugged at his pants as if to draw my attention, but it was unnecessary because they had already slipped lower, a hint of his curve escaping. "If you keep looking at me like that, I won't be able to stand over here alone. I know you simply wished to see me, but it's too much. Please, Sellah, tell me to go. Make me go."

"No." I stepped closer, made bold by the fear of losing him to the darkness. Kaid hissed as if in pain, but my one step altered the course of our future. That single movement rewrote our destiny, and he released his pants.

They fell into a wet heap on the floor, and he snatched them up to hang out the window, but I didn't see his movements. All I saw was him, bare and glorious. So impossibly tall. Chiseled as if made of stone, and when my sight dipped to his legs, I saw just how magnificent he was.

"Sellah," he groaned, as if he was suffering. "Please, my love, grab me a blanket. I don't want to hurt you, but if you don't stop drinking in the sight of me like that, I'll take you until you know who you belong to. Please don't tempt me."

"I want to belong to you."

"Sellah, stop." I watched his control snap thread by frayed thread.

"I already belong to you."

"Sellah…"

"I always have. I always will."

Kaid's restraint snapped, and he lunged for me so fast that I barely inhaled before his lips crashed against mine. This kiss wasn't like the others. It was rough and hungry. He was dying, and I was life, and he pushed his tongue into my mouth. I moaned at the claiming, not bothering to stifle my cries. No one could hear us over the war in the heavens, and I finally let him experience my voice.

"Gods forgive me for this request, but will you let me take

your clothes off?" he asked against my lips. "I feel like a thief for asking, but I need to see you before you leave me. We don't have to do anything besides look, but will you grant me this memory?"

"You're here to take and plunder and own," I said with a smile. "But what you want, you can't steal. A man cannot steal what's already his." I grabbed his hand and placed it on the collar of my dress. "Can you do it, though? I'm nervous."

"I don't want this if it scares you."

"Good nervous, Kaid," I assured him. "Please, don't stop. Just help me."

Kaid kissed me gently and then slipped his fingers below the dress' neckline. He stood to his full height, smiling at me as he pulled the fabric off my shoulders. I had the sudden urge to fold my arms over my chest, but I took a deep breath and placed my hands atop his. I squeezed him tight, and together we slid the garment off my body. I was too nervous to look down and see my nudity, so I watched Kaid's awe instead. He studied every inch of me as if I was priceless gold. Love and longing filled his eyes, and after a long minute, he lifted his gaze. His smile grew wider, and the kiss he pressed to my mouth was devoted adoration.

"I'll never love another woman," he said. "I'll wait for you. I'll swear a vow of celibacy, and when your spirit returns, I'll be here because I don't want anyone else." His fingers drew abstract designs on my clavicle. "Thank you for trusting me. Would you like me to help you put your dress back on?"

"No." I stepped into his gravity, pressing my bare chest against his as I wrapped him in my embrace. He froze at the sudden contact, but I didn't let go. I moved until our hips touched, until I felt every inch of him against my belly, and I gazed up at his impossible height with bold purpose. "I want you to wait for me. I hope you're here when I reemerge, and I selfishly don't want you with another woman, but don't swear a vow of celibacy just yet."

Kaid's eyebrows pinched at my words, but the second understanding hit him, his eyes widened. He stood frozen in my arms, as if trying to process the moment, and I couldn't stop the laughter from bubbling out of me. I rose onto my toes and kissed him, and that unlocked him from his shock. He hoisted me up against his chest, capturing my lips with a burning need, and strode across the room until my calves hit the mattress. He released my waist, and I toppled onto the bed, my form gloriously on display for his eyes to feast upon.

"Goddess," he growled as he stepped between my legs, nudging them wider with his knees. "For that's what you are," he continued, his eyes devouring me. "There's nothing on this earth or in the heavens as perfect as you. Your beauty is unmatched, and it's mine. Say it, Sellah. Tell me you're mine."

"I always have been," I whispered. "I always will be." Instinct screamed for me to be ashamed of his brazen lust and my nakedness, but my spirit reveled in his pleasure, drowning out any thoughts of shame. This was how Kaid and I were meant to be. This was what was right. What was good and pure and holy.

Kaid cursed as he knelt between my thighs, but I captured his face, all nerves and resolve. My hands pulled him until he hovered over me. His eyes were wide with nervousness, and the urge to cover myself with a blanket grew stronger. Nothing separated us, save a few inches of air. I was rarely nude even in my solitude, so my unprotected skin not only on display but seconds away from being changed forever terrified me. Not because I didn't want this, but because I'd finally taken control. After twenty cycles, I decided my body, my life, and my future were mine. I claimed the right to choose, and the beautiful man hovering above me was that choice. He would always be that choice.

"Are you sure?" he asked.

"With every fiber of my being."

"I don't want to hurt you."

"I don't care. Hurt me. Love me. Undo me. Take everything because you own me."

"No." He kissed my mouth with a fire that would never die. "You own me, and I'll worship you until your pleasure is so great, you can't contain it. I want you to scream for me, my goddess. No one can hear you, and I need to know what you sound like when you come undone wrapped around me."

Kaid kissed me again, hot and desperate, as his hand lowered to my core. His fingers slipped between my thighs, and my hips lifted off the mattress at the contact. He'd never touched me there, and the sensation was overwhelming. It was as if lights and colors and sounds had mixed together, creating a storm of magic in my soul, and I loved it. I wanted more.

"Gods." His finger pushed inside me as he held my gaze. The pressure was slightly uncomfortable through the pleasure, and if that was how he stretched me with only his fingers, I couldn't imagine how all of him would feel. The thought should have frightened me, but it only assured me I belonged with him.

"Please, Kaid." I ground against his hand to increase both the pain and the bliss.

"Eyes on me." He smiled wickedly as he settled between my thighs. "I want to watch you."

My breath hitched as he eased into me, and the sting increased. I grabbed his shoulders, stilling him for a second, and he lowered his lips to my breasts, worshiping my body as if I was the altar he prayed upon. Only once I was writhing below him did he push deeper.

"You're so big." I tensed as he sank inside me.

"You can take it." He pushed further. "I know you can, goddess. I want nothing to separate us."

His words unleashed something within my soul, and I spread my thighs wider to offer him more room.

"Good girl. Relax as you take me."

I released the tension in my muscles, and with a sharp

pain, he thrust in to the hilt. I practically screamed at the contact, but he captured my mouth in a searing kiss, stilling to allow me time to adjust.

"Gods, Sellah. You feel like death and salvation and euphoria all at once."

"I love you," I whispered as he moved, and I focused on that truth instead of the discomfort.

"I don't love you," he growled as he angled his hips to hit the spot that unleashed the stars. "This isn't love. Love is too simple a word for what I feel. The world could end. Ages could pass. The gods could die, and I would still adore you. You've been braided so deeply into my heart that I no longer exist without you."

"Kaid," I cried, and he slowed, afraid he was hurting me, but I wrapped my legs around him so he couldn't escape. My response encouraged him, and his body slid against mine with such intensity, it became my new obsession.

"You're mine. Not Hreinasta's. Mine." Kaid lifted, pushing his fingers between us to stroke the fire coiling in my center, and the bundle of nerves exploded with delicious beauty. "Scream for me, Sellah. I want to feel you unravel."

"I…" I moaned.

"Now, goddess," he growled.

Something about his demand sent an electric current between my thighs, and his skillful fingers pushed me over the edge. I saw stars and blackness and the heavens, and I let my voice pour out of me as I rode wave after wave of euphoria.

"Good girl. Eyes on me," Kaid commanded, and I obeyed, which only prolonged the delicious ache. "You're exquisite. You're the most beautiful thing to grace my life."

"Please." I wasn't sure what I was begging for. For more of him, both the pleasure and the pain? For him to bring me the stars? For him to join me in this floating sensation?

"Gods, Sellah," he cursed, pulling out of me with an unsteady jerk. Losing him made me whimper, but he gripped my thigh as he knelt, coming undone on the soft skin of my belly. His face was beautiful in his bliss, and I wanted this to happen again and again and again. I understood why he hadn't spilled inside me, but his enraptured expression made me long to do it again so he could.

"I only say I love you because I don't know how else to describe this emotion." He collapsed onto my chest, pressing me into the mattress with his comforting weight. "I want to steal you from here and cherish you every day for the rest of your life."

"I love you," I said, hugging him tight to my breast as I kissed him fiercely. My legs found their way around his waist, but the movement made me flinch.

"I'm sorry if I hurt you." Kaid held me as if he was trying to absorb my body and keep me forever.

"Don't be. I want to remember that I had you. That our love was real."

"It is real, Sellah. Not was. Is."

Tears spilled from my eyes because, despite the sting, I would heal. I would wake up one day and no longer sense him inside me, and then I would forget when my body was claimed. I didn't want to forget. How would I survive without him? How could I leave him in just a few short weeks?

"I will love you until my death," Kaid promised. "And then I'll love you from the grave until I'm dust. When your consciousness returns after she abandons your vessel decades from now, I'll be here waiting for you."

"I don't want this, Kaid." A new and primal fear grew in my chest. "I don't want her to take me. I want us." I gestured between our chests. "Again, and again and again. I want to grow old with you. Not die here alone." For that's what I'd be with Hreinasta. Alone for decades, locked inside my own body.

"Then let me take you from here." Kaid leaned back just enough to look me in the eye and grabbed my thigh, hiking it over his hip so that our bodies remained joined. "I've been wanting to ask if you'd run away with me, but I was afraid to voice my desire."

"Why?"

"Because I know you love me, but I didn't want to force you to choose between me and the gods. Being bound to Hreinasta wasn't your decision, but wishing to leave her service and abandoning your faith in her are two vastly different things. I won't pressure you. I want you more than life itself, but I'm not your family or Hreinasta. If you're going to be with me, I need you to decide that on your own and be happy with the person you'll become and the future you'll live.

"Besides, if we run, our lives will no longer be safe. They'll hunt us down for our blasphemy. I've lived among the poor and the destitute, but you haven't. Fleeing with me means that for all our days, we'll need to keep one eye looking backward. We may go hungry. We'll have to work until we bleed, living in lands harsh enough to hide us from the gods. If I take you from here, our life won't be soft mattresses, luxurious clothes, and rich foods. It'll be dirt and toil and fear, but I'll do it. I would do anything for you, even sacrifice my own life, so if you say yes, I'll live in the dust beside you."

"Kaid." I brushed his black hair back and kissed his lips before drifting to kiss his cheeks, his nose, his forehead. "I was forced into this servitude, told my body, my future, and my love weren't my own. You're the only thing I've ever chosen. To help you, to trust you, to love you. We aren't two people, but two halves of the same soul. I belong to you, so take me far away so we can build a life and a family."

"Family?" Kaid pressed his face into my neck as if I'd gifted him the greatest treasure this world had to offer.

"My thief, I want a future with you, for you have stolen my body, mind, and heart." I kissed his ear, thankful he couldn't see the blush coloring my cheeks as I finally admitted the desire that had been growing inside me for weeks. "My parents often avoided me when I lived in their home, and I never played with my siblings. I used to observe them in the courtyard from my window, longing to join them, but it was forbidden. If I fell and scarred my skin, I would be unworthy of Hreinasta. If my brothers accidentally touched me while passing me the ball, I would be tainted. Do you know how painful it is to watch your siblings play feet from you and not be allowed to participate? They ignored me even though I hung my torso out of the window, hoping they would at least speak to me, but they pretended I didn't exist. I was so alone as a child that I didn't understand what family meant until you. You're my family, but I want more. I want everything this life has to offer with you."

"Then I'll take you far from here and give you a family," Kaid promised, sealing his oath with a kiss. "I need time to plan, so be patient while I make the arrangements, but I swear on Varas' holy flames that when you're old and grey, you won't be here in this temple returning to a body you don't recognize when Hreinasta abandons you for another, but in my arms with our children worshiping the very ground you walk on."

NINE

"*You've climbed in the dark before,*" I tell myself, choosing to ignore the glaring differences between Szent and the Verdens Kant. Even on the darkest nights, Hreinasta's temple was bathed in light. As the capital of the realm, Szent's holy fires burned eternally. Torches lit the streets, and the moon illuminated the building I'd memorized every inch of. Night at the end of the world is absolute. This is not the same.

But I tell myself it is.

"Slow down, my child," The Stranger speaks into my mind. "There's no need to rush."

"I don't know how much longer I can hold on," I say through gritted teeth. My limbs are ready to give out, and my bloody fingers are raw.

"You'll hold on as long as needed," he answers. "I will not watch you fall."

"Then help me."

"I can't."

"Why not?"

"You must do this alone. You must have faith."

"I do have faith." I spit. "I've spent over a cycle trusting your promise. My body aches. I've lost so much weight that my bones stick out, and I'm covered in sunburns and scars. I have faith, but I'm exhausted. Why can't you help me?"

"I wish I could."

"That's not an answer!" My anger echoes off the eternal cliffs.

"Yet it's all I can give. Climb, child. Do not despair, for I am with you."

"You're always in my mind." I take a deep breath and slip my fingers from their crevice, hoping to locate another hand-hold in the blackness. "I sometimes wonder if my grief invented you."

"You've seen my face."

"Twice." I almost laugh with relief when I find a sturdy grip. "That hardly proves my sanity."

"I am here and real. Your faith tethers me both to you and this world. You'll see me soon."

"I would prefer if I could feel your hands again, like at Death's temple."

"I would carry you if I could, but for now, you must climb alone. You're almost to safety. Don't surrender now."

I grunt as I pull myself up the rocks. I can't see the protruding ledge, but a section of the air is darker than the rest, and I hope my aim is true. I speak his name instead of a prayer. I say it a second time, then a third. When my knuckles finally reach the ledge, I've repeated it seventy-three times, and I clamber to safety. For long minutes, I sit against the cliff wall in exhausted relief. I didn't die. I can climb in the dark.

I fish through my pack for a strip of dried meat and the waterskin. I eat every bite but drink sparingly, and then I say his name again as sleep claims me against my will.

"SELLAH?"

His voice is wrong. It's not deep enough. There's no thunder to the tone.

"Sellah? My Child!"

I jerk awake, and my scream catches in my throat when nothing but air fills my vision. I'm hanging precariously at the edge of the ledge, and I scramble backward to safety as I realize it wasn't Kaid's voice but The Stranger's.

"Thank you," I gasp.

"You refused to wake up," he answers in my mind.

"How long was I asleep?" I ask, for the sun is well overhead.

"At least twelve hours. I planned to let you rest longer, but I reconsidered once your arm fell over the edge."

I rub my face, and now that my alarm has receded, I notice the ache in my muscles. Sleeping on this rocky surface did nothing to ease the soreness from climbing. Part of me wants to sit here for the rest of the day and start my ascent in the morning, but I can't waste supplies. "Do you think there's another ledge above?"

"Who knows what nature has created?"

"Do you hide your face from me because you know these half-answers annoy me?"

"Who knows my reasons?"

I roll my eyes as I grab a handful of nuts and seeds from my pack. My hunger isn't satisfied by the meager meal, but rationing is more appealing than starvation.

"If you climb, the gods will provide," The Stranger says.

"The gods have forsaken me."

"Not the ones who truly care."

My mind flicks to Lovec and Udens, to Elskere, the wed gods. I'm like the first two in my loss, the last two in my vows. Perhaps Elskere still favors me. Look at all I've done in the name of love and marriage.

There's something different in The Stranger's tone, though, a tenderness that makes me wonder if his words hide another meaning. Is someone else looking kindly upon me? Hopefully, a secluded god sits atop the Verdens Kant, watching me with favor as I climb the edge of the world.

"The sun's shining," The Stranger continues. "The path is clear."

He says nothing more, but as I stare heavenward, I cannot help but think that he's guiding me again, just as he did with the ledge.

With pained fingers, I begin, and my raw skin bleeds instantly. My muscles shake with exhaustion, my mouth is parched despite the drink I washed down my breakfast with. I regret not remaining on the ledge for a second night, but I sense him. He's close. I'll find another scattered bone soon. I have so few left to recover that I can practically taste his kiss. That memory spurs me on as I whisper his name, remembering how his dark hair hung over his eyes, how his large hands always located the perfect grip when he climbed, how, despite the ash coating his forehead, he was still the most beautiful thing to grace this world. I miss his scar and the way it twisted when he smiled, how it felt rough against my soft skin and molded to my fingers when I caressed it. I miss everything about him, from the way his body moved against mine, to the deep voice I've forgotten, to the smile that eclipsed the sun. It hurts to think about him. It brings me peace to remember him.

Tracing his muscles in my memory helps pass the time and blocks out the sight of the blood dripping down my knuckles. My knees are scraped, and my toes are bruised, but taking inventory of everything I love about him erases the now and leaves me in the past. It grants me the strength to find another crevice, another handhold, another footrest, and I'm shocked when I suddenly come across a vast indent in the cliffside.

I couldn't see it from below, for the jagged protrusions hid it, but as I haul myself up between two pillars, I notice a path that's been carved into the mountain. Excitement fills my chest. It's wide enough for me to walk on, the open air above me allowing light to spill in. This is why The Stranger encouraged me to climb. This path winds on a small incline up the cliff face, disappearing into the clouds, and I cannot stop my feet from following its call. Have I passed the test? Did I ascend high enough that the Verdens Kant deemed me worthy and offered me aid?

I race along it as the day dies, hours passing peacefully, but the sudden end of this path dashes my hopes. It was merely a reprieve, like the ledge below, and I stare at my mutilated fingers. I can't do this again. I cannot bring myself to shove them back into the minuscule crevices.

"Help me," I whisper. To him? To the gods? To the empty air? I don't know.

I should camp here for the night, but if I sleep, I fear I'll never climb again. So I place my hands on the rocks and haul myself up. I don't know how long I scale the harshness. I've lost track of the time, and all I know is I made a mistake. I should've camped on the path and rested, but I ignored my body's warning, listening to desperation instead. As the blood on my palms causes me to lose my grip, I realize I've made more than a mistake. I've killed myself, for my fingers keep slipping, slipping, slipping. I try to hold on, but it's too little too late, and I fall.

THE WEDDING

K aid climbed through my window, looking rough around his edges. The holy ash on his temples was smudged, black stubble covered the normally shaved sides of his head, and dark circles clung below his eyes, visible despite the soot from Varas' fires. He looked both older and younger as he stood before me, exhaustion fighting his limbs as he caught his breath from the climb.

"Three days," he said, pulling me into a hug, my face burrowing into his powerful chest as his nose pushed into my hair. "I have a contact willing to smuggle us south on his ship if we can make it to the coast. It'll be tight, but if we leave sooner, that'll give them too many opportunities to cut off our escape."

I nodded against his shirt, and his arms tightened around me. Those three days couldn't pass fast enough. My birthday was two weeks away, and Hreinasta would waste no time claiming me. The moment I turned twenty-one and came of age, she planned to possess my body. The priestesses had already started preparing for the ceremony. They cleansed me daily in fragrant waters. They called me to endless prayer at their side. A cycle ago, I would have bent an obedient knee and submitted wholeheartedly to their purification, but now it was all I could do not to scream. Fear was my constant companion as the acolytes bowed reverently when I passed. Dread was my dearest friend as I sat elevated in the temple's inner sanctum for all the devoted worshipers to see.

My mother visited often, my father remaining in the outer courtyards where the men prayed. They worshiped at the busiest hours, not there to visit me or to repent, but to garner the respect of their peers. How holy their family was, how sacred. Hreinasta had chosen their daughter as her next host, and how they bathed in the praise and envy of Szent's upper class. Watching my mother preen and squawk and strut strengthened my resolve to flee this place with Kaid. Not once during her worship did she look at or speak to me. All my parents cared about was how my sacrifice and suffering brought them status and wealth. It wasn't devotion or religion. It was a performance. My faith meant nothing in this temple. Their faith meant nothing at all. They abandoned me cycles ago, though, so their disregard shouldn't have hurt as acutely as it did. I was never their child. I was their thing, and I wondered how much shame my escape would bring them. How the tables would turn on their arrogance in three days.

The guards had doubled as well. It surprised me they let me sleep alone, but I assumed they thought me safe so high off the ground. No one accounted for a thief. Thank the gods, otherwise, our plan would never work. Those three days couldn't pass fast enough.

Kaid rarely visited since our decision to leave, and while I understood, it only heightened my anxiety. Sneaking into my room had become almost impossible because of the increased security, and he'd been too busy as he both served Varas and planned our escape. We had to disappear, running fast before they caught our trail, but there would always be a chance they would find us. We weren't escaping oppressive parents or abusive masters. We were fleeing the gods, the all-powerful rulers of the realm. Even with Kaid's meticulous planning, we might never make it beyond Szent's city limits, but neither of us cared. We would try. We had to. I refused to let Hreinasta possess me without a fight.

"I didn't think I would see you until our escape," I said as Kaid finally loosened his strangling grip on me. His hold was tight, almost uncomfortably so, but those were my favorite hugs. His love and devotion bled through his limbs into my skin as he held me, reminding me of just how intensely he wanted me with him. "I assumed you would come for me when it was time. The guards are too many to risk a visit."

"I know." He caressed my cheek with hesitant fingers. His expression was filled with nerves, and I noticed how flushed he was.

"Are you well?" My hand flew to his forehead to test his skin, but he caught my fingers and brought them to his lips.

"I am." He kissed my knuckles. "I should stay away, but Sellah, my goddess, there's something I want to do. Something we won't have time for once we flee Szent." He released my hand and cupped my face in his calloused palms. "Once we escape, we'll always be on the run, looking over our shoulders. We may find sanctuary in the presence of a lesser but sympathetic god, but it's not a life I would have chosen to give you. It's the only one I can, though, so I'll embrace every hardship with gladness. Our first months together will be filled with fear and struggles. We won't have time for what I wish to do. We'll weave through humanity, becoming new people, and losing all traces of this life. I cannot wait to live the rest of my days with you, but I need to do this right. So, will you climb with me one last time to our roof?"

I nodded, wondering what he had in mind, but I followed without question. He'd tell me when he was ready, and his urgency told me to be patient. The climb took longer than usual since we had to avoid the constant patrols, but we eventually reached the roof. The moon bathed us in her ethereal light. The crisp harvest air brushed against our skin, and I shivered at the coolness.

"Most travel to their temples to recite their vows, but we can't. The gods aren't bound by flesh and blood or stone, though, so while it's tradition to pledge this at their altar, some still speak their promises in the old way." Kaid smiled nervously, taking both of my hands in his, and I stared at him with curiosity. "Before the birth of mankind, two deities fell so in love they forsook their own names, choosing to be called by one name instead." My heart stumbled in my chest when I realized what vows Kaid was referring to. "Elskere, the wed gods, became husband and wife under the moon's light in that first age. They vowed their undying love with both their words and bodies, with only the heavens as their witnesses. Centuries later, they are still one, still lovers, and all who wish to marry journey to their shrines. But there are those who still wed below the moon and stars with both their words and bodies, praying for Elskere to bless their union." Kaid paused, as if to gather his strength, and then he reached out, brushing a thumb over my cheek. It was only when his skin touched mine that I realized I was crying.

"Sellah, my best friend, my entire soul, marry me? When we flee this place, I want it to be as husband and wife. I want to wed you in the name of Elskere and make you mine until death claims me." A tear rolled down his cheek, and I leaned forward, capturing it with a kiss.

"I'm already yours," I whispered against his skin. "Of course, I'll marry you."

Kaid wrapped me in his arms, almost strangling the breath from me.

"I've never seen a wedding," I said between suffocated breaths, and he loosened his relieved grip.

"I have," he said. "I know the words, but even if I didn't, I don't think Elskere cares how we say it. They abandoned their first names to become one. No one remembers what they were called before they joined, not even the gods. I trust they only care if those evoking their blessing have the same fierce love they do."

"They already know I love you like that," I said, and Kaid kissed me, unable to stop himself. When we finally broke apart, I was breathless and panting, yet so full of bliss.

"Come." He knelt in the moonlight, pulling me down before him, and clasped both of my hands in his. "Are you ready?"

"Marry me, Kaid."

"Elskere, I call upon you to bless my vows," he said with a smile bright enough to challenge the sun, and then he nodded at me.

"Elskere, I call upon you to bless my vows," I repeated.

"I am your humble servant Kaid."

"I am your humble servant Sellah."

"And from this day until the end of my days, I forsake that name so that I might be called husband."

"From this day until the end of my days, I forsake that name so that I might be called wife."

"As you became one, so will I become one with Sellah."

"As you became one, so will I become one with Kaid."

"With your blessing, my love for her will be unending."

"With your blessing, my love for him will be unending."

"In the name of Elskere, Sellah, you are my wife, my love, my present, and my future. I reject all others for you, and I pledge my body, my soul, and my being to you and only you."

"In the name of Elskere, Kaid, you are my husband." I paused, trying to recall the vow, and Kaid mouthed the rest of the oath with me.

"With this kiss, Elskere." Kaid released my hands and cupped my jaw, his face never so beautiful as it was under the moonlight as we wed. "I seal our vows."

He kissed me, and my arms wound around his waist as I poured all my love into our embrace. I meant every word of our promise. Kaid was my husband, and I was his wife, and as we married beneath the moon, a strong wind blew through Szent, extinguishing every torch in the city. As the world plunged into darkness, I pulled at my new husband's shirt. Elskere had blessed us with this blackness, I was certain of it. It would take time to relight every torch and fire, granting us perfect secrecy. No one would see us as Kaid and I completed the vows of our words and began the vows of our bodies.

TEN

I wake with a scream on my lips as my brain registers the agony radiating from my right thigh, and with shaking muscles, I struggle to sit up. My strangled cry is inhuman at the sight, for the outside of my thigh is ripped open and pumping blood onto the stone. The crimson pool spreads alarmingly fast, and I yell as my fingers force my gaping flesh together.

I'm sitting on the hidden path, but I must have hit a protrusion as I fell, blacking out temporarily as the stone sliced through my leg. The wound is deep. Too deep, and my shaking hands don't slow the blood spurting from my veins. This wound will kill me, and I already feel the effects of the blood loss. I've nothing in my pack to stop the bleeding, and even if I did, there's no way I could climb on this ruined leg. My vision blurs, unable to focus on my weak fingers failing to pinch my flesh closed, and my cries echo off the edge of the world. I didn't even find him. If I must die, I want to hold a part of him, but I'm alone, always alone. I have been since the day I was born, kept separate and untouched until him. I guess it's my fate to perish lonely, too.

I say his name as my fingers lose their grip, my thigh

gaping open. I say it again as I lay back, unable to sit up. I say it a third time as my pooling blood spreads below me.

My vision goes black, but I see him above me. My eyes can't distinguish his features, though. All I see is a shadow, but I know he's welcoming me to death. I shall finally join him in the nothingness. I wish Death hadn't been banished. At least then I could find him in the afterlife, but Hreinasta stole everything from me. My childhood, my faith, my husband, my eternity.

With weak fingers, I reach up and touch his shadow, the skin surprisingly warm for a ghost. I say his name again, but even my dying ears hear how garbled my words have become. Perhaps this fate is best. I don't know how much longer I can survive without him. I've already forgotten the sound of his voice. I only remember that it was deep as thunder and thick as smoke. How long before I forget his face? His scar? His friendship?

"Sellah!" the shadow yells as darkness claims me. My, how my memory distorted his voice, for as he speaks, nothing about the tone sounds familiar. I hate that I'll die knowing I forgot pieces of him.

The shadow shifts closer. Death closes in faster.

"My ch—"

I'M VAGUELY aware of movement, of a solid warmth against my chest. I can barely open my eyes, but the world comes to me in flashes. A black cloak draped over whatever is warm and moving before me. Clouds, endless clouds. Something grey and razor sharp. A familiar voice, a presence I think I recognize. And pain. Unending pain.

Pain and warmth and endless sky.

Then the darkness comes again.

INTENSE PAIN LANCES MY LEG, and I jerk awake, sitting up violently fast. A broad palm gently catches my chest, stopping my momentum from propelling me into the dark figure crouching before me. I stare wildly at the featureless face, a groan slipping from my lips as I attempt to gain my bearings.

"There you are, my child," the figure says, and at the term, I know whose hand presses against my clavicle.

"Stranger," I croak, my vision finally clearing enough to make out his features. I've not seen him since Death's ruined temple in the jungle, and I forgot how alarming his white eyes are, how dark his aura is.

"I worried I lost you," he says, and I realize the pain in my right thigh is coming from his other hand. I glance to where his fingers rest against what I thought was a gaping wound but is instead a series of neat stitches.

"What…?" I start as he pulls his palm from my chest and returns to bandaging my leg.

"It's not infected, which brings me relief," he says. "For many days, I worried the fever might take you."

"Days?" I rasp, my throat as dry as The Sivatag, and The Stranger hands me a water skin.

"You've been lost to me for almost a week," he answers, binding my wound, and I seize the opportunity to scan our surroundings. We're on a massive plateau, the flat rock extending as far as the eye can see, which isn't far since the clouds swallow us whole. We must be higher on the Verdens Kant, and my lethargic brain cannot reconcile this waking reality with my last memories.

"I didn't die?" I ask. "Where are we, and why are you helping me? I thought you couldn't help?"

The Stranger chuckles at my spewed questions. "You did not die, but you came very close. And we're at the top."

"Top? The top of the Verdens Kant? How?"

"Drink your water, my child," he scolds. "I strapped you to my back and climbed the edge of the world. I believe this is the pinnacle, but the clouds never clear, so perhaps I'm mistaken."

"You helped? Why? You told me you couldn't?"

"I helped because if I had not, you would've died." A change comes over The Stranger. His cloak grows darker, his voice deepens, and the air surrounding him oozes black. "I cannot let you die, my child. You are my only hope, my only way, and I do not suffer what is mine."

I recoil as he calls me his. It's not how Kaid used to utter the word, with reverence and adoration. The Stranger claims me as if I'm his possession, his property, and fear pricks my skin. In truth, I know very little about the man who insists he can return Kaid to me if I find his scattered bones. In my sorrow, I believed his promise, but I don't truly understand the darkness I've allowed to latch onto my spirit. I don't even know this dark man's name.

The Stranger looks at my pale face, his white eyes seeing into my soul. I can't breathe at the intensity in his gaze, and then as suddenly as he darkened, the blackness slips away, returning him to his usual self.

"Do not fear, my child. You must do this alone and have faith in my promise, but there are always loopholes." He brushes my hair behind my ears. "How can you have faith if you are dead? I am not aiding you in your quest. I am only aiding your life. It is why I could not intervene until death threatened you. I cannot deliver you to his bones, but I cannot stomach the thought of leaving your corpse on these rocks."

I nod, realizing for the first time that a small fire burns beside us. I don't know where he found wood to burn in a land of stone, but I don't question him. I'm simply thankful to still be alive.

"I may have little power in this world." He grips my chin gently. "I cannot save you from everything, but I can stitch your leg and carry you to safety. I have grown fond of you, and your death would put an end to our plans."

The way he speaks makes me wonder if there's another reason he promised to return Kaid to me. He sought me out a cycle ago when devastation crippled me. I clung to his oath out of sheer survival, but now I question his motives. Why is my faith so significant? Why am I so important to this stranger?

"Rest." He takes the water skin from me. "When you are well, you'll find his bones, and we shall leave this edge of the world behind us."

"There's truly nothing up here, is there?" I ask as I lay down.

"It would seem that way."

"How disappointing." I yawn. "I'd hoped this climb would be worth it."

And it is, in the end. I rest for three more days, and then, on aching legs, I wander the shrouded plateau, The Stranger never far behind me, until I find his thigh. I hug what used to be an impressively powerful part of his body to my chest as The Stranger makes me swear to remain among the clouds until I can make the descent alone. Now that I have his severed limb, my dark protector cannot aid me, and so he leaves me with a full waterskin, his pack of dried meat and nuts, and a fire burning in the mist. I stay atop the edge of the world for as long as my supplies allow, and then with a leg that may ache forever, I scale the Verdens Kant, the descent more excruciating than the climb.

THE VOWS
SEASON OF THE HARVEST, CYCLE 78920

Kaid raised his arms, letting me peel the shirt from his body, and the second his skin was bare, the air fled my lungs. He was perfect in his imperfection, and my fingers traced his chest down to his chiseled abs. It was as if the gods had sculpted him themselves, and I would never tire of looking at him.

"I love your face when you study me," Kaid said with an unsteady voice. "This must be how the gods feel when worshiped."

I lifted my eyes to his and then lowered my lips to his chest, seductively kissing his smooth skin. "Because it is worship."

"My wife." Kaid gripped my hair and yanked my mouth up to his, devouring me with a hunger I'd never experienced from him. He'd called me by many names over our time together. Friend. Sellah. Goddess. But Wife? Wife was my favorite.

Kaid's tongue licked the seam of my mouth, and I opened, granting him access to every part of me. His groan sent a shock of electric desire to my core, and my fingers dug into his chest.

"Husband," I moaned, his kiss swallowing the word. "Please."

A feral need consumed Kaid at my plea, and he ripped my dress from my body, the delicate fabric shredding at his strength. He threw the ruined garment behind me and laid me down on it, his movements rough and desperate yet impossibly gentle. His lips never left mine as he pressed our bare skin together, and I kissed him with urgency, desire building in my chest.

"Eyes on me, wife." He kicked his pants free, and my feet wrapped around his legs to help push them off. "I want to watch your face as we make our final vows."

His name escaped on my breath as I met his hungry gaze. Everything in me broke apart and reformed, new and whole, at his expression, and when he pressed against my entrance, I gasped with pleasure, my back arching against the roof.

"Gods, Sellah." Kaid pushed into me slowly, inch by delicious inch.

"Please." I was all greed and love and happiness.

"Patience, goddess." He gripped my chin roughly, forcing my gaze to his. "I want to savor this moment as I make you mine. I want to watch your face; feel every ounce of pleasure you take from me." He thrust hard as his voice died, and unlike our first time, where the sting distracted from my enjoyment, this was nothing but pure bliss. It was the most delicious sensation to grace my body, and every part of me came alive.

My legs locked around his hips, forcing him further, and I moaned, thankful that the whistling wind hid my screams. I could shout at the top of my lungs, and not a soul would be the wiser. Yes, it seemed Elsker had blessed our union.

"I can barely control myself, wife," Kaid growled into my mouth. His grip tightened on my jaw in a possessiveness I would never tire of, and he thrust harder, letting me know who I belonged to.

"Then don't." My legs already caged him against my body, but I slid my hands down his muscled back, severing his restraint.

"Gods, Sellah." He seized my waist and rolled to his back, hoisting me on top of him, and the unbridled desire in his eyes almost pushed me over the edge, my arousal coursing through me like a forest fire.

"More," I moaned into the wind, letting the wed gods witness our vows. "I want more."

"And I want to watch you." He lifted my chest off his, guiding my movements as he reveled in the sight of my moon-kissed skin. "Do what you will to me, wife. I am yours."

Our gazes met, and his eyes revealed every emotion in his heart. He worshiped me as he studied my face, my breasts, my belly, and then where we were joined, and I glanced to where he stared. The sight was more than I could bear, and I gripped his chest, leaning forward so that I could watch our bodies pledge our marriage vows. We became one as my hands clutched the muscles containing his thundering heart. Neither of us spoke, our heaving breaths words enough, and Kaid covered my hand over his heart with his broad palm as he lifted his other to cover my heartbeat. We moved together, savoring the vision of our joining, feeling the power of two hearts beating as one. We were married. I was no longer a vessel for the Pure One. I was Kaid's wife.

"I can't hold on much longer," Kaid groaned. "Please let me feel you."

My gaze lifted to his face, loving how I ruined him, and I leaned forward to capture his jaw. I kissed him as he wrapped me in a powerful embrace, joining every inch of our skin together. We were slick with sweat. Our breaths were erratic, the bliss flowing between us almost unbearable. We moved faster, our rhythm so perfect, so in tune, that it was as if our bodies had memorized a choreographed dance. The sensations were too much, my body more fire than flesh, and by Kaid's grip on my waist, I knew he intended to keep his promise. He would give me a family, and the realization that he might gift me a child on our wedding night undid me.

I screamed, unable to contain my voice. My vision blurred, my heart exploded, my blood burned, and it did not end. It rolled endlessly through me; the wind carrying away my ecstasy so that we remained hidden.

"Wife," Kaid groaned as he found his release. I gasped at the sensation, and it drew out my euphoria until my entire body was almost too sensitive to touch. "We cannot be undone now." He moved lazily as we enjoyed the aftershocks of our climaxes. "We wed in the eyes of the gods, and these vows cannot be broken. You are mine, my goddess, but more importantly, I am yours."

"I love you, husband." I propped myself up on his chest, my thumb finding its way to his scar, and I caressed it adoringly.

"I don't love you, my wife," he answered, and I smirked at his declaration. "For what I feel is more than love. There are no words to describe my devotion to you."

"Three days," I said as Kaid traced lazy circles on my back. "I have to survive three more days, then I can have you for the rest of our lives."

"It will be a good life, Sellah." His rough fingertips contrasted my soft skin, and I loved how different we were. At first glance, we made no sense, but when fit together like puzzle pieces, we became whole, each one complimenting the other. "You believe me, right?" he continued. "I'll do everything within my power to give you a good life."

"I do." I reverently kissed his scar. "If we spend every day together and each night like this, I'll be happy."

He laughed, and the sound was so beautiful it hurt my chest. "I'm yours for as long as you want me."

"I'll want you until the day I die."

"I'll want you even in death, Sellah. There's no afterlife, but that doesn't matter. I'll love you until I'm dead in the dirt, then I'll love you until my body is nothing but bones. And when my bones fade to dust coating the earth, I'll still want you."

ELEVEN

The grass grows taller than a man here, and exhaustion poisons my limbs as I stare at the rippling fortress of greenery. Who knows what hides within the grasslands of the Mitte Midagi, waiting for unsuspecting prey to wander until they're lost?

My leg aches with such ferocity that I worry it's a punishment for my sins. His scattered bones were supposed to be left untouched, unfound, unwanted, but I disobeyed the gods. I've found all but an arm and his head, and the pain in my thigh reminds me of his severed body. The Stranger stitched my flesh closed with skill, but the misery of climbing down the Verdens Kant and then walking endlessly to the Mitte Midagi pulled the stitching raw and ugly. The scar will be brutal, but I don't complain. His scars are worse, for he is in pieces.

I never open the chest unless it's to add another piece of him, but this new exhaustion, this new wariness of The Stranger, has me unlocking the chains. I lift the lid and stare uncomfortably at the severed limbs and torso that used to be my breathing husband. I detest seeing him this way, but my warm fingers find his cold ones and lace together with their stiffness. For a few seconds, I linger against his skin, ignoring the curse's bite. The last time I felt his hands, he made me his wife. It's been well over a cycle since our wedding, since I've seen his eyes or heard his voice. I'm so close to the end of my quest, so close to finishing this journey, yet I feel so far from his love. I am no longer the beauty he married. I'm too thin, too bruised, too scarred. My hair is dull. My skin is cracked and dry. My mind is spiraling. What if he returns and cannot love the broken girl I've become? What if he never returns, and this madness was for nothing?

That's my greatest fear, and it's why my wariness of the Stranger has increased now that only two severed parts remain. Ever since he claimed me on the Verdens Kant, I cannot ignore the realization that I pledged my faith to someone dark enough to claim he can return the dead. No one can do that, not even the gods. There's no afterlife, not after Hreinasta banished Death. There's this painful existence, and then nothing. The Stranger is either lying, or he's a darkness I should have no part in, and I cannot decipher which I fear more. That his lies sent me to suffer these quests in the most treacherous parts of the realm for nothing, or that I willingly opened my soul to evil? I always knew his promise was dangerous, but my desperation clung to hope. I refuse to live in a world without Kaid. I don't want to survive for decades knowing our marriage lasted only a night. I need The Stranger's promise to ring true, but I dread what it means.

"You should go before you lose the light," The Stranger says in my mind. "The grass is tall. It will blot out the sun, but you do not want to see nightfall in the Mitte Midagi."

"I know." I clutch his poisoned fingers harder until the pain of the black magic makes me forget the ache in my stitched thigh.

"Do not lose faith now, my child," The Stranger says.

"I can't remember his voice. Yours is the only one I hear."

"Are you doubting? Have you lost hope that you'll hear it again?"

I say nothing. What can I say? That I need Kaid, but I fear what the end of this journey means? I don't know The Stranger. What price will he extract from me to perform the impossible?

"It pains me to see your despair," he continues. "I thought you were different, Sellah. I hoped you would have faith when no one else would. I have not forsaken you."

"I'm afraid."

"You should be... but not of me." His voice sounds so close that I can almost imagine him behind me. "I've grown fond of you, my child. You should fear your task at hand, but never me."

I lock the chains around the trunk and peer at the towering grass.

"Everyone I've trusted betrayed me," I say. "My parents. The priestesses. Hreinasta."

"But not him. Not me."

"When this is over, will you abandon me?"

"You are mine, child. I do not suffer what is mine."

"I want to believe you."

"So, believe."

"It's hard when you promise the impossible."

"For others, yes, but not for you." I sense a warm presence at my back as he speaks. "You survived the Sivatag when its heat kills all others. You reclaimed Lovec's temple when his faithful could not. You climbed the Verdens Kant and returned when most die on those rocks. You faced Udens and gained his favor. He is a brutal god who takes his vengeance in blood, yet he did not spill yours. I don't understand how you struggle to believe my promises when you yourself defy the odds, the gods, the darkness. Now go before the sun falls from the sky," he orders when I hesitate. "I won't abandon you."

He's right. I should be dead one hundred times over, yet my broken body still fights. Perhaps it's not The Stranger I should fear, but myself.

"Watch over me?" I step into the towering grass, its height making me dizzy.

"Always, my child."

THE GRASS IS SURPRISINGLY SHARP, the ground below me uncomfortably soft, and I can barely see more than a few paces ahead. The reeds are taller than me in some places and come to my breasts in others, but no matter where I walk, it's too thick to see where I'm stepping.

The wind rustles the grass, forcing it to bend, and anxiety settles in my chest. Moving stalks are my only warning of the predators hunting this endless nothing, but if the wind doesn't stop, I won't see danger coming. Even the smallest insect can be deadly, especially in the presence of black magic. That's why I'm here. I sensed the draw of his bones, the darkness thick about him, and I'm sure I'm not the only one to feel its effects. How many poisonous creatures hunt these grasslands, fueled by this oppressive evil?

Something wet slides across my skin, and I yelp with an undignified squeak. I faced the evil that consumed Death's abandoned temple. I fell from Verdens Kant and killed tigers bred from dark magic, yet the slimy trail left by a small hidden creature disturbs me the most.

"Are there predators here?" I ask The Stranger.

He doesn't answer.

"Stranger?"

"Do you truly want to know?" His voice is a warning.

"Yes... no." I fall silent, the sharp grass stinging my arms as I push through it. "Yes."

"They say it has a taste for human flesh," he answers. "It's grown impossibly large, its teeth able to rip apart skilled soldiers. It's said he started small and innocent, wandering among the grass and mud. His home is a cave hidden in the nothingness, and while it never appears in the same place twice, he finds it each night. Legend tells of a vast treasure lost inside his lair, but all who seek its entrance must first kill its inhabitant. In the first age of men, warriors tested their skill against the Mitte Midagi, and the creature killed them in self-defense. Their blood on his tongue changed him, though, transforming him into a monster. He swelled to an unnatural size and craves human flesh. He may already have scented you."

"Why didn't you tell me about him?"

"Would it have stopped you?"

"No."

The Stranger huffs with self-righteous satisfaction.

"What is he?"

"A beast you don't want to meet. Follow the call, my child. Find his bones before the creature finds you."

"He's in the cave, isn't he?" I don't have to ask. I know Valka hid him there, in the home of a monster to hide the magic.

"If that's what you think."

"It's what I know. He's always left in the darkness, always in pain and suffering." The ache in my thigh worsens with each step, souring my mood. "I wonder if I constantly sense him because the gods abandoned me. In their anger, they wanted me to know they scattered him to the worst parts of the realm."

"That's not why, my child."

I cock my head, wishing The Stranger was here so I could look at his dark visage and ignore the fact that my own feet have disappeared below the mud.

"You say the gods abandoned you, yet your face burns with Lovec's mark. You're welcome to return to the Vesi, and you always hear the call of his bones. You swore your marriage vows in the way Elskere did, and the wed gods blessed your union. They accepted your faith, and despite

Hreinasta's claim on you, you no longer belong to her. You belong to him, even in death."

When my bones are nothing but dust coating the earth, I'll still want you.

"Elskere didn't protect us," I argue. "Our marriage lasted hours."

"But they protected your bond. It has not broken. It's why you always find him."

When my bones are nothing but dust coating the earth, I'll still want you.

I say his name silently, for it'll never break. "I will find him."

"And the wed gods will guide you."

I open my mouth to respond when the reeds ahead shift, and I freeze. That was not the wind. That was something in the grass. Something large. Something fast, and it's aimed at where I stand.

TWELVE

The hidden predator surges toward me, and I force my aching legs to run. The creature is moving too fast for me to outrun, but gods be damned, I refuse to be easy prey. I've barely eaten these past few days, my energy waning as the scar on my thigh aches, but the rustling behind me urges me to flee faster. My burning lungs can't maintain this pace, though. The mud sucks at my feet, and the reeds beat my limbs. Every direction looks the same in these grass-lands. I don't know which way to run, and the unseen predator grows closer. Closer. Closer. And then the grass falls still.

Panic forces me to skid to a halt. It's as if whatever was chasing me vanished, and I try to slow my breathing enough to listen for movement, but all I hear is my own thudding heart. The fear was cruel when I saw the monster's move-ments, but the stillness is worse. It could be anywhere, waiting for me to make a mistake.

I worry my breath will rattle the grass, giving away my location as I search the nothingness. I don't move, but neither does it. Prey and Predator locked in a stalemate, and only one wrong move will determine which of us is which.

Another slick body slides across my ankle, and a strangled hiss slips past my lips before I clamp my mouth shut. The grass rustles to my left, and I burst into a run, berating myself for being so weak. I'm too exhausted to outrun whatever monster hunts me, but I can't let it catch me. I can tell by the thunder of its steps that it's more than triple my size. It's a fight I won't win.

My ankle twists, and I yelp as I crash to the marshy water, mud splattering my teeth as my face smacks the earth. I scramble to stand, but the sludge sucks at my hands and feet. I fall again, chest slapping the ground with a loud thwack, and the creature changes direction, aiming for the sound.

I frantically search for something other than the sodden grass roots to help pull myself out of the mud, but as I lift my eyes, I come face to face with a forked tongue tasting the air. I freeze as the small black snake hisses, but then it darts to the side, its slimy body caressing my arm. The familiar feeling dawns on me, but I fight down the scream. Snakes. They were what kept brushing my ankles, and a terrifying notion worms into my brain. Is this how the monster keeps finding me? Are the snakes signaling their master?

That thought burns fear into my chest, and I find the strength to haul myself out of the swamp. I can barely run, but I push my muscles to their breaking point. I won't die here in the mud. I won't let snakes devour me whole. I won't—

Something fleshy and damp wraps around my ankle and yanks. I fall so hard that my stomach cramps at the impact, and the mud forces its way into my mouth. I gag as it hits the back of my throat, no longer caring to keep quiet as I thrash against the grasp on my leg. Glancing behind me, I instantly regret that decision, for a massive tail is choking my limb, scaly and greenish brown. Its end is tapered, but the further into the grass it winds, the thicker it grows until it's as wide as my waist. I strain to catch sight of the hidden body it's attached to, but the monster shifts, yanking me backward.

My chest drags over the earth, my fingers trying to find anything solid, but it's no use. There's nothing but grass here. No stones, no branches, and the tail cuts harshly into my ankle as if to prove it's the only power in the Mitte Midagi.

Snakes dance about me as the unseen beast drags my helpless form through the grasslands. They slip over my limbs, coil around my torso, twist against my skin. I cannot scream. I cannot fight. The fear's overwhelming, and I may not know what kind of creature owns this scaly tail, but I know who found me. The monster with an appetite for human flesh, and I am its next meal.

I don't know how long it drags me, but suddenly the ground changes from mud to dry dirt and then to rock. The pain increases as my chest grates over stone, and then the world plunges into darkness. The Cave. The pull of his bones is so intense that I know he's here, but I won't find him. I cannot escape this monster's hold, and soon I'll be nothing but flesh caught between its teeth.

I struggle even though I know it's useless. The grip on my ankle is too strong, my foot turning blue from the lack of blood flow, but I'm too stubborn to surrender. I've survived too much, fought too hard to give up now, so I thrash and scream and pray. My skin bleeds as the monster hauls me further into the cavern. The air is dark and musty. The ground is hard and damp. I don't know how far we descend, the stalagmites and stalactites growing increasingly threatening. If only I possessed the strength to rip them from the earth and plunge their sharpened ends into the beast.

Eventually, a dim light illuminates the cavern, but I barely register my surroundings before I'm drowning. I cough and sputter, treading water until I break the surface. I choke as the creature tows me through an underground lake. The water is freezing, and my teeth are chattering by the time the razor-sharp tail drags me to the opposite stone shore. It's inexplicably lighter here, but before I can take stock of the environment, it releases me.

I scramble backward, my ankle leaving a trail of blood as I lunge for the water's edge. Light from tiny crevices in the cave's ceiling reflects off of piles of gold, and I realize that's why it's brighter here. The Stranger was right. The monster of the Mitte Midagi guards a treasure horde of unprecedented glory. But despite the endless wealth, the likes of which not even Hreinasta has seen, I'm blind to it. I cannot focus on gold and silver, the coins and jewels, for in the dimness I finally see the man-eater, and my stomach drops.

The creature is unfathomably large, taller than me as he stands on four scaly legs. Vicious teeth protrude from an angular snout, and its tail whips behind it, knocking coins from their piles with echoing clatters. Its hot breath bathes my skin, the stench of death thick in the air, and I'm paralyzed by the reptilian monstrosity before me. It must have once been a crocodile, but black magic swelled him to an unnatural size. My entire torso could fit in his jaws, but by the gleam in his yellowed eyes, he has no intentions of starting with my head. No, this monster will want to hear me scream as he eats.

I frantically search for an escape, but with the water at my back and the beast at my front, I won't make it more than five steps. The pull of Kaid's body is so strong, I know he's here, but I'll never locate him among the piles of gold before I, too, am ripped to shreds.

Stranger, help me, I don't know what to do.

The creature lunges, and I throw myself to the ground to avoid its fangs, my shoulder slapping the stone with bruising force as I roll. The pain drags a scream from my throat, but I don't stop until my feet are back under me. My scarred thigh burns as I push to a stand, but the crocodile's tail thrashes out with a speed an animal that large shouldn't possess. I barely see it before it slams into my gut, tossing me across the cavern. I land on my side hard enough to dislocate my shoulder, and I scream as my left arm pops out of its socket. My vision blurs, but nothing can hide the size of the monster stalking toward me. I wish the blow had rendered me unconscious. I don't want to feel my bones crack between its teeth as it consumes me.

I'm in too much agony to fight, but even if I was healthy, the scales of battle are tipped in his favor. Perhaps that's why The Stranger didn't answer me. He knows as well as I that my life was forfeited the moment the tail captured my leg.

The creature's thundering footfalls shake the earth, and while I should force my aching body to stand up, to flee, my blurred eyesight fixates on the gold. It glitters in the pale light, and I stare, mesmerized by its beauty. I can't look away. It won't let me. Perhaps it's my mind avoiding the inevitable, or—

My vision focuses on it, and The Stranger's words flood my memory. *You say the gods abandoned you, yet your face burns with Lovec's mark.* The Stranger did answer me. He showed me my deliverance, and I launch myself at the towering gold. It's taller than the monster, rolling hills of treasure that extend endlessly, but my eyes are drawn to the one object that might save my life. It's an exquisite work of craftsmanship, studded with priceless jewels, but they aren't what capture my attention. The polished blade extending from its hilt does. A sword, as sharp as the day it was forged, protrudes from the top of the third golden hill. And if I can get to it…

Lovec, bless my hunt. I am not the prey. I am the hunter.

Left arm useless, I scramble over the coins, using my right hand to force myself up. The unstable surface gives way below my feet, but I do not relent. The creature launches onto the gold behind me, but the slipping treasure can't support its weight. It collapses beneath him, sending him sliding back to the stone. The loosening avalanche threatens my footing, but I'm nearly at the first ridge. Not caring about my injured arm,

I throw myself over to the other side and roll down, dislocated shoulder alive with agony.

Lovec, guide my steps.

I scream in pain, in resolve, in violence, and I'm up the second swell before the beast crashes through the gold. The sliding piles disrupt my climb, and I slip backward, but I keep moving, keep living.

Lovec, grant me strength.

My face burns where he marked me, and I feel the hunter's power wrap my bones in warmth. The reptile behind me barrels toward his meal, but I roll down the second hill without falling victim to his fangs. One more swell, and I'm at the sword.

Lovec, do not abandon me.

My lungs burn. My muscles cramp. Sweat coats my skin, and the monster's foul breath is hot on my neck. Its snapping jaws rattle the air, and on slipping legs, I vault over the coins to the weapon. My fingers grip its hilt, and I rip it free from the horde. My hips crash hard against the gold as I land, but I ignore the bruising as I roll onto my back, swinging the sword just as the monster leaps for me. Its jaw unhinges, readying to swallow me whole, and I barely have time to position the blade before me.

I scream as the beast's fangs slice into my arm, but with a surge of energy and a burning face, I thrust the sword into the creature's mouth. Metal meets flesh, and as its fangs carve into my biceps, my blade carves into its brain. I roar as my blood runs thick and hot, but I keep pushing, forcing the weapon further into its skull. For a moment, I fear my fight is too little, too late, and the reptile will devour me, sword and all, but with a shudder that shakes the entire cave, the creature dies.

I stare in disbelief as its eyes fade into death, and then its body collapses. His protruding jaw lands on my stomach, and I jerk underneath its bloody weight until I'm free. I scramble backward, pulling the weapon with me, but as I extract my arm, the monster inflicts one final wound, slicing through my forearm. My entire right arm is a gory, mangled mess, but I'm alive. I am the hunter, not the prey.

I stand on unsteady feet and hold my bleeding fist over the beast's skull. His death is offering enough, but I add my blood to the worship.

Lovec, accept my sacrifice.

I lift my bloody fingers to my face and trace the mark the god of the hunt made on my skin. My flesh burns excruciatingly, but I savor the pain. It's Lovec's mark, his acceptance of my offering, for I am his. We are much the same. The gods have not forsaken me.

IT TAKES three excruciating tries to force my shoulder back into its socket, and then I slide down the gold to the lake's edge. I clean my arm as best as I can, but the blood won't stop flowing. The deep punctures worry me, but I've no way of treating them here. Removing my shirt, I bind the many wounds as tight as the fabric allows. At least in the nothingness of the Mitte Midagi, there's no one to judge my nakedness. I would remove my pants and shred them into bandages as well, but the thought of trekking through that grass without protection on my legs keeps them firmly in place. The Stranger stitched my thigh with skill. Perhaps he'll grace me once more with his presence to prevent me from bleeding out.

Wounds bandaged, I dip my hand into the lake to drink when I see them. The bones. Hundreds of them line the bottom, and I let the water drip through my fingers, suddenly not thirsty. Remains of all the monster's prey lay in white heaps below the surface to pile in the silt, but there's one limb with flesh still perfectly preserved. An arm. His arm, the black magic preventing him from decaying.

I dive, exhausted lungs aching as I hold my breath, and

the second his skin touches mine, the poison burns my fingers. Two punctures mar his biceps from where the crocodile must have tasted him. If the monster wasn't dead, I would kill him for desecrating his body, but if the sting of the black magic against my skin is any indication, the creature's mouth probably burned with an unholy vengeance.

When I surface, I set his handless arm down on the stone and search for something amidst the treasure to carry it. This dark poison hurts worse than his other limbs, and I'm not sure if it's because it's one of his final pieces or if it's because my body is so weak. Thankfully, I find a sack filled with gold and priceless jewels, and I start to dump them out before I freeze. If the sheer number of bones is any sign, hundreds before me tried and failed to steal this horde. I've no interest in greed, but if The Stranger can do what he promised, Kaid and I will need coin. So, I shove his arm atop the wealth and then slip back into the lake to return to the grasslands above.

It takes the rest of the day and some of the night to escape the Mitte Midagi, but when I finally locate my horse, I can barely stand. With weak triumph, I throw the bag of treasure onto the cart, and I hear The Stranger laugh in my mind.

"Well done, my child. Well done."

THE END
SEASON OF THE HARVEST, CYCLE 78920

K aid slipped his shirt over my head since my dress was in tatters, and after he pulled on his pants, we climbed down from the roof. An ugly sorrow filled my chest on the descent. I dreaded saying goodbye to my husband on our wedding night. I longed to curl beneath the sheets with his body gloriously bare against my overheated skin and sleep in his arms to greet the sun together, but he'd already stayed too long. And what were three days compared to a lifetime? I could survive three days, and then my true life would begin. I would be Kaid's wife, our children's mother, a woman who decided her own fate, who pledged fealty to a god of her own volition.

We reached my window, and as Kaid helped me into my room, I read the same sorrow in his eyes. My new, beautiful husband lifted his hand and cupped my cheek, and I leaned into his caress. "In three days, I'll come for you no matter the obstacles," he said reassuringly. "Then I'll never leave your side. I swear it."

"I love you," I whispered through my tears.

"I'll never tire of those words." He smiled, stepping closer until we stood chest to chest, and I had to crane my neck to meet his gaze. No matter how many times I looked at the thief, his beauty stole my breath.

Kaid slid his other palm against my jaw and leaned in for a kiss, but before our lips could join in farewell, our world exploded.

The door flew open with such force it shattered into splinters. The hinges ripped off the wall, and before I realized he was moving, Kaid shoved me behind him, throwing out his arms as a shield. Fear pulsed through me, and I watched in disbelieving horror as guards poured into my room.

Only they weren't guards. They were soldiers, their uniforms unmistakable. Valka's acolytes, and if his followers were here, death would follow. Kaid backed me against the wall, trying to shove me out of the window, but the soldiers were too fast. Ten men swarmed my suddenly too-small bedroom before we could take more than two backward steps.

They wordlessly seized Kaid as he tried to shield my body. He fought and kicked and raged, splitting one soldier's lip open and breaking another's nose before they subdued him. It took four men to contain the powerful man I called mine, but his rage over his own capture was nothing compared to the feral monster he became when two soldiers gripped my arms.

"Get your gods damned hands off her!" Kaid screamed, bucking forward. He was so strong two soldiers lost their grips, the others dragging across the floor as he lunged for me, but the four remaining acolytes burst into action, all eight of them struggling to keep my husband in check.

"Let go of her, or with Varas as my witness, I will kill you." He head-butted the man before him, and the shorter soldier fell. I never realized how tall and powerful Kaid was, how dangerous the thief I trusted with my life was until that moment. It took eight men trained by War himself to contain him, their violence no match for a husband's rage.

"Shut him up," the soldier holding me growled, and one

of Valka's men punched Kaid so violently in the mouth blood sprayed through the air.

"Stop!" I shouted, flailing against my captors. "Don't hurt him, please." No man beside Kaid had touched me, and now strangers groped my body, restraining me as I fought. My brain told me I should panic at their hands soiling me, but all I could see was my husband's abuse. He bit a soldier, drawing so much blood he had to spit it onto the floor. He kicked a man in the shins and kneed another in the gut, but the larger soldier punched him in the mouth again, snapping his head back so hard that I screamed.

"Get him out of here," the acolyte holding me continued, ignoring my pleas.

"Sellah!" Kaid garbled through the blood as they hauled him from my room. "Sellah! Do not touch her. Don't you dare touch her!"

The soldier punched him for the third time, and he fell silent while I cursed obscenities that had never left my tongue before.

"Kaid?" He didn't answer me. "Kaid?"

"Shut up." My captor clamped his fingers over my lips, and with all the ferocity within me, I bit him. He swore, and before I could register his movements, he struck my temple. Pain exploded, and my hearing dulled. I think I heard Kaid spewing violence and rage, but the ache in my head deafened me to all as Valka's acolytes dragged us to the inner sanctum.

Hreinasta sat on her throne at the rear of the Holy of Holies, but she wasn't who I noticed. This place was for the purest souls, for those who didn't tempt the priestesses. No man was allowed to set foot inside this room, yet the largest male I'd ever laid eyes on stood beside the goddess, his size monstrous compared to Kaid's looming height. I'd never seen a true god before, Hreinasta hiding within the bodies of mortal women, but there was no mistaking the monster clothed in ornate armor. His eyes were pure white, his irises the faintest tint of grey. His black hair was trimmed with military shortness, and his muscles were as much of a weapon as the wicked sword hanging at his hip.

Valka. God of War.

If he was here. Death would follow.

His acolytes threw me before Hreinasta's throne, Kaid's shirt barely covering my nudity as I fell to my knees. She was significantly smaller than Valka, her human host approaching forty cycles. She wore the same vessel as she did when I was offered to the temple, her tanned skin still smooth and lovely, her braided hair beginning to show the signs of age. The only reason she held onto this body was because she was waiting for me. Otherwise, she would've discarded it the moment her hair grew white. And I hated her for it. This haughty woman stared down at me, her hatred bleeding through her aura, but it wasn't her. The mortal shell had no idea what was happening. A selfish goddess lacking self-control had stolen twenty cycles of her life, and if I could kill Hreinasta without harming her innocent host, I would do it with my bare hands.

"My vessel," she said, her voice melodic in its disgust, "how you have disgraced me."

"I am not your vessel," I spat, all thoughts of self-preservation vacating my body in my rage, but then Valka stepped forward, and I froze, the magnitude of our situation suddenly dawning on me. Valka, a male, the god of war, was here in the temple of the pure primordial goddess. In the inner sanctum where no man was permitted entrance.

Blind with panic, I lunged to my feet, aiming for my husband, but a soldier caught me before I made it a single step and threw me to the floor. My body slapped the unforgiving tiles so hard that my skin burned red, and Kaid roared in rage. Our gazes met, and the eight soldiers could barely contain his violence.

"Don't touch her!" he bellowed as he kicked and writhed and punched. "Keep your hands off my wife."

Valka strode unbothered to Kaid and drew his sword. The blade was an unholy monster, an impossibly large length of metal, and my stomach heaved.

"What are you doing?" I shouted, scrambling over the floor, but a soldier grabbed my hair, yanking me to a stop. "What are you doing?" I was inconsolable, my voice more fear than words.

"It was Varas' ashes that gave you away," Hreinasta said calmly behind me. "The smudge on your white garments, my vessel. Proof that you were no longer pure. Proof of your disobedience."

"Don't touch him!" I screamed, ignoring her. "Don't you touch him!"

"Your sins will not go unpunished. Humans do not get to disgrace the gods," she continued.

"I'll kill you if you touch him." I surged against my captors, their fists ripping hair from my head as I lunged, and one of them had to climb on top of me to keep me from escaping.

"Get off her!" Kaid didn't care that War approached him with a blade sharpened for the slaughter. His eyes were on mine, always on mine, and the pain etched on his face was too much to bear. "Get your filthy hands off my wife."

Valka wordlessly stepped before Kaid and pressed an unnaturally large palm against my husband's chest above his heart. Power pulsed through the room, the shock wave almost visible, and Kaid stumbled at the force.

"Your soul is now tied to every inch of your body," Valka said with a cold and ruthless voice. He was unlike anything I'd ever experienced, and the dread coiling in my gut threatened to kill me.

"You will remain awake until the end," War continued, and Kaid stopped struggling for the first time as he stared in terror at the hulking god.

"Don't touch him!" I screamed, fear and horror and bile

clogging my throat. Kaid started thrashing again at my voice as the soldiers held me down, and his shirt bunched up to reveal my bare body.

"Get off her!" he cried as they manhandled me, his shirt ripping as they struggled to contain me.

"If you don't stop resisting, thief, I will carve her up as well," Valka said, and Kaid froze, all the fight leaving him.

"Let her up." Tears rolled down Kaid's cheeks, but I couldn't stop screaming. "Let her up and cover her. I'll accept my fate without a struggle if you just unhand her."

"No!" I surged forward, the shirt covering nothing as I thrashed, but I didn't care. Gods be damned, let them see all of me, for my vows to Hreinasta didn't matter. My wedding vows had replaced them.

"Sellah." Kaid gazed at me as if we were the only people in the world. "Don't be afraid. Nothing they do can erase my love for you." He looked at Valka, bravery and defiance coloring his aura. "I will accept what must be done, but let my wife go. Don't hurt her. Please."

Valka stared cruelly down at Kaid, and then, surprisingly, he nodded. Hreinasta gasped behind me, but War bristled at her outburst, and she fell silent. A small part of me felt unnerved that the primordial goddess cowered before another. She was the first, the greatest, yet a single shudder from Valka silenced her. It spoke of just how terrifying War was. Of how fragile her human hosts were.

Kaid nodded at Valka, and with tears streaming down his face, he fell still. The god reached down, pulled off my husband's pants, and then walked to me. With a single nod, Valka dismissed the soldiers pinning me to the ground and handed me the pants. I lay prostrate and half-naked before Valka while the man I loved stood completely bare, but I didn't want his pants. I didn't want what this gesture meant, and I couldn't move as my stomach threatened to heave itself onto the floor.

"Put them on, wife," Kaid said, his voice so beautiful and soft despite his tears. "It's all right."

With a wet and ugly sob, I sat up, tugging his shirt closed around my exposed breasts, and accepted the pants from Valka. I slid them on, pulling the strings tight, my body too dressed as Kaid stood too bare.

"You've been found guilty of defiling a vessel of the Pure One, thief," Hreinasta said, too haughty for the gravity of this horror. "Your soul has been bound to your body, and you will remain awake until the end. Then you shall be scattered to the far corners of the realm."

"Scattered? What are you talking about?" I looked wildly up at Valka, but he simply gazed at me with cold indifference before returning to my husband. Kaid shook uncontrollably, but he didn't fight, determined to keep War's threats from me.

"What are you going to do to him?" My voice was hysterical.

"Sellah," Kaid's deep rumble cut through my terror. "Sellah, my love, look at me." I obeyed, barely able to see through the tears. "I will love you until I am nothing but dust, and even then, I'll still love you."

"Don't." This wasn't goodbye. It couldn't be goodbye.

"My goddess," he said loud and clear, his beloved term for me a defiant slap to Hreinasta's ego. "Look away. Don't watch this."

"No," I sobbed. "I'm not leaving you."

"I love you, Sellah."

"I don't love you." He gave me a sad smile as I repeated his words back to him. My feelings were too infinite to be contained by a simple word, and I was losing it, losing him.

"Until I am dust, wife."

"Until I am dust."

Kaid looked at the violent god, and his bravery in the face of his punishment surprised even War. The room stilled for a moment as everyone stood in awe of my husband, and Valka nodded. His soldiers moved to Kaid, stretching his arms and legs out at his sides, but Kaid did not fight. He did not struggle. He did it for me so that I might not endure Hreinasta's wrath.

And then Valka raised his sword and swung.

I screamed in horror as my beloved thief roared in pain. The blade slid through his shoulder, slicing his arm clean off his body. Blood exploded from the wound, and with a terror that wouldn't stop, I understood Hreinasta's words. He would remain awake as they cut him to pieces.

I bolted to my feet, racing for him as if I could stop War.

"Sellah, no," Kaid cried, spitting blood. "Please."

As if to reinforce his threat, Valka turned to stare at me, and I crumpled to my knees before my husband, his blood already pooling on the stone. I felt Hreinasta's satisfaction polluting the air at my back, but Valka seemed impressed by Kaid's strength.

"I'll make it quick," War whispered so that the Pure One couldn't hear his small mercy before moving to Kaid's other arm. "For your bravery, I will not prolong your suffering." With the bloody sword, he severed the limb. Kaid screamed. I vomited, but I wiped my mouth and turned my gaze to my husband. I told him I wouldn't leave him alone. Until death. Until we were dust.

A soldier laid Kaid's arms on the floor, and Valka slashed his hands from his wrists. War's acolytes then bound them in cloth and carried them from the temple as the god returned to Kaid.

He made good on his promise, working swiftly as the soldiers gripped Kaid's torso to keep him upright. Valka carved through Kaid's knee in one swift stroke and then sliced his thigh off at his hip. Blood poured from his severed body, the crimson pooling around my knees, but I didn't move, letting its warmth bathe me. The tears wouldn't stop as I watched, as I forced myself to stay with him until the end, for

Kaid showed no signs of passing out as the god's power kept him awake.

"I'm so sorry," I mumbled as War separated his other leg at the hip, leaving that one whole. "I'm sorry. I'm sorry. I'm sorry." It was all I could say as the soldiers lowered his limbless torso to the floor.

Kaid couldn't speak, his skin growing pale, but he held my gaze with unwavering conviction as the acolytes wrapped his limbs and carried them away. But his dulling eyes spoke volumes. *Until I am dust.*

Without realizing I was moving, I crawled through his blood until I crouched before his face. Valka lifted his sword but froze as I moved into his blade's path. Hreinasta mumbled her annoyance at the delay, but War ignored her, granting me a final moment with the man I loved. I gripped Kaid's chin and kissed him. He could barely move, his lips limp against mine, but his fading eyes spoke for his mouth. *Until I am dust.*

Valka grunted, and I retreated through the blood. I did not abandon my husband, though. I only withdrew enough for the blade to swing without catching me. That moment between us stretched out for an eternity. I saw every experience we would never have, each word I would never speak to him. We stayed locked together in a wordless conversation, dread for the end thick, but not as heavy as the love. In those last seconds, there was no hate in my husband's eyes, no regret. Only unbearable pain and unending love.

I lifted my fingers to my lips and kissed them, his blood staining my mouth as I said goodbye, and then War raised his blade and beheaded Kaid.

THIRTEEN

The forest is still. Normal. Serene. Not the darkness I've come to expect. Not the chilling oppression that usually accompanies the call of his bones. The towering foliage is vibrant and thick, the gnarled branches and rough bark rich with an ancient knowledge that only comes from decades of undisturbed growth. The underbrush is understatedly magnificent, and as I push through the peaceful trees, I worry my intuition has finally led me astray. I have one more scattered part to find. Only one piece until his body is whole, and I always knew reclaiming this one would be the most difficult. His head won't be found willingly, and I wonder if these woods are here to mock me. They're too beautiful and green to house the black magic of a soul bound to flesh and then carved into pieces.

Yet the pull of our marriage bond led me here. Somewhere in this dense forest, his final piece lies in wait, despite how easy this last task appears. I'm almost afraid to hope that this is the end, that I've finally completed my quest. This past cycle and a half has been nothing but pain and strife, a struggle I barely survived. I'm no longer the beauty worthy of

Hreinasta I once was. My body is too thin, my bones stick out, my flesh is scarred, my skin peels from the sun, and my hair's brittle with malnutrition. It's been a cycle since The Stranger set me on this path, the Thaw cool this far north. Seasons have passed since I saw Kaid, the details of his face blurring together in my memory, the sound of his voice lost in the past. I say his name as I walk so I don't forget. I won't abandon him to history. His death cannot be in vain, cannot be because the Pure One is too weak in her conviction to live among us and follow her own demands.

I come to a small creek, and its clear, blue water sparkles in the sunlight that filters through the leaves. My desire to bathe and drink wars with my need to find him and end this torment. I pause, standing on the bank for long, undecided minutes, but it's my stench that wins the struggle. The scar on my leg is mostly healed, my arm scabbing from my fight in The Mitte Midagi. I feel inhuman, more beast than girl, so I strip off my clothes. I scrub them in the cool stream and then wash myself. My skin is pink and chilled by the time I'm done, so I sit on the grass in the strips of sunlight, enjoying this rare moment of peace. Perhaps it's my fear that's begging me to stall. Maybe I'm afraid of this torture ending. In a matter of days, or maybe even hours, I'll face The Stranger's promise. Before the Season of the Thaw comes to a close, I'll know if this has been for nothing. And even if it wasn't, even if The Stranger holds true to his vow, I'll see Kaid for the first time since our doomed wedding. He'll have been dead seasons, his last memory one of blood and suffering, and I'm no longer the wife he remembers. I am her shell; her withered bones. What if our marriage was only meant to burn for a moment? It was more than I ever expected, but it wasn't enough. It will never be enough. I'm forgetting him instead of spending my life memorizing him, and I want to drown in that pain. If The Stranger cannot return Kaid to my arms, I worry it'll hurt worse than his death. Hope is dangerous when left to fester.

I shove those thoughts down as I test my nearly-dry clothes. As tempted as I am to remain in this serene pocket of the realm, I must push forward. I drink from the cool water after I dress, and as I walk along the creek bed, I notice plump berries growing red and inviting on a nearby bush. Recognizing them as edible, I eat my fill without hesitation. I eat until the sweetness is almost sickening, but I don't mind. It's been so long since I found food so easily. These green and vibrant woods are a blessing, and that renews my fear. Every place deemed worthy of hiding his bones has been a hell of violence and evil. I'm either mistaken about the call to this northern forest or this is a trap I'll pay dearly for entering.

I scrub the sticky juice from my fingers and force myself to leave the comfort of the creek. The further into the trees I venture, the more the serenity unnerves me. These woods are too beautiful, too vibrant, too peaceful. The birds chirp, the sun shines, the wind drifts softly. I'm walking into something; I can feel it. There's no reality where finding his head is this simple. No, Valka wouldn't have hidden Kaid's skull with such little thought. I've never heard of this nameless forest, and The Stranger has been quiet. This stretch of earth isn't known for monsters or turmoil, so I have no clue what darkness waits for me. A devil? A beast? The land itself? I prepare for the worst, but when I finally step into the outskirts of a clearing, I realize I wasn't prepared. Not for this. Not for what stands before me, guarding Kaid's final scattered bones.

"No." I can't breathe. "No. No." I can't stop saying that two-letter word that's too large on my tongue. It makes sense. Everything makes sense. This is why the gods never stopped me from reclaiming his bones. At first, they assumed the barbarities of the realm would break me, but when I met every challenge with success, I often wondered why they didn't descend upon me. I told myself it was because without Death, no one governed the afterlife. Even if I found his limbs, they would be nothing but useless flesh in my hands. But I was mistaken. This… this is why they never deemed it necessary to stop me. My survival in the desert and on the cliffs didn't matter. Nor did my triumph in the jungle or my victory in the Vesi. This was always what awaited me in the end, and I won't survive this.

"Tell me this isn't true," I beg. "Tell me my eyes deceive me."

"They do not, my child," The Stranger speaks into my mind, his voice finally present after his long absence.

"Did you know?" I shout. "Did you know his final piece was here?"

"No." His answer is both the truth and a lie.

"Did you know this was here? In the woods?" I feel dizzy from lack of oxygen, but I can't calm down. I can't go in there. I cannot come face to face with the object of my hatred.

The Stranger doesn't respond.

"Is this why you were absent? Did you leave me without your voice because you knew what I would find?"

Again, he is silent, and I curse him with violence.

I understand why the forest is peaceful, beautiful, welcoming. It wasn't harboring a great and ancient evil. Its secret is something worse, an enemy I despise, but not an evil recognized by this world. No, the realm sees him as an object of worship and honor. As someone demanding respect. I haven't stumbled into a monster's lair or a witch's hovel. No, I'm standing before a temple. It's smaller than the ones housed in Szent, but it doesn't matter. This is a house of prayer. A consecrated holy place. This is the dwelling of a god. His visage is carved in stone at the shrine's entrance, but even if it wasn't, I would recognize his acolytes. Their uniforms are burned into my memory, visions I'll never forget. I understand why Kaid's head was laid to rest here, for no one, perhaps not even Varas the Great Thief himself, could steal it.

This temple is dedicated to Valka. This is an altar to War, and the god who carved my husband into pieces guards his last resting place.

FOURTEEN

"I can't." I double over, stumbling into the safety of the tree line. "I can't. Don't make me."

I'm no longer in a forest but back in Hreinasta's inner sanctum, Kaid's blood bathing my knees as it pools hot on the stone floor. Trees don't stand before me, but soldiers, cruel and emotionless as they carry his severed body away. The memory I tried so hard to suppress floods to the surface with a vengeance, and I hear Kaid scream in agony. I see the impossibly tall Valka slice him to pieces with a dripping blade. I sense Hreinasta at my back, victorious in my husband's punishment. The repressed memories are too much. I cannot face Valka again. I cannot relive that day.

I stumble as I pick up my pace, racing blindly through the trees. I've been so alone. No family, no parents, no husband, no friends. I've endured everything in isolation, and his death rushes back in painful waves, crushing me under its weight. *Someone, help me, please. I can't do this.*

"Sellah." A voice cuts through my fog of panic, but I keep running. "Sellah!" The voice is firmer, closer, deeper, and I slam into a solid wall of muscle. "Breathe, child."

Strong arms wrap around me, and I collapse against The

Stranger's chest with gut-wrenching sobs. I cry with all the heartbreak I never allow myself to feel, and he holds me tight, his incredibly powerful body hard against my withered one. He whispers compassion into my hair, which only makes me cry harder, and I lean deeper into his embrace. This is the first time The Stranger has touched me other than to save my life. This is the first affection he's shown me, and in my haze of grief, I realize that, besides Kaid, he's the only person to hug me since my mother abandoned me to Hreinasta's control. Before that, she only touched me occasionally, but it never held warmth and tenderness like this, and I cling to his black cloak with shaking fingers. I didn't realize how badly I needed comfort, and as Kaid's final moments play on brutal repeat, I listen to the thunder of The Stranger's heart. I hold him close, and for a few agonizing moments, I wish he was my father. He's a dark and deadly being, one who might not be human, but I don't care. I want Kaid back in my arms, and I want this stranger to be my father. I crave a life filled with love. Not the obsession with beauty or prestige, but genuine affection. I never considered it, but as The Stranger holds my convulsing body, I suddenly understand. He cares about me. Truly cares. I wonder if he loves me. I hope he does because I can't be alone anymore. The loneliness is too oppressive.

It takes a long time for my tears to stop, and even longer for my breathing to steady, but The Stranger clutches me to his chest until I fall still. The sun begins its descent before I finally find the courage to speak.

"The gods never intervened in my search for Kaid's body because they knew Valka guarded his head. They knew no matter my success or failure, this last leg of my journey would be impossible. War may reside in Szent, but he's not bound by mortal flesh like Hreinasta. One hint of my presence, and he'll be here."

"So, you intend to give up?" The Stranger asks into my hair. His voice is soft, neutral, but I sense the accusation. "All these hardships, all these trials, and you emerged the victor, but now that you're at the end of your journey, you'll abandon all hope?"

"This is Valka." I pull back to look into his pure white eyes. "How can I defeat a deity of violence? Even with Lovec's blessing, I stand no chance. What is the Hunter to War?"

"You don't have to meet Valka on his terms."

I squint at The Stranger.

"Your husband trained you for this very moment, my child." He cups my cheek gently. "Kaid taught you to steal, to hide, to slip through the darkness unseen. He was a skilled thief, blessed by Varas himself, and he prepared you for this. You need not greet War on the battlefield, only steal from him."

"Stealing from War is no simple task."

"Gaining access to Hreinasta's chosen vessel in her fortified tower should've been impossible, yet your husband found a way without fail for a cycle. Surely, he taught you well enough to manage for one night."

"Hreinasta's temple was not the fortress Valka's is," I argue. "And Kaid was blessed by Varas himself. He earned the Thief's ashes. I have no such protection."

"Do you truly believe that?" The Stranger lowers his palm from my cheek and steps back. "Do you truly believe the Thief won't bless you?"

"Why would he?"

"His greatest acolyte was executed in secret without his consultation at the hands of Valka and the order of Hreinasta. His head now sits preserved by black magic in War's temple. Varas claimed Kaid. Do you think his servant's demise didn't anger him? That he isn't enraged by the Pure One's disregard? She murdered your husband in the dead of night, refusing him a public trial and denying him the last chance to face his sworn god. Would you not feel disrespected if you stood in Varas' shoes?"

"I never considered how the Thief might have taken the news of Kaid's punishment." They'd kept his bloodshed silent, and I shiver, remembering the reason for the privacy. "Do you truly believe Varas will bless me?"

"I think you've learned the gods haven't forsaken you, my child." He tucks my hair behind my ear so gently it surprises me. "Most blindly follow Hreinasta's ways. They fear the primordial goddess and bow to her corruption, but you are special, Sellah. You had the bravery to choose your own path. To see through her hypocrisy, and while most gods won't openly claim you, they notice the spark in you. A spark that will change the realm. You began this journey believing you were abandoned, disregarded and shunned, but it's time you face the truth. You are not alone. The gods that matter see you. I see you."

He says the last part so strangely that my stomach pitches. I suspect he's trying to tell me something. Something important, but I'm unsure what. My head is spinning, and my gut churns too fiercely to make sense of it all.

"Help me build a fire," I say as I turn to search for kindling. It's easier to focus on a task than the idea that the gods haven't forsaken me. That a primordial goddess who refused to cultivate enough self-control to live purely in her own form bullied them into corruption. Kaid always wore the holy ashes of Varas' temple, and while these woods are not the Thief's inner sanctum, the gods are not bound by walls and stone. Just as we wed under the stars, I'll pray under the canopy. I'll burn a prayer to the Great Thief and paint my face as my husband once did. Then I shall see if Varas is as angry at Kaid's punishment as I am.

THE FIRE FADES as the sun dies, stealing all light with it. As the last embers lose their color, I kneel before them and pray to the god who witnessed my husband being brutalized in the streets and saved him when he was only a boy. I pray to the Thief who blessed Kaid after he stole my white and golden dress as an offering. I pray to Varas who lost a devoted acolyte in the dead of night, and then I smear ashes onto my fingers. I paint my eyes and forehead just as Kaid used to, and while I don't sense a divine blessing descending upon me, I feel closer to him. How often had I stared at his gorgeous face, the black soot only enhancing his perfection? I say his name. It's my mantra, my prayer, my security. It's all I have left, and with ashes like his to guide me, I move through the trees toward Valka's temple.

I have the advantage of darkness, but the soldiers have the advantage of familiarity. They know every room, know where each hallway begins and ends. They've been tasked with guarding Kaid's head, which means it won't be easy to find, and just because night has fallen doesn't mean their defenses have loosened. *Kaid, help me. Varas, protect me. Elskere, guide me.*

The moon reigns high in the cloudless sky, and I move through the trees, circling the vast temple. It's a large fortress, and that it's so far from any town tells me this was constructed for one purpose. To defend his skull from me. The faithful do not pray here as part of their daily routine. They pilgrimage here to stand watch, to serve War with their swords. I don't doubt their eagerness to kill, and if they find me, my head will join Kaid's.

I take my time circling the temple, letting Kaid's teachings govern my observations. The entrances will be impossible to breach, as are the lower windows, but an open one hovers high on the second floor. It sits above a sheer wall, rendering a climb to its ledge hopeless, but if I could drop in from the roof?

I circle the temple again, and I spot a tree with a long hanging branch. The jump is significant, and there's a chance I'll miss my mark, but it's my only option. They designed this fortress to be impenetrable, ripping every tree and bush from its proximity, but it seems this single branch escaped their notice. I thank Varas for his provision and slip through the darkness. The thick bark offers generous handholds, but my arms shake from the beast's puncture wounds, and my legs struggle from the still-tender gash. When I used to climb after Kaid, the impressive heights were easy for my muscles, but now, a simple tree threatens to be my undoing. It takes far longer than it should, but eventually, I'm perched on the outstretched limb. I close my eyes for a second and visualize my husband before me. My mind watches his agile form balance on the branch and leap onto the roof with ease. I map his movements, memorizing where each of his footfalls would've landed, and then, with a deep breath, I race forward and fling myself at the temple.

The instant my feet leave the tree, I know my angle is wrong. I don't have Kaid's height or his power. I don't even have my own strength anymore, and I bite my lip to keep from screaming. If I fall, this height will break my legs, and I hurl a desperate prayer to anyone listening as my ribs hit the edge.

I fight my scream as the sharp stone slams into my abdomen, my knees cracking against the side of the building. My armpits scrape over the jagged ledge, leaving layers of skin behind as I slide, and my fingers claw for purchase. I can't breathe through the sharpness in my chest. I worry I broke a rib.

"Did you hear that?" a soldier below asks.

"Sounded like something hit the wall," a second voice answers him.

Kaid, help me. Don't let me fall.

My toes suddenly find traction against the smooth side of the temple, and I push myself up. I imagine my husband's powerful fingers gripping my shirt, hauling me to safety, and I scramble over the edge, collapsing just as the guards walk below where I'd been hanging.

"Probably the wind rattling the tree," the first man says, and I twist to see the branch shaking dangerously.

Varas, please, don't abandon me now.

I lay on my back as I catch my breath, the pain in my ribs lessening to a dull ache, and when the footsteps fade around the corner, I crawl to the edge. I locate the second-story window and wait, counting the intervals between the circular patrols. There's no pattern to their timing, which shows their dedication and foresight, and after long minutes go by, I come to terms with the fact that I'll just have to jump and hope Varas shields my shadows. I take a fortifying breath, and like Kaid taught me, I swing down and through the opening. I land with a graceful thump, praying I didn't drop into a room filled with guards, and as my eyes adjust to the darkness, I realize my prayers are only half answered. The room is teaming with soldiers, men and women of immense size and power, but they're all asleep. I must have dropped into their barracks, and I freeze in my crouch, hoping my fall didn't wake any of them.

The man on the cot beside me grunts and rolls to his side, his face coming to rest inches from mine. I stop breathing, fear pumping my heart faster. His eyes flutter, and my muscles coil so tight they hurt. For an agonizing second, I wait to be discovered, but then the soldier snorts in sleep and burrows deeper under his blanket. I'm paralyzed for endless seconds as I listen to his snoring increase, and it takes almost a full minute for me to gather the courage to move. I wonder if this was how Kaid felt when he hid in my room. He didn't know if my sleeping form would be friend or foe, but I was merely a girl, the Pure One's naive and pampered vessel. These soldiers are trained killers, forged by Valka himself.

I don't dare stand, so I crawl hands over knees to the door, pausing with my finger on its latch. I've never been inside this temple, but if it's anything like Hreinasta's, the Holy of Holies will sit at its center, the most guarded place within these walls.

That's undoubtedly where Kaid's head waits for me, and if I was Valka, I wouldn't leave it out in the open. I would lock it away in an impenetrable vault underground. *Varas, help me. I don't see how I'll survive this.*

"Calm, my child," The Stranger says into my mind.

"Stay with me." My whisper is barely audible, but I know he hears me.

"I always have. I always will."

I lift the latch, begging the hinges not to squeak, and I push the door open. Torchlight floods my eyes, but to my relief, no soldiers patrol this upper corridor. I silently click the door shut behind me and pause in the dimness. I wait for the call, for his bones to pull at my soul, and a gentle tug shifts the air to my right. Based on the layout of this sprawling temple, venturing to the left will lead me to the main staircase, but the calling is urging me to venture deeper into Valka's place of worship. I obey, keeping to the shadows, but I meet no living soul. Only flickering flames.

As I approach the rear of the temple, the hallway makes a sharp left turn. Rooms pepper my journey, but none of them call to me, so I ignore them and make for the bend in the corridor. Ascending stairs greet me as I round the corner, and the pull at my chest grows stronger. I take the stone steps two at a time until I reach a wooden door. I can go nowhere but forward, so I lift the latch and slip inside.

The sight takes my breath away. Valka's inner sanctum. His Holy of Holies. I've only ever been inside Hreinasta's temple, which was all pale marble and glittering gold. Bright and soft and white. Pure and feminine, a gorgeous backdrop for her beautiful vessels. I stood briefly in Lovec's abandoned house of worship, its grey stone unadorned, but time and snow and beasts had tarnished any grandeur it once held. But this? This is a room of power. The stairs lead to a small balcony that wraps around the circumference of the chamber, and my guess is that when Valka blesses his acolytes with his presence, they stand watch up here over him as if he's a warrior in the arena below. Rich, opulent tiles and golden artifacts decorate every inch of the floor and walls. His sacred fire burns at the head of the room, the flames spouting from a massive, ornate shield. Carved pillars hold up the balcony, and exquisite murals adorn the walls, each scene depicting the enormous god in the throes of battle. Each portrayal is more violent than the last, but it's the one behind the altar that steals my breath and chills my skin despite the flame's warmth. It's of a nude man stretched out before Valka as the god severs his arm. The limb is falling through the air, blood spurting from the wound. Valka is painted in striking detail, his muscles bulging, his skin shining, his short hair almost lifelike. His victim is less detailed, a nearly featureless dark-haired man, but in the pit of my stomach, I know. It's Kaid. This is his execution.

Anger floods me, and my fear evaporates. This is why I felt the pull. I know where Kaid is. He's behind that mural, and so help me Stranger, Varas, Lovec—whoever is listening—I will break that wall to pieces.

I search the balcony for a way down, but there are no steps. I'm trapped up here, the fall to the floor high enough to break my legs. It seems to enter the Holy of Holies, one must use the heavy, ornate, gold-plated doors below, but entering that way would surely get me killed. The inner sanctum is oddly empty, and I suspect Varas has intervened on my behalf, the ashes shielding me. Perhaps the Stranger was right. The Great Thief wants revenge for what was done behind his back, and what better way than to help me steal his acolyte's remains from under War's nose?

I swing over the balcony railing and aim for a pillar. I drop with a painful thud against it but manage to use its circumference to slide down. The descent is awkward and too fast, delivering me to the tiles with a sickening crack of my ankles, but after five minutes the pain recedes, and I'm alone in

Valka's inner sanctum. After fleeing Hreinasta, I avoided all temples save Lovec's frozen one, but his was in such disrepair, it almost didn't count. Curiosity begs me to gawk at this lavish chamber, but I don't have time. I've been blessed with solitude so far. I won't push my luck.

I scan the room for anything that'll help me destroy Kaid's mural, and I grin in triumph when I see the garish display of ceremonial weapons. They're studded with jewels and fine metals, intended only for worship and not battle. Against blades of steel, they would be useless, but against painted tiles?

I lift a golden axe off its mount. It's beautiful, and it's almost a shame that I plan to use it as a bludgeoning tool, but Kaid is more precious than any wealth. I pull two more weapons from the wall as backups. Once I begin, the sound will echo, and the soldiers will undoubtedly descend upon me. I'll have to work fast, and I won't have time to find a new tool if this ceremonial axe breaks. I most likely won't have time for more than the first blow, but I ignore that reality as I move to the painting.

If I squint, the featureless man morphs into Kaid, and an overwhelming longing floods me. I miss him so much. More than the sun misses the moon, the lover she shares a sky with but never at the same time. More than the desert misses rain. All the physical pain I've endured on this journey is nothing compared to the ache in my heart from missing him, and standing before a mural that depicts the last time I saw him alive is torture.

The pull of his bones is so strong that I force myself to gaze at the painting, and the moment my eyes land on the painted victim's head, it hits me. Kaid's final resting place is not a vault locked away below the earth. Valka walled his head in behind the depiction's skull. I can't stop the laugh that pushes past my lips at the obviousness. A vault would have been more secure, but it seems War enjoys his humor. It also seems he expected no one to make it this far without his soldiers' knowledge. Valka created a fortress, an unseizable temple, but he made a mistake. He prepared for an army, for a battle won with brute force. He should have been preparing for a thief's wife.

With renewed hope, I climb atop the altar, careful to avoid the flames licking the air in their shield behind me, and I raise the axe. *Kaid, I'm here. I'm coming for you.*

And then I swing with all my strength.

THE ESCAPE
SEASON OF THE HARVEST, CYCLE 78920

Kaid's headless and limbless torso lay before me in a warm pool of blood. I was too numb to move, to cry, to feel. I was hollow. Kaid was dead. My husband was dead.

We'd just promised our wedding vows in the eyes of Elskere. In three days, we were to flee Szent for the sea and sail south. He'd just been alive, a living, breathing man of impossible beauty with a voice so deep it rattled my chest. But now? Now he was nothing. They had carved him into pieces like cattle, forever silencing his voice, and that thought ripped a hole in my soul. I wouldn't survive this. No wife could.

I registered movement beside me, and to my shock, Hreinasta's vessel slipped through the blood and placed a slender palm on my shoulder. Her tanned skin was smooth and unblemished, the expensive lotions and oils keeping her vessels gorgeous until she shed them. I gagged at the scent of her hands. The fragrance she wore was floral and delicate, and mixed with the stench of death, they made my stomach roil.

"To defile an acolyte of mine, especially my chosen vessel,

is an offense that cannot go unpunished," she crooned, and I hated her. I despised her voice, loathed her beauty, abhorred her softness.

"He did not defile me," I spat. "He made me whole."

Hreinasta tsked disapprovingly. "This is why I don't dwell among mankind, choosing to inhabit the bodies of my priestesses instead. Men cannot be trusted. They are vulgar, disgusting things. Fickle and cruel and driven by their baser needs. I cannot allow my primordial body to be tarnished, which is why this body serves me now... as will yours."

"What?" I balked at her words, flinging myself backward so fast that Kaid's blood splattered my face. Surely, I'd misheard her. I was no longer pure in Hreinasta's eyes. A man had taken me, but it had been my choice. I'd given Kaid my love, my body, and my trust willingly, and while I'd never felt so whole as when I was in his arms, the goddess only saw my disobedience.

"You are my chosen vessel," she said. "And your beauty is unrivaled. Yes, I demand purity and righteousness from my devotees, but my spirit does not reside in you yet, therefore your sin was against your own soul, not mine. I claimed you as my next host when you were but ten cycles of age. If I were to recant that decree, I would have to admit that a man entered my sacred temple and violated my priestess. That will not do. The trespasser has been brought to justice, and we shall proceed with the transference as planned."

I couldn't have heard her right, but as I scanned the sanctuary, I suddenly understood the scene. No trial, no priestesses, no city magistrates. Varas was absent, despite it being his servant's execution. Only Hreinasta and Valka bore witness to his death, along with the few soldiers War trusted with his secrets. No witnesses to this treachery. No pure acolytes to observe my sin. Hreinasta wanted my beauty so fiercely, to save her own image with such intensity, that she murdered my husband in the dead of night and planned to take me as her vessel. No one would be the wiser. Only I would know, but my consciousness would fall dormant for the coming decades once she possessed me, and her current host would remember nothing when her spirit left her. No one would ever learn the truth.

My body went ice cold, and bile burned my throat. That couldn't be happening. I wouldn't let it.

"Come, come, acolyte," she said. "It is a great honor to be chosen as my vessel. Think of the glory, the prestige, the pride. This thief was nothing, a rat to be put down. He wanted to destroy you, but I will elevate you to grandeur."

"I would rather die than allow you to inhabit my body," I growled.

"But I'll make sure you don't." She turned to Valka, and my stomach dropped at their silent exchange. For a second, their eyes remained locked together, and then War strode to the holy fires. He dipped a torch into the flames, then aimed for Kaid's torso. With a horrifying sickness, I understood. He meant to burn Kaid's chest, and rage consumed me. The soldiers were gone, having carried his limbs and head away into the night. Both gods stood at my back, the path to the door unobstructed, and my legs were moving before my brain had time to process my decision. With a speed I didn't think myself capable of, I launched myself off the floor and raced for my husband's bloody torso. I scooped his remains up in one graceful movement, and then I was running for the exit. I half expected Valka to shove his blade through my spine as Hreinasta screamed for my apprehension, but the blow never came. War might revel in executions dealt in secrecy, but it seemed he wasn't a lapdog to be ordered after a girl. I heard Hreinasta's feet slapping the tile as she sprinted after me, but I knew she couldn't catch me. In her primordial form, she would have captured me before I made it two steps, but her human vessel was older than I was, accustomed to the comforts of a worshiped and served woman. Kaid's training had forged me into a warrior in my own way, and clutching his disfigured body and wearing his blood-stained clothes, I disappeared into the night, never looking back.

FIFTEEN

The blow cracks the painted victim's face down its center, and I cannot describe the joy that washes over me. I do not stop. I do not hesitate. The soldiers will come for me, but I don't let that deter my violence. I repeatedly slam the mural until my limbs ache and the golden axe deforms. Crack by crack, the wall shatters, and the fissure becomes a gaping wound as the axe snaps in half. I seize the ceremonial sword and continue hacking at the painting until it crumbles to the floor. I'm sweating uncontrollably from the fire at my back and shaking from the exertion, but the destruction is done. The spray of dust assaults my face, and I cough violently, the debris stinging my lungs. But when it settles, I see it. I see him.

Kaid's expression is preserved in suffering, the skin unblemished but pale from the lack of blood. I stumble forward, climbing through the rubble to reach him, but the second my fingers trail over his scarred lips, I gag. Kaid. My Kaid. His final scattered bones. Blind to anything but him, I pull his head from its resting place and clutch it to my chest. Even in death, he is beautiful to behold. I found him, all of him. My journey is at an end, and I don't know whether to be relieved or terrified.

Metal rings behind me, and I freeze. I may not be a great warrior, but I recognize that sound. A weapon is being drawn. Many weapons. Valka's soldiers have discovered me, and if they know I'm here, so does he.

With careful movements, I place Kaid's head in my pack and then grip the ceremonial sword. For a terrifying moment, I brace for the attack, but the men don't move. They don't speak. They simply stand frozen behind me, and I realize it's because they're confused. A slender, feral girl appeared in Valka's Holy of Holies and defaced his image while his trained acolytes stood guard. No one saw me enter. They believe their temple to be an impenetrable fortress, yet here I stand as if I materialized from thin air to desecrate their altar and misuse their weapons of worship.

My face burns white hot, but not down the center where Lovec marked me in blood. It's my eyes and temples that sting… where I painted the prayer ashes just as Kaid once did. Lovec isn't lending me his strength. It's Varas. Whether or not he has claimed me, the Great Thief is with me now. He wants me to avenge his faithful's execution, and a reckless idea floods my mind.

Until War carved my husband apart, I'd never seen a god besides the one I was pledged to, but Hreinasta was housed in human flesh. I'd never seen a deity in their true form until my twenty-first cycle. Valka is a monster in size, his eyes almost white save for the faint grey in his irises, and I didn't realize that was a trait of the gods until I met Lovec with his ice blond hair and pale eyes with their hint of blue. The Stranger's pure white eyes flash through my memory, but I shove him aside. I have no time to consider what that means, and my thoughts turn to the men at my back. Have they ever encountered a god other than Valka? Do they know what the deities look like? Here in the solitary North, they cannot travel with ease between multiple temples like in Szent. If I'm right, they have no clue what Varas the Thief looks like. Even married to Kaid, I never heard the god described. Perhaps he keeps his appearance hidden so he may plunder unnoticed in the night, and here I am, wild and unhinged in War's inner sanctum. I'm disheveled and painted in ash, sweaty from hacking apart the visage of a god. The soldiers haven't attacked because they aren't certain how I got in here. Not a single guard witnessed my entrance, so my arrival must be by divine intervention. They don't know what I am, and I grin with wicked intent.

I hoist the decadent ceremonial sword over my shoulder and spin toward the soldiers, eyes crazed and mouth curved in a deranged smirk. My face burns again, and I take it as Varas' approval of my plan.

"I wonder if my brother knows how easily his defenses can be breached," I say, praying that these men have never met Varas. "I had to create such a racket to get your attention."

I laugh as their grips tighten on their weapons, but they make no move to attack. I start to pace before the holy flames, kicking a chunk of debris with chaotic energy as I saunter through the chamber.

"I wonder. Should I tell him when I return to Szent?" I whirl on the men with aggression, and they collectively flinch. I fight a smile. It seems they don't know what Varas looks like, and my sudden appearance is enough to convince them I'm the Great Thief.

"Should I tell my brother how his acolytes slept while his inner sanctum was ransacked?" No one makes a move, and I lunge forward so fast that the ceremonial blade is against the frontmost man's throat before he can even blink. "Do you make it a habit of refusing a god? Do you find it wise to ignore their questions?"

He swallows, the sword's tip bobbing against his Adam's apple.

"Perhaps I should kill you all so that Valka knows the quality of men who serve him. That they let the Thief into their midst to insult their god," I snarl, leaning closer to the soldier, enjoying how his muscles stiffen. His eyes bulged the minute I alluded to myself as Varas. I was right. These soldiers have met no god besides War. Battle forged their massive deity, so to them, it's realistic that Varas could be a small woman, a creature agile and slight enough to slip through defenses and steal unseen.

"Or perhaps I won't kill you." I yank the sword back so fast that it nicks his skin, sending a thin trickle of red down his throat. "Valka would be angry with me, and I am not the god of war. I prefer to plunder what I please in the dead of night, not to fight bloody battles. I've stolen from my brother while his faithful stood unaware, and the punishment he'll inflict on you for your failure will be far greater than any violence you might suffer at my hands."

I saunter through the crowd, and the soldiers step aside, letting me pass with uncertainty. I channel Kaid's confidence as I stroll seemingly unbothered through the throng. I mimic Hreinasta's haughtiness as I sneer at their shocked expressions.

A young soldier snaps out of the group's trance and moves to cut off my escape. Everything within me panics, and I almost stumble, but then my face burns so painfully, I understand. Varas won't let me back down now, so I launch myself at the charging man.

"Are you so foolish that you would raise your hand against a god?" I snarl, swinging the golden sword in a harsh arc. It slices through the soldier's uniform, the tip coming to rest against his heart. "I am the Thief, and you dare to defy me?" I scream. "I should flay your flesh from your bones for this insult. My presence here is between my brother and me. I have no intention of slaughtering Valka's acolytes, but to raise a blade against a god is to wish for an agonizing death." I step so close to him that my breath hits his cheek, and he flinches. "What say you, boy?" My voice suddenly sounds different, as if Varas is truly speaking through me. "Will you challenge me?"

The soldier backs down, and I lower the weapon with a smirk. "Smart boy," I say deprecatingly as I push past him, my shoulder knocking him forcefully aside. Varas must be granting me his strength, for the young man stumbles, nearly crashing to the floor. I stifle the look of surprise and swing the ceremonial sword casually over my shoulder as I stride for the exit. Just a few more feet and I'm free. I cannot believe I pulled this off, the only explanation for my success, the stinging of my skin. I barely breathe until I depart the inner sanctum, and I don't slow as I move toward the temple's exit. No one stops me, and when I step outside into the cool night air with Kaid's head strapped to my back, my knees lock to stop me from collapsing in relief. I did it. I found his final piece and escaped with my life. This moment is surreal, and tears fill my eyes as I force myself to keep walking. I need to disappear into the trees. I need to—

The ground shudders with such thunder that I almost fall to the dirt, but I don't need my vision to know what shook the earth seemingly to its core. I don't need sight to understand who just landed before me, blocking off any chance of escape. My face goes cold, the burning evaporating from my eyes as Varas abandons me. His aid won't extend to what stands before me with brutal purpose.

"Such beauty and performance might fool men, but I am not so blind, thief." His authoritative voice rattles the air, and fear pulses through me in scorching waves. I stood a chance when my enemy was mortal, but now? Now I will die, for blocking my escape is the god of this temple himself.

War.

IT HAPPENS TOO FAST. A blur of motion, an explosion of pain, and suddenly I'm on the ground, certain every rib in my chest has cracked. I lay on the dirt, unsure how my face came to be pressed against the earth. One second, I was standing, and the next I was sprawled on my belly, my body breaking. I was foolish to believe I could steal from Valka, that I could escape with Kaid's final piece without garnering the attention of the very god who executed him.

"I must say, I'm impressed with you, little vessel," War thunders as his footsteps draw closer.

"I am not her vessel." I spit blood onto the grass as the horde of soldiers at my back slowly circle the fight.

"You found every bone I hid," Valka continues as if I'd said nothing. "I was tempted to remove his head from my temple, but I wanted to see if this beautifully defiant sinner had it in her to challenge me. If I'd known a warrior's heart beat within your breast, I would have taken you from Hreinasta and claimed you as my own. Despite your beauty, which still shines through your brokenness, your determination and strength are your greatest assets. Your talents would have been wasted as a human shell."

"At least that we can agree on," I slur, pulling myself to my hands and knees, but before I even register his movements, Valka's fist slams into my chest. I fly through the air as something inside me fractures, and I land with a scream on a soldier. We tumble to the ground, and the world blurs around me from the pain.

"'Tis a moot point, though," Valka continues. "Hreinasta is a primordial being, the goddess even I must bow to. Despite my desire for you, your treachery knows no bounds. I was content to let you live in quiet freedom after you fled, but you were so determined to find your thief that you forced my hand." He bends before me, capturing my jaw in his crushing fist. "What is it you plan to do with him, anyway? You cannot bring him back. Is burying his bones together worth all this pain? Your lover is dead. His soul is in pieces. Are you really so foolish as to incur both mine and Hreinasta's wrath over a corpse?"

I try to speak, to curse him, but all that escapes my mouth is blood.

"Pity," he snarls. "Such beauty. Such bravery and determination. I had hoped to avoid this, little vessel, but you have forced my blade."

He unsheathes his sword with deliberate movements, his soldiers stepping back to escape his blow, and that's when I see it. Darkness flutters in the trees. It's barely visible, only a faint blackness winding against the night, but I know what it is. I recognize the familiar pull.

Lovec, grant me your strength as the hunter. Udens, your strength as the protector. Kaid, I love you. Until we are both dust.

Valka draws back his sword, and my vision blurs again as blood pours from my mouth. I can feel the broken bones inside me as I bleed internally. The pain is too intense, but as his blade cuts through the air with the whistled song of death, I launch to my feet.

I scream in agony, my limbs faltering, but I do not stop. Valka's sword carves into the earth where I'd lain, the wind from his blow hot on my back, but I do not slow as I vault for the trees. My vision darkens. I have seconds before I pass out, seconds before Valka slices the life from me as he did my husband, but I do not stop.

I say his name one time, two times, three as I run. Valka's body heat washes over me, his powerful legs hunting me down with ease. He grunts as he raises his sword, the sound too close. He's on my heels, confident there's no escape for me, but I'm almost there. The darkness hovers mere feet away. If I can just—

War swings his weapon, the whistle of air like a scream,

and with my last ounce of strength, I leap. I soar weightlessly, my consciousness slipping, but as the tip of Valka's razor-sharp blade cuts deep into the flesh on my back, I slam into the waiting darkness. The Stranger catches my agonized body, his power whisking us into the night as I black out.

THE STRANGER
SEASON OF ICE, CYCLE 78920

S now coated the realm, and it was the first time I understood the true savagery of the Season of Ice. For twenty-one cycles, I'd been sheltered, guarded, protected, but I finally experienced the brutality of life beyond the temple walls. The cold ate at my skin and settled in my bones. It burrowed into my soul and corrupted my body from within. I would die in the darkness, in the frost, but I didn't care.

Those first weeks were nearly the death of me before I learned the world's harsh truths. I knew nothing of the world, of people, of men, and I was a ghost. For a month, I wandered in such a daze that I didn't even remember which cities I slept in. I huddled in alleys and survived on discarded scraps. My filthy skin hung from my bones in malnutrition, and then my blood came.

I'd woken alone in an abandoned alley, my pants stained and wet, and when my fingers brushed my thighs, I saw the damning crimson. My cycle had come, just as it always had, and as I stared down at my legs, a darkness I'd never tasted devoured me. I'd prayed that Kaid had left me with a child on our wedding night. If I was forced to spend the rest of my days without him, I longed for a baby to remind me of the man I loved. The hope that I carried a part of him inside me was the only thing that kept me from surrendering to my despair, but as I sat there in my blood, my will to survive evaporated. Nothing remained worth living for.

Something broke inside me that day. Something that might never heal. Using the skills Kaid taught me, I stole what I needed without remorse and purchased a trunk with my illegal gold to carry his dark magic-preserved torso. I freed a horse from a wealthy merchant's stable, and we wandered the realm as the ice came. The empty numbness plaguing my chest didn't care if I lived or died. I learned through town gossip that Hreinasta had publicly shunned me. She hid her execution of Kaid, choosing instead to proclaim my blasphemy and treason. She chose another girl to inhabit as her vessel, and the last I heard before I turned my ears away from the news was my family had lost everything in their shame. I wanted to feel sorrow for them, to be ashamed that I brought destruction upon their heads, but every time I contemplated repenting, I saw Kaid die all over again. Remembered Valka condemning him to remain awake until the end, and I cursed them instead. I cursed my parents for sacrificing a child to a selfish god. I cursed Hreinasta for her weakness in following her own decrees and Valka for his cruelty. The gods had abandoned me, and while I was acutely aware of their absence, I didn't care. I wanted nothing from them.

I remembered little after that. All I knew was cold and loneliness, but one fateful night as I sat before my meager fire, a shadow drifted toward my flames. I watched it swirl in on itself, taking shape, and when a man made of darkness emerged, fear gripped my chest. For a moment, I contemplated defending myself, but a glance at the locked trunk Kaid lay inside convinced me to accept my fate.

I prepared to greet death as the stranger approached, but instead of greeting me with violence, he merely crouched before my fire, letting the flames light his face. He was incredibly handsome, both old and young, his body too tall and strong. Long, midnight-black hair framed his haunting features, and the whitest eyes I'd ever seen stared out at me. I flinched at their eerie blindness, but the visitor simply smiled at my movement. We sat, eyes locked in silence, and then he lowered the hood from his head.

"Sorrow should not mar such beauty," he said. "Come, child, tell me of your troubles. Let me share in your burden as thanks for allowing me to share your fire."

I'd given him no such permission, but I let his statement slide. I lacked the energy to fight a stranger wandering in the dead of night.

"Surely, you can speak?" he pushed.

"I can." My voice sounded harsh, and I realized just how long it had been since I'd uttered words.

"Excellent, my child. Now tell me what ails you."

"No." I could barely manage the single syllable.

"No?" He cocked his beautiful head at me, the flames reflecting unnervingly in his bone-white eyes. They had no pupils, no irises. They were expressionless, yet so full of wisdom and emotion that I struggled to hold his gaze. "I suppose I judged wrongly, then." He stood gracefully, pulling the hood of his black cloak back over his head. The garment hung in long tatters, ethereal in its smoke-like fabric. "I apologize for the inconvenience. I mistakenly believed you were the one who I could help. The one who could help me."

He turned to vanish into the darkness, but I had the sudden urge to stop him, to tell him everything he wished to hear.

"They killed him," I blurted, and the man froze with his back still to me. "The gods killed my husband."

"The gods?" he twisted, his eyes meeting mine with both horror and anticipation. "Which ones?"

"Valka." My answer didn't seem to surprise or interest him. "By Hreinasta's order."

The stranger flinched at her name, suddenly enthralled by my words, and he sat before the fire, folding his hands in his lap. He remained silent, but something about the way his black hair was the same shade as Kaid's, the way his eyes saw nothing and everything, the way he studied me as if I were his entire world, opened my floodgates. I haltingly recounted my love for my husband and his horrific death. He listened intently to every detail of my past, but his interest intensified when I spoke of the ritual that bound Kaid's soul to his flesh and how Valka carved him into pieces and scattered his bones.

"I can help you, my child," the dark man said as he moved closer, staring at me with those unblinking eyes.

"How?"

"I've witnessed this punishment before. The soul is bound to the body so that it, too, becomes severed and then trapped within the cursed flesh. You were smart to save his chest from the flames. If you had allowed him to burn, part of his soul would have been destroyed, and I could not help you."

"How can you help?" I looked at him with confusion, my entire being aching from reliving Kaid's death.

"I have a task for you, my child," he said in earnest. "One, you must complete alone without my aid, but if you overcome the trials set before you, I swear to return your husband to this life."

"That's impossible," I whispered. Dying was a final and inescapable nothingness. No afterlife, no punishment or reward, no resurrection. Death was the end, the abyss, the ultimate slumber. It's why humanity clamored for the god's favor. They wished their lives to be blessed before the great darkness stole them, and my parents had aimed high, attempting to garner Hreinasta's approval. It was almost a pity that their selfishness had led to disgrace and not blessings.

"Perhaps." He stared at me with such intensity that fear coiled through my gut. "Or perhaps not. Faith, my child. That's what I need from you, and if you place yours in me, I'll grant you your greatest wish. If you can trust my promise and complete the tasks at hand, I shall return your husband to you."

"What tasks?" I knew he was lying. Kaid would never come back to me, but I needed that hope. My soul longed to believe this dark stranger, and grief conquered my reasoning.

"Valka scattered your husband's bones to the far corners of the realm. His final resting places are lands of great evil, but if you find them, if you can gather them all, I will return him to you."

"How is that possible?"

"You must believe. That's all I'm able to tell you."

I shouldn't have believed him. I should not have granted him my blind trust, but all rational thought vanished the moment he promised me Kaid.

"My child." He took my frail hands in his strong palms. "Give me your faith, and I'll return to you what was lost."

His fingers felt warm despite the darkness diving deep into my muscles, ensnaring my organs, flowing within my veins, and I realized that this was only the second time a man had touched me. The second time I'd experienced kindness in connection with another being. I didn't count Valka's soldiers, for their hands had been violent, their touch intrusive. I could not accept their violation, and if the promise of Kaid's return did not convince me, the dark man's gentleness sealed my fate. No one, not even my family, had ever offered me such affection, and I swore my oath to him before the flames.

When I woke the next morning, he was gone, and for a moment I thought I'd dreamed our encounter until his voice flooded my mind.

"Remember to have faith, and you shall find him. Listen to your heart. Your love will guide you."

"Who are you?" I asked. My chest ached, begging me to walk south, and little did I know its tug would lead me to the Sivatag.

"I am no one, my child. I am but a stranger in this world."

SIXTEEN

My eyes blink open, heavy with disorientation, and as the blurred world comes into focus, the first thing I see is The Stranger's dark hair hanging over his forehead as he hunches close to the flames. I can't tell what he's doing. The pain radiating from every bone in my body is all-consuming. My mouth is as dry as the Sivatag, which makes me wonder how long I've been unconscious.

I struggle to sit, but my aching muscles protest the movements, so I lay still, watching The Stranger work in the early morning light.

I WAKE WITH A START. The sun dips dangerously low in the sky, and I realize I've slept the entire day. My throat is parched and my body sore, but the pain has faded some. I wonder if I have The Stranger to thank for the relief. My gaze finds him, and he sits hunched in concentration in the same spot I last saw him, dark hair hanging in front of his sculpted face.

I part my lips to speak, but then I notice what he's doing. My entire body goes stiff, for laid out before him is Kaid's fragmented and bare corpse. I almost gag at the sight of him arranged in pieces on the dirt. I haven't seen his full form in one place in over a cycle, and seeing it positioned together yet separate like a puzzle makes me numb.

I'm lightheaded and sore, dehydrated and starving, but I ignore my needs as I crawl to Kaid's side. The Stranger's eyes flick to mine. He says nothing. His expression remains blank, but I feel his affection all the same. He knows the storm raging within me. He understands the magnitude of this moment.

He resumes his task, and I realize he's stitching Kaid back together. His attention to detail is impeccable, the thread delicate, his stitches uniform. So far, he has reattached Kaid's head and left arm, and is working on sewing his left thigh to his hip. That's the leg that Valka split in two, so his shin rests below the knee, waiting its turn. The right side of his body is still detached, and while The Stranger's skill is more refined than mine, I cannot sit idly by. He seems to sense my need to help and stares at the dirt beside him in expectation. I crawl to the spot, and The Stranger passes me a sharp needle and strong but elegant thread. He then lifts Kaid's wrist into my lap and places his severed hand next to it. He says nothing as I thread the needle, content to simply watch me, but when I pick up Kaid's hand, the black magic stings my skin, and I drop it in surprise. The Stranger catches his lifeless fingers and returns them to my thighs with a gentle expression. That he managed to sew this much is a testament to his strength. I can tell by the tenderness in his eyes that he'll gladly accept the burning pain for me, but I need to help. So, I inhale a deep breath and grip my husband's flesh.

I work carefully in silence beside The Stranger, determined to make my stitches as beautiful as his. At some point, a water skin and food appear next to me, and I use the excuse of eating and drinking to rest my hands. The bite of the magic is unbearable; my progress slowed by Valka's beating, but I don't give up.

The air is warm as night falls, and I realize The Stranger must have transported us south. Judging by his unhurried movements and lack of concern, I doubt Valka is coming for us. I don't know where we are. Perhaps neither does War, but that's not why we're safe. I stare at my friend, the dark man who saved me even though he swore he couldn't lend me aid. He's why no god hunts me. Why we're free to take our time with my husband's limbs. I don't know how I didn't see it sooner. Maybe I didn't want to acknowledge it, but I'm no longer afraid. I should be, but I'm not. In truth, I love The Stranger. In his own way, he has become my father, my true and only parent. There's a deeper meaning to his term of endearment. He rarely refers to me as Sellah, but always his child, and I finally understand why. I once had a family who abandoned me. It seems I now have a family of my own making.

The sun sets, but we don't stop until I've reattached Kaid's hand and he has finished with his leg. I want to continue working, but I can barely keep my eyes open. My fingers burn from the black magic, and my body aches from Valka's beating. I should be dead. War's blade had split open the flesh on my back, but I'm surprisingly whole. I realize there's so little I know about The Stranger as he wraps my blistered palms in salve-coated bandages. His hands look far worse, bloodied and raw from the curse, but when I attempt to bandage him, he silently shoves me away. He says nothing as he forces me to eat. He builds up the fire, covers Kaid's nudity with a blanket, and then tucks me protectively into his side while I sleep. I'm surprised by his affection. He rarely spent time with me face-to-face while I searched the realm, but something has changed. The Stranger seems stronger, taller, darker. His eyes are whiter yet full of life, of compassion, of danger, yet he holds me against his chest with the innocence of a parent comforting their child. Not even my own mother cradled me when I lived in her home, and I don't care who this dark man is. He could burn the world to ash, and I would still love him.

———

THE STRANGER IS ALREADY WORKING when I wake. I silently move to help him, but he shakes his head and points to the food and water with authority. I don't argue. His expression warns me I won't win, and I doubt my blistered hands could hold a needle. So, I obey, gathering the dried fruit and nuts before crawling to Kaid's head. I scoop it into my lap, my pants protecting me slightly from the magic, and I eat as The Stranger works. I pretend my thief is merely sleeping, that he laid down on my thighs after a long day to rest. I try not to stare at the stitching on his neck or the pallor of his bloodless skin. My husband is sleeping. That is all.

Eventually, I fall asleep, my healing body exhausted and poisoned by black magic, and I spend the next night in a feverous fit. I'm vaguely aware of The Stranger tending me, my injuries burning with infection. I think two days pass while I suffer through delirious sweats, but when I finally wake, Kaid's body is whole, and I can't stop myself from scooping him into my arms. The stitching is so fine, so immaculate, that I can hardly believe he was once scattered throughout the realm, and I'm suddenly terrified. I've been hoping for and dreading this moment. This is when I'll learn if I placed my faith in a liar or a power capable of returning the dead. Either way, the outcome weighs heavy on my shoulders. If The Stranger fails, I'll have fought for nothing, but if he succeeds? It changes everything, and not just for me. For the realm.

"I must warn you," The Stranger says gently, and after so many days of silence, his voice sounds odd. "I shall return him to you, but he may not be the same man you remember. He has been dead for seasons. Not only was his body carved into pieces, but so was his soul. The body is easy to mend, but the spirit? It will never be completely whole." He stares at me as if he needs me to acknowledge my understanding, but all I can do is gaze at him numbly.

"And then there's this." He points to Kaid's arm where the Beast of the Mitte Midagi bit into his flesh. "Valka's cuts were clean and precise, sliced by a god's weapon while he yet lived, but this injury was inflicted after death when the soul was stagnant. I cannot say what damage happened to him in the mouth of that creature."

"What…" my voice breaks. "What are you saying?"

"He may not be the man you remember." The Stranger clutches my hands sympathetically.

"I don't care," I say with conviction. "I'll love him no matter what."

"That's what I needed to hear, my child." He caresses my cheek with fatherly affection. "Are you ready?"

"No." It's the truth. "But I refuse to live one more second without him."

"Then I shall begin."

He kneels beside Kaid's corpse and places his broad palms over his heart. A tidal wave of fear crashes into me, and I feel like I'm choking. I'm afraid to watch, but I force myself to as darkness emanates from The Stranger. My heart has stopped. Or is it beating too fast? I can't tell.

The smoke swirls around him in pulsing black waves as he begins to speak in an ancient and guttural tongue. The ground shakes. The sky darkens. The world ceases to exist except for him and those words. Those horribly dark and violent words. His voice is demonically cruel, and his white eyes flash in the blackness. The smoke dances around him in thick pulses, then with a vicious command, it shoots for Kaid's body.

I yelp as his corpse jerks unnaturally. This brutality is unlike anything this world has suffered. The darkness is so oppressive; I worry I'll pass out under its weight. It's too much. I want him to stop.

Lightning electrifies the sky, and the thunder that follows is so loud, it cracks the earth. The dirt collapses as the land splits apart, but still, The Stranger calls to the darkness. I want to snatch Kaid's body away from him as it convulses at awkward angles, but I can't move. The Stranger's power roots me to the ground, and all I can do is watch in horror.

When it feels as if I've been trapped in this hellish storm for days, the black shroud collapses onto Kaid, burrowing deep into his body. His corpse jerks, and I want to scream for The Stranger to stop. My husband has been violated enough, but just when I open my mouth to demand he end this, I realize the darkness didn't move Kaid. He did that of his own volition, and he scrambles backward on unsteady limbs, putting distance between himself and the Stranger before his arms give out.

I gasp as I watch him surge to life, and his eyes snap to mine like a cornered animal as he collapses in the dirt. They're wild with alarm, and I can't tell if I'm overjoyed or horrified. He's alive. My Kaid is breathing, moving, seeing, but he stares between The Stranger and me as if we're monsters come to devour him.

His pale chest moves awkwardly fast as panic consumes him, and a new fear settles over me. There's no recognition in his gaze. Only terror. Has he been dead for too long? Has he forgotten this life? The Stranger said he might be different, but has his resurrection erased me from his memory?

With slow movements, I snatch the blanket from the dirt and move to cover his nudity. He flinches, chest heaving as he fills his empty lungs, and his fear feels like an accusation. What have I done? He was dead, nothing but severed limbs for over a cycle, and I forced him back to the land of the living with a darkness I don't understand. Did I do the right thing? Have I made his suffering worse?

Kaid watches me warily as he struggles to breathe, and I gently place the blanket over his legs. He studies me with uncertainty, staring deep into my eyes without recognition. I love him more than words can convey, and I long to pull him into my arms, but his panic has paralyzed me.

His gaze remains on my face, never turning toward The Stranger, who's the more terrifying sight. It's undoubtedly because the dark man frightens him, but my heart longs for it to be because he finds comfort in my features. With that hope, I find my voice.

"Do you know who you are?" My words are barely a whisper. I don't want to spook him.

"Yes." His voice is rough from disuse, but its deepness resonates in my chest, and I can't stop a smile from curving my lips. I forgot how glorious that sound was.

"And..." I falter. "Do you know who I am?"

"Yes." He pauses, and I hold my breath until my lungs hurt. "You're my wife."

SEVENTEEN

You're my wife.

Three simple words. Three words to undo me, and he's in my arms before I realize I'm moving. He grunts as we collide, and I recoil, ashamed I hurt him, but his weak arms wrap around my waist before I can pull away. We collapse to the dirt, his body unable to hold us upright, and he groans as my chest lands atop his. The sound is heartbreaking, and for a moment, I fear I've damaged his stitching, but then I feel dampness against my throat. Tears. His tears.

The sound comes again, and I realize it isn't agony flooding his tongue. It's sorrow and joy and love, and I break into a thousand pieces. I pull him tighter, burrowing my face into his neck, and for what feels like forever captured inside a moment, we cry together. His skin no longer stings, and while it's still cool to the touch, it isn't dead flesh. My husband isn't dead. He's here and whole and alive. He's in my arms.

Unable to wait any longer, I twist in his embrace and kiss him. He tries to reciprocate, but his lips are awkward from disuse. It doesn't matter, though, because it is the most beautiful kiss we've ever shared.

"I told you," Kaid says against my mouth, his words

garbled as he struggles to use muscles that lay dormant for seasons. "I would love you until I was dust."

"I don't love you." I cover his entire face with kisses until he attempts a weak smile. "Because love isn't enough for what I feel. It is too much. It's everything."

Kaid grunts as my lips find his but this time it's from the pain, so I peel myself off his body. Unwilling to be parted from him, I cradle his torso until he's leaning against my chest, his head resting on my thundering heart, and I tuck the blanket securely around him so he's no longer lying on the dirt.

"How am I here?" he whispers against my breasts, his voice exhausted.

"Someone special promised that if I found you, he would return you to me." I meet The Stranger's gaze, and I swear tears brim in his white eyes.

"Hmmm," Kaid grunts, his eyelids heavy with sleep.

"Rest, husband." I kiss his hair, pulling him closer. "I'll tell you all about it when you wake, but rest now. I'm not going anywhere."

Kaid falls asleep, his breathing steady in my embrace. I still throw The Stranger a wary look, though, but his comforting smile assures me everything will be all right. Kaid's no longer dead, no longer scattered bones to be found. He's resting, but he will wake, and every day for the rest of his life, I'll be there when he does.

I WAKE to the sound of dirt crunching beneath boots, and I blink, forcing my vision to focus. Kaid had woken at midday, and with The Stranger's help, I dressed him and fed him some broth. The movement exhausted him, and he fell asleep in my arms after an hour, but it was a glorious hour. The brightness in his eyes burned a path straight to my heart, and I've never been so content just to sit and hold something. I hadn't meant to fall asleep. I wanted to remain awake, to trace the lines of his face with my eyes, but the fiery sunset tells me I'd slept for a few hours. Kaid's head still rests on my breast, his breathing steady, and I kiss his brow before searching for what woke me.

The sound comes again, farther away, and my gaze finds The Stranger. He's walking into the sunset, and with anxiety crowding my chest, I slip out from under Kaid's peaceful form.

"Wait!" I race after him, skidding to a stop in the dirt as he turns. "You're leaving?"

"You don't want me here, my child." He smiles, cupping my face. "Not for this reunion."

"I…" I trail off, knowing he's right, yet his departure still nags at me. I haven't gone without his voice for more than a few days, and I'm not ready to lose him. "Are you leaving me?"

"Sellah, my Sellah." He pulls me into his embrace, hugging me tight. "I will never leave you. I swear it."

I heave a sigh of relief against his chest, and he leans back to stare into my eyes. He says nothing, but an understanding passes between us. He isn't my birth father. He's not Hreinasta. He won't forsake me.

The Stranger holds my gaze for a moment, then with a smile, he turns to leave.

"Who are you?" I capture his wrist, forcing him to face me.

"Have you not figured it out?" he smirks, his white eyes flashing. His are colorless, unlike the others with their faint irises, but they're the same. The eyes of a god.

"Death," I whisper, and he nods. "How? Hreinasta banished you. She eradicated your cult. How are you here?"

"Because of you, my child. Because of your faith."

"I don't understand."

"I had no standing in this world or in the gods' realm after she exiled me. Without the faith of the gods or mankind, I had no foothold," he explains. "I wandered for centuries in the nothingness, searching for a crack, for an escape from my exile, and I found that in you. Your despair was so great that in the darkness, you longed for a way to undo your pain. You didn't realize it, but your longing was almost a prayer, and I heard you. I was but a whisper when you first met me, but as your faith grew, so did my presence. My footing in this world is complete. The moment Kaid remembered you, your belief in me solidified. I now have an acolyte, and because of that, Hreinasta's banishment has ended. It took but one believer to open the door. Although I suspect your husband will soon follow your lead."

"Why…" I swallow, my throat suddenly dry. I'd unleashed Death. Had I made a mistake? Would the world burn for my actions? "Why did she abolish your cult? Have I condemned the realm by freeing you?"

"Oh, my child," Death laughs. "You, of all people, should know Hreinasta isn't the goddess she claims to be. When Lovec claimed you, you believed it was because you were both the same." He trails his fingers down my nose where Lovec marked me in blood. "He had lost his wife, and you, your husband. When Udens granted you safe passage through the Vesi, you believed it was because you were not so different. You both understood the pain of losing those you care about." He cups my jaw, and I realize what he's about to say will break my heart. "You and I are the same. We understand what it is to lose love at Hreinasta's hands."

"No." I shake my head, dreading his confession.

"I am a primordial god, as is she." Death brushes my cheek with a long finger. "Life and death. The beginning and the end. Light and dark. Good and evil. We were the first, but at the dawn of time, there were three primordial deities, Hreinasta's twin completing the trinity."

I pinch my eyebrows at his revelation. The Pure One has

no siblings. I served in her temple, yet none of her priestesses knew this.

"They embodied life, and in life, there is good and evil," he continues, sensing my doubt. "Many believe I am darkness and evil, but I am simply death. The end of life. Only the living can be evil, and Hreinasta and her sister manifested the scales of morality. Hreinasta believed she was goodness and purity and her twin the expression of sin, but I didn't see it that way. Both sisters were light and dark in their own ways, good and evil trapped equally between them. Hreinasta loved me, and trusting she was the holier sibling, she felt I belonged to her. I never did. I couldn't. One look at her sister, and I was hers.

"Our love was unbreakable. It consumed everything in its path, but in her jealousy, Hreinasta killed her twin, hoping it would force me into her bed.

"I am death, though. Killing her wouldn't keep her from me, so Hreinasta forced Valka's hand. He bound my love's soul to her body and carved her into pieces, her trapped spirit shredding as they cut her apart. Then he scattered her bones to the corners of the realm and burned her chest and heart to ensure I could never resurrect her."

I inhale a horrified breath. Kaid hadn't been her first victim. Hreinasta has done this before, murdering her own sister. "That's why you told me it was fortunate I saved Kaid's torso from the flames when we met?"

"Yes." Sorrow paints his features as he speaks. "I can never return my love to life because they burned part of her soul. In death, a person's spirit moves on, but if it's bound to the body and then destroyed, there's nothing I can do. Hreinasta knew that, and she wanted to ensure I never saw her again."

"I…" I trail off at a loss for words and settle for slipping my hand comfortingly into his.

"Hreinasta hoped her sister's death would force me to choose her, but my disgust only grew. I threatened war and

243

carnage, and to save her image, the Pure One banished me with lies. I ceased to exist until you pulled me from the nothingness."

"Why did she kill Kaid that way?" My anger at the pure goddess doubles with each passing second. "You were gone from this world. Returning the dead was impossible."

"Because death is not cruel enough. Without her sibling, she now embodies both good and evil, yet she considers herself better than us. She believes herself so righteous that she became the very evil she loathes. Hreinasta despised you for choosing Kaid over her, as I loved her sister instead of her. She wanted you to suffer."

I look back at my sleeping husband with fear. "If she hates me that intensely, will she come for him again?"

"You're safe, my child." Death tightens his hold on my hand. "You are mine, and I protect what's mine. She won't lay a finger on you or the family you two will build. Lovec claimed you, and he won't allow suffering to befall you. Neither will Udens, and I suspect Varas still cares for Kaid after how he aided you at Valka's temple. Elskere blessed your marriage. The wed gods won't wish to see you parted since your bond pledged in their name helped you find his bones. Hreinasta won't touch you."

"I'm glad I returned you to this world." I fling my arms around his neck, and he laughs as he hugs me close. "What will you do now?" I ask as he releases me.

"First, there's a temple of mine that needs to be purged of a dark entity." He smirks, and I shiver at the memory of the jungle where I found Kaid's hands. "Then? Then I'll do what I must to stop Hreinasta from inflicting harm on her people. Perhaps she'll remember the good in her, but if not, I shall rise to challenge her. Now, enough talking to me." He grabs my shoulders and twists me with a chuckle to where Kaid sleeps. "I will see you soon, and I swear to never be far. Merely speak my name, and I'll answer. Now, go to your husband."

I squeeze his hand before striding toward our campsite but only make it halfway when a thought pops into my head. "Stranger?" I smirk at my misstep, but he simply smiles. We've grown fond of that term, and in my heart, Death will always be my Stranger. "Lovec's wife. Could you return her to this world?"

"I could."

"Would you? For me?"

"For you, my child?" He laughs. "Anything."

Then The Stranger… Death vanishes into the night. I smile, thankful he hasn't abandoned me, but glad he granted us our privacy. I want to be alone with Kaid until we're sick of the sight of each other, and I run until I'm at his sleeping form. He wakes as I settle next to him, his eyes instantly finding mine.

"I finally get to wake beside you," he mumbles with a smile, and I kiss his forehead softly.

"Are you hungry?" I ask, offering him some of the fresh fruit The Stranger gathered for us.

"I don't know." He stares at the melon without moving. "I… I've forgotten how to be alive. I don't know if I'm hungry. I don't know if I'm thirsty or tired or in pain. All I know is I love you, and I think that's enough for now. I'll need help to remember how to live. Will you help me?"

"You don't need to ask." I shift so I can use both arms to prepare the fruit without letting go of him. "My wedding vows have not ended. I'll be with you every step of the way." I slice the melon and feed him a few bites. The juice drips down his chin as he struggles to chew, and I can tell by his flushed cheeks his failing embarrasses him, so I kiss it off his skin until we both ache from laughter.

"You're different," he says, as I encourage him to drink some water before continuing to eat.

"It's been a long cycle," I say, concealing just how hellish these past seasons have been,

"Not bad different," he adds quickly. "You look the same, if not more tanned and scarred, but you know I don't mind scars." He smirks, or at least he tries to. "I meant your spirit. When we first met, you were a shell. It was as if you didn't know how to be alive, and perhaps it's my ego, but I like to think I helped you, much like you'll have to help me now."

"You're too modest. Everything good about my life is because of you."

He laughs and then groans in pain, falling silent for a long minute as he catches his breath. "Over our first cycle together, I watched you blossom from a girl who thought she deserved nothing to a strong and vibrant woman. A woman who didn't accept abuse because those in authority told her she should. It was impossible not to fall in love with you. I tried. I really did. I swore I would be your friend and nothing more, but your appetite for life spoke to my soul. You wanted so much more than your family had condemned you to, and I fell hopelessly in love with both you and the idea that I could give you that future. When I died, your refusal to leave my side proved you were the strongest woman I knew, but looking at you now, I realize I only experienced a fraction of the goddess you are. You're different, but in a good way, Sellah. I want you to tell me every single detail I missed. Not now because I'm tired, and I worry hearing of your suffering will be too great a strain on my heart, but I have no doubt your stories will prove how incredible my wife is. I can't wait to relearn everything about you."

"If we weren't already wed, I would marry you again," I say, brushing his hair off his forehead.

"Marrying you was my greatest joy, so I would do it again in a heartbeat. Perhaps when I am well, we can find a temple to Elskere and pledge our vows in a traditional ceremony. I'll steal you a dress, an obscenely ornate and expensive wedding dress, and then marry you properly."

"You won't need to steal me anything." I gesture to the

cart where my horse rests comfortably. Since Kaid no longer lies in pieces inside the chest, I placed the sack of gold and the ceremonial sword from Valka's temple in it for safekeeping. Seems when The Stranger saved me from War, I still had the expensive blade clutched in my fist, the object of worship worth more money than the riches my parents boasted. Between the weapon and the bag of treasure, we'll never want for the rest of our lives.

"I'll tell you all about it when I tell you of my travels, but I managed to steal us enough gold for a lifetime," I continue, and his eyes snap to mine.

"I cannot wait for that story. Varas would be impressed with that haul."

"Varas may have helped," I say with a twinkle in my eye, and Kaid's mouth practically drops open.

"Wife," his teasing voice is a warning. "I am too tired for this excitement, but now I'm anxious to hear."

"Don't be," my voice saddens, and I pull him closer. "Most of my stories are filled with pain. I'll tell you, and while some moments were good, most will sadden you."

"I still want to hear. I want to share everything with you." Kaid kisses the bare skin on my chest, and his uncoordinated movements tickle. "Remember at the beginning of our friend-ship when I asked you to tell me your stories?"

"But I told you I had none, so I listened to yours instead," I answer.

"Well, now the tables have turned, and I'm here to collect." He gives me a struggled smile. "You made a promise to give me a story if I gave you mine. Looks like you're finally going to keep your end of the bargain."

He lifts his head, barely able to make it more than a few inches, but I understand his request. I lean down, capturing his lips, and we kiss until we can't breathe. His movements are slow and uncoordinated, but my husband doesn't let that deter him as he tastes my mouth, my cheeks, my throat. We live eternally in those kisses, our words and breaths and adoration melding together, and it is perfect in its imperfections. As his lips meet mine stroke for stroke, passion for passion, I decide everything I endured was worth it. Every scar, every hunger pang, every fear. I would suffer through all the pain life inflicted on me again, because I've loved my thief from the moment I found him in my room, and I'll love him until I am dust.

THE FAMILY
SEASON OF HARVEST, CYCLE 78929

I shut the door gently so I don't wake them and creep down the hall to my room. With the excitement of the day, neither girl wanted to sleep, and it was a battle of wills to see who would break first. Exhaustion won in the end, and with soft kisses to their small tanned brows, I left them to dream of swimming, tropical fruits, and pink fish.

Kaid sits on our bed as I round the corner to our bedroom, but he's staring off into space, oblivious to my presence. I smile at how beautiful he is and lean against the doorframe to wait for him to wake from his trance. The first time this happened, it terrified me. It was almost as if he stopped existing in this world, his mind somewhere else, and when he finally snapped out of his daze, I was nearly inconsolable with terror. It happens less now than it used to, but occasionally my husband's consciousness leaves this plane of existence. All these cycles later, though, it no longer frightens me. Death warned he might be different when he woke, but to our relief, Kaid is the same man I married. These small moments of absence are the only change, and I embrace them instead of fear them. I let his soul find its way back to me as I study his beauty.

NICOLE SCARANO

His scars are almost invisible now, his sun-kissed skin and rippling muscles hiding Death's flawless stitching. He no longer limps, his body fully functional, but at the beginning, he was as unsteady as a newborn. After Death left us, Kaid could barely stay awake for more than a few hours at a time. I kept him warm and fed, but as we sat around the fire for days, my request to return to the Vesi flooded my mind. Udens had given his permission for me to bring Kaid to his waters, and as soon as my husband was strong enough, I packed up our camp. It was a quiet journey as Kaid slept on the cart, but he was alive and not in pieces in the chest. I smiled the entire trip, but it was nothing compared to the grin that split my lips when my husband saw the Vesi for the first time.

It was on those shores that I recounted the story of The Stranger and my journeys. It took us days to get through the tale, his body unable to stay awake for long, but he didn't let me forget a single detail. I told him about every horrifying moment, including those that occurred in these waters. He hated hearing of my suffering. I could feel the rage wafting off him, and I worried that learning of my time without him would harm his healing, but he bore it with the same bravery he met his death with.

The following weeks were decidedly more enjoyable. We ate tropical fruit, worked his muscles in the shallow water, and slept naked under the sun. The fish swam with us as I helped him grow stronger, and when my eyes caught sight of the pink one, I couldn't stop the tears. Udens had come to meet Kaid, and the way he swam around my husband confirmed the god of the sea had claimed him just as he had me.

We both gained much-needed weight on the sun-kissed shores of the Vesi, and after a month of never donning clothes, Kaid laid down beside me one night and dragged my body atop his. We made love for the first time since our wedding. It was awkward and exhausting. We laughed and fumbled as Kaid tried to control his still-weak muscles, but I've never loved anything more.

We left the Vesi after that, and true to his promise, we found a small shrine to Elskere. I wore an elaborate gown, and Kaid wore the finest fabrics, and we pledged our marriage vows again. The southern village prepared a wedding feast for us, and we danced and ate and drank until dawn, celebrating our love with strangers who felt like family. Amidst the revelry, I noticed a dark stain watching me with fondness among the sea of vibrantly dressed guests, and while he never came close, my heart surged with joy. Death had come to bear witness. Like a father, he came to his child's wedding, and as the sun heralded the new day, Kaid and I completed the vows of our body. When we finally emerged from the wedding suite at midday to continue our journey, the villagers showered us with gifts. Some were small and humble, some were homemade, and others were tiny fortunes, but all were presented with kindness. That's when we knew. We were home, and with the gold I stole from the Mitte Midagi, we purchased a fertile farm.

The weather was bright, the land rich and fruitful, and Sato surprisingly offered us her favor. Within a cycle, we had a harvest beyond our wildest dreams, but it was overshadowed by the birth of our first daughter. She came into this world with gorgeous black hair and a powerful set of lungs, and I never knew how much love I held in my heart until I saw her. She was mine. She was Kaid's. We had our own family, and I would never abandon her like my parents deserted me. Kaid would never reject her like his father had dismissed him. We would love her until her life was overflowing, and then we would love her more.

Death and Lovec, along with his newly returned wife, traveled to us to celebrate our first daughter and then again two cycles later when our second girl was born. We wanted Udens to bless the girls as well, but we waited until they were old enough to visit the Vesi and swim with the pink fish. This was the cycle we finally journeyed to the sunken city, and after an entire season of sun and salt water and fruit, I'm thankful to be home. Our daughters were in their glory, though, and are less excited to be home. They hated leaving the colorful fish, playing with Udens in his innocent form every day until we had to drag them out of the waves for meals. Shortly before we left, a whale presented himself, and the green hint in his white eyes told me Udens had plans for us. We swam to him as a family, and he carried us through the sunken city, the school of fish sending air bubbles our way so we wouldn't drown. When we resurfaced, Kaid and I told the girls a simplified story of how their mother found one of their father's scattered bones in these waters. We have yet to tell them the full truth of our history, but they've started to question Kaid's scars and his moments of absence. They didn't fully understand what we said, but they knew enough to cry and hug their father, Udens carrying us on his back to offer his support. When their tears finally dried, Kaid launched them into the water one by one, and we spent the rest of the day with laughter in the presence of a god. No, our daughters did not want to leave the Vesi, but with the harvest fast approaching, we had to return. Kaid still quietly prays to Varas, but the thief in him died when his body did, and he's content to live his days chasing his children through the grain and vegetables.

"Did it happen again?" His voice interrupts my reverie, and I smile as he finally registers me standing in the doorway. I nod, and he extends a hand. These moments used to bother him as they did me, but now he accepts that they're a part of who he is. He knows I don't love him any less because of them. If anything, I love him more because of how precious our life is. This is the future we weren't supposed to have, and neither of us takes it for granted.

He grabs my hand as soon as I step within reach and pulls

me atop his lap. I straddle him with a laugh that he swallows with a greedy kiss.

"I'm so glad to be home," he moans into my mouth.

"As am I, but the girls hate it." I thread my fingers through his hair, tilting his head to gain better access to his mouth, and his groan at my force sends a bolt of electricity to my core.

"We'll take them back next Season of Growth." Kaid's hands find my thighs, and he pushes my nightdress up my legs until my lower half is bare against him. "But I'm going to enjoy that we're no longer living in a tent and can shut the door."

I laugh as he grinds against me, and the delicious pressure steals my humor, replacing it with an unholy need.

"Kaid," I moan.

"My goddess." He rips my clothing from my body. His mouth finds mine again, and my soul ignites, loving that even all these cycles later, he still calls me that. His love has never once faltered, his devotion to me stronger now than it was at our first wedding.

"Wife." He bites my bottom lip, his teeth applying just enough pressure to drive me to madness. "I need you."

I'm already moving before he can finish speaking, my frantic fingers trailing down his chiseled abs to his pants. I'm clumsy as I undo them, suddenly starving for this man. We would sneak down to the water to be alone at the Vesi, but those moments were always rushed so we wouldn't leave our daughters unattended for too long, and while I never regret our time with our girls, our family, I crave Kaid so badly it hurts. Our love for each other hasn't waned, our need never dying. With each cycle, we grow closer, and while I want to savor this moment, I'm too desperate.

I grip his length and push him against my opening. His breath catches as he realizes just how deeply I desire him, and I slip my fingers into his dark hair, forcing him to look at me.

"I want you to watch me," I say as I lower myself slowly

onto him. Kaid curses so loud that I clamp my hand over his mouth so he doesn't wake the girls, and fire burns in his eyes at how I seized control. He revels in my desperation for him, so with my palm still clamped over his lips, I lean forward, my bare body brushing seductively against his chest.

"Sellah," he growls, gripping my hips. "Stop teasing me. I need you."

My arm wraps around his neck, my hand still covering his mouth. "I want you hard and loud," I say, rocking against him as we become one. "I'll capture your cries, but it has been so long since I've had you on a bed, I want to feel you lose yourself."

Kaid grips my hips harder, and I know there'll be bruises there tomorrow. The thought floods me with arousal, and he slides inside me without resistance.

He takes my request to heart and thrusts with wild abandon, my pleasure growing out of control. He moans obscenely into my palm, and it's the most arousing thing I've ever heard. His groans are deep and filled with longing, beautiful and full of passion, and it's the sound of his voice rough with desire that sends me over the edge.

I slam my mouth to his, kissing him so he can contain my screams, and my climax lasts and lasts and lasts until I am boneless and blissfully happy.

"Don't even think about it," Kaid growls as he forces me to continue moving. "I'm not done with you yet. I'll never be done with you, wife."

His pace increases until I'm the one unable to hide her voice. "Oh gods, Kaid, please."

"There are no gods in this bed but you," he says as he kisses my throat. "You are my goddess. You are who I worship."

"I love you, Kaid."

"I don't love you, Sellah." He looks at me with all the

adoration coursing through his veins, and I lose control at the knowledge of what those words truly mean.

"Please," I beg, needing him to fall over the edge with me, and as my body convulses with the most exquisite bliss, he follows me off the ledge with a roar. I kiss him to muffle the sound I adore. I crave his voice. After forgetting what it sounded like while he lay in pieces, I need to hear him often. I enjoy listening to him speak or sing, but in these moments, I love to listen to his pleasure, and he grants me my every wish, letting me hear just how much he loves my skin pressed against his.

We ride out the receding waves together, and when I finally stop panting for breath, he gently lays me on our bed. He helps clean me up, and then he settles his gorgeous, bare body beside mine in the darkness. I curl against him, and my fingers find his scars. He likes it when I touch them. By tracing them, my fingers have turned the things he hates most into his—

"Mother!" I was so exhausted that I didn't realize I'd fallen asleep until our youngest daughter's call breaks through the night.

Kaid and I jerk awake, realizing her small voice is coming from the other side of our door, and we jump off the mattress, laughing as we scramble for our clothes.

"Yes, my darling?" I open the door, pulling my arm into my nightdress, and find both of our girls standing there in the darkness. "What's wrong?"

"We got used to sleeping with you and father." The youngest rubs her drowsy eyes. "Can we please sleep in here with you?"

I turn back to Kaid, who laughs, his plans to have me all to himself flying out the window at the sound of her adorable request. "Of course." He smiles at our daughters. "Just for tonight."

The girls squeal with delight and crowd into our bed

between us, and while I know this wasn't his plan, he can't stop himself from beaming. This was our dream all those cycles ago in Hreinasta's temple when I believed I couldn't have a future of my own. This was what I wanted. Kaid as my husband, my best friend, my partner in this life, and the father of our children. I dreamed of a family we could build better than the ones we came from. It was a fantasy then, but as we curl around our daughters and join hands over their small bodies, I'm overwhelmed by my reality. Kaid stares at my misting eyes, and I know he understands. He has the same look of happiness and peace in his expression, and we hold each other's gaze as our girls fall asleep. We stay awake for a long while, watching them, watching each other, our hands remaining locked together, and then when our eyelids become too heavy, I squeeze his fingers softly.

"I love you," I mouth over our daughters' heads, and he lifts my hand to his scarred lips, kissing my palm reverently, adoringly, worshipfully.

"And I, wife." His eyes twinkle in the darkness. "I don't love you."

LIST OF THE GODS

- **HREINASTA**: The Pure One, the divine goddess. One of the primordial gods. Lives in Szent.
- **THE STRANGER**: SPOILER - God of Death. One of the primordial gods. Banished.
- **VALKA**: God of War. Lives in Szent.
- **ELSKERE**: The Wed Gods of Love. Lives in Szent.
- **VARAS**: God of Thieves. Lives in Szent.
- **LOVEC**: God of the Hunt. Lives in the North
- **UDENS**: God of the Sea. Lives in the Vesi.
- **SATO**: Goddess of the Harvest. Lives in Szent.

ALSO BY NICOLE SCARANO

ABOUT THE AUTHOR

Nicole writes fantasy, sci-fi, mystery, & romance as Nicole Scarano & steamy fantasy & sci-fi romance as N.R. Scarano. She doesn't like to box herself into one genre, but no matter the book, they all have action, true love, a dog if she can fit it into the plot, swoon-worthy men & absolutely feral females.

In her free time, Nicole is a dog mom to her rescued pitbull, a movie/tv show enthusiast, a film score lover, and sunshine obsessive. She loves to write outside, and she adores pole dancing fitness classes.

For all book links, socials, & to sign up for her newsletter visit:

linktr.ee/NicoleScarano

Made in the USA
Middletown, DE
06 September 2024

59824887R00163